THE MISSING NURSE

An enthralling crime mystery full of twists

(Yorkshire Murder Mysteries Book 1)

ROGER SILVERWOOD

JOFFE
BOOKS

Revised edition 2019
Joffe Books, London
www.joffebooks.com

First published as "In the Midst of Life" 2004

**Please join our mailing list for free Kindle
crime thriller, detective, and mystery books
and new releases.**
www.joffebooks.com/contact

ISBN: 978-1-78931-185-3

CHAPTER 1

*Moorside Hospital for the Criminally Insane, Pontylliath, Wales, UK.
13 May 1981.*

It was 9 a.m. Nurse Derri Evans, aged twenty-five,
loaded a hypodermic with one millilitre of equinox.
Holding the syringe upright in front of the pharmacy
window, he pressed the plunger until the yellow liquid
squirted out of the tip of the needle. He let the empty
ampoule fall and clatter into the waste bin and placed the
hypodermic in a stainless steel kidney bowl on the worktop.
He reached up into a cupboard and pulled out a square of
lint from a navy blue wrapper and draped it over the bowl.

He carried the bowl and contents out into the corridor to
the cream door opposite. It had the number sixteen painted
above the observation grill. Silently, he opened the eyehole
and peered into the room. The shapeless mound in the bed
indicated that Gavin Meredith was still asleep.

The nurse selected a key from a bunch fastened to a
chain round his waist and pushed it into the door. The smell
of camphor and perspiration came strongly to his nostrils as
he entered the room. He wrinkled his nose.

'Come on, Gavin. Wake up,' he said brightly as he crossed to the barred window to open it. The fresh cool breeze wafted onto his face, and he heard the rustle of leaves on the trees. He smiled, 'That's better.'

He looked at the bed. There was still no movement. The sheet was pulled up and over the pillow. 'Come on, Gavin,' he said coaxingly.

He crossed the room and peeled back the bedclothes to discover only pillows and clothes where the patient should have been. Suddenly, from behind, he heard a slight noise. He turned to see the tall figure of Gavin Meredith in blue-and-white striped pyjamas. His face was scarlet, his mouth open dripping saliva. He was in front of the open wardrobe door holding an iron bed-side above his head and aiming it at him.

'Gavin!' The nurse yelled and put his arms up to defend himself.

It was too late. The iron bed-side hit him on the forehead. He fell backwards, the kidney bowl and contents went up in the air and blood spurted from the wound. As Derri fell, he hit the back of his head on a radiator pipe protruding from the wall. His eyes closed and he slithered down the white plaster wall onto the maroon linoleum.

Seconds later, there was some loud knocking on the door. And frantic calls. More knocking followed by the rattle of keys. 'Are you all right, Derri? Are you all right?'

The door opened and three nurses, a male and two females, burst in. They saw Nurse Derri Evans lying unconscious by the bed in a pool of blood. The iron bed-side was across the corner of the room, the kidney bowl and hypodermic were scattered under the bed and there was blood splattered down the wall and on the floor.

Gavin Meredith was crouching in the corner of the room his hands around his head, his big eyes looking alternately upwards and then at the nurses. His wet mouth turned up at the corners.

Nurse Derri Evans' heartbeat was irregular and his breathing shallow. They removed him to a side ward where a doctor and three nurses worked on him intensively for forty minutes. At 10 a.m. he was dead.

Police Station, Bromersley; South Yorkshire, UK. 17 June 2002.

Detective Inspector Angel growled something unintelligible as he purposefully closed the door with the words 'Chief Constable' painted on it. Although a heavy man, he bounced down the stairs as fast as the youngest policeman in the station. He strode along the olive green corridor and stuck his pug-shaped nose into the CID room and surveyed the occupants. His eyes came to rest on a slim, twenty-two-year-old Asian man. He was smartly dressed in a dark suit, white and blue striped shirt and tie.

'Hey, boy,' Angel bellowed.

The young man stood up, breathed in hard and stared at him, his chin and eyes set like granite.

Angel ignored the show. 'Find DS Gawber and tell him to come to my office, pronto.' He turned away and then turned back, 'And you'd better bring yourself along as well. See what you can learn.'

Angel turned swiftly away and moved on to his office. He had just sat down when there was a knock at the door.

'Come in.'

A tall, lean man with a tanned face, close-cropped hair and a gold earring glinting from his earlobe came in. He was wearing jeans, trainers and a white t-shirt with 'Bromersley Bitter' printed in red on white across his chest.

Angel looked up. His jaw dropped. 'Who are you? What do you want?'

'Morning sir. I'm DS Crisp. I've been assigned to you while DS Gawber's away.'

Angel pursed his lips and breathed out loudly. 'Oh no you haven't, lad. There's some mistake.'

The DS stared hard at him. 'There's no mistake, sir. The Super said…'

'I'm sure Superintendent Harker wouldn't assign a man off the dustbins to me.'

The DS touched his worn jeans and smiled. 'Oh, yes, sir. I've just come off an obo, sir. Drugs squad. Had to dress the part.'

Angel wasn't smiling. 'Aye. Well, go home and dress for *this* part. And take that earring out. And get a wash and a shave. And be quick about it. We don't deal with druggies in this department; we deal with a smarter, craftier, more evil set of crooks, in the main, and they *all* dress better than you. We need to be at least as smart as the public we serve. And for goodness sake, stand up straight.'

The young man turned to leave and then he turned back. 'Yes, sir.'

'Be back in thirty minutes. And where has DS Gawber gone to?'

'Er. He's gone on a course.'

'What sort of a course?'

'Profiling, sir.'

'Profiling? What the hell's that?'

'Well, sir, it's where…'

'All right, Sergeant, all right. I can *guess* what profiling is quicker than you can tell me.'

DS Crisp was glad to be out of the room. He closed the door quickly.

Angel grunted as he reached over for the phone and dialled a number. 'Hello. It's Mick Angel. I want to speak to Superintendent Harker. Oh. Morning, John.'

'Aye. What is it?'

'I've just had a lad in here telling me that DS Gawber is away.'

'He's on a course. Hendon.'

'Short notice, isn't it, sir?'

'You've got Crisp, Mick. Just for the week.'

'Right, sir. Who is he? What is he?'

'A transfer. Spent most of his time in the drugs squad in Manchester. Came here as sergeant. Good report.'

'Right, sir. Well, I'll have to manage, won't I?'

'Yes.'

The phone went dead. Angel shook his head and replaced the handset.

There was a knock at the door. 'Come in.'

It was the young Asian. He came in, closed the door and walked smartly up to the desk.

'I have to tell you, sir, that Detective Sergeant Gawber is not in the station.'

'I know that *now*, lad.'

'Also, I have to tell you, sir, that there is a lady to see you. Superintendent Harker said that you were the only senior officer available.'

Angel screwed up his face as if someone had trodden on his corn. 'A lady? What lady? Who is she? What does she want? Do I know her? What's going on in this place today? The organisation has gone to pot. And it's Saturday morning. Don't you realise that, lad? I'm not even supposed to be here!'

Ahmed's eyes opened wide. 'I don't know anything about that, sir. And I don't know anything about the lady. She's in reception. That's all I know, sir. I'm just passing on a message.'

'When am I supposed to do my own work? I've known tins of spaghetti in better order than this. What's the Duty Officer doing? I've more cases than the baggage handlers at Heathrow, and I am not canvassing for any more.'

Angel stood up and sat down again. He shook his head and blew out a long sigh. 'Well, you'd better show her in, lad,' he growled. 'And bring yourself back in here, then park yourself discreetly in yon corner.' He pointed to a chair at the side of the steel cupboard.

'Right, sir.' Cadet Ahmed Ahaz went out and closed the door.

Angel muttered something, squared up the papers on his desk and dropped them into a drawer. He threw a paper

5

cup at the wastepaper bin, then produced a small notebook in a leather cover from his coat pocket. He found a ballpoint pen and clicked it ready. He stood up and turned to look in the mirror, he straightened his tie and ran his open hand through his dark brown hair. He turned back to the room and pulled up a chair to be as near the end of the desk as possible, angling it towards the window. He always sought to see people's reactions as clearly as possible.

There was a knock on the door. 'Come in.'

Cadet Ahmed Ahaz ushered a small lady of about forty-five, into the room. Her small, bright, busy eyes looked around the room. Then she stared at the tall, bulky figure of the Inspector.

'Miss Miriam Thomas, sir,' Ahmed closed the door and went over to the chair beyond the metal cupboard.

Angel smiled down at her and held out his hand. 'Ah, yes. Come in. Please sit down.'

Miriam Thomas came forward to greet him. She had small features, a needle-shaped nose and sharp chin. She was not wearing any make-up and had the slightest growth of fair hair around her mouth and chin. Her hair was dark brown. She was dressed in a long, navy blue raincoat, black stockings and low heeled, black shoes. Strips of the blue dress she was wearing underneath showed around the neck and where the coat dropped open at the knee.

'I'm Detective Inspector Angel. Now, what can I do for you, Miss Thomas?'

She lowered a big black handbag onto the floor and brought her hands together on her lap. 'I am in need of help, Inspector.' She spoke positively and forthrightly and her pleasant sing-song voice soon identified her as being Welsh.

'That's what we're here for, Miss Thomas.'

'Thank you. I don't know quite where to begin.'

Angel smiled encouragingly at her. 'In your own time.'

'Well, er, I am a nursing sister at the Moorside Mental Hospital for the Criminally Insane at Pontylliath. That's in Wales.' She paused and was pleased to see the Inspector making notes.

'Please go on.'

'Well, Inspector, my sister, Fiona, has gone missing.'

'Oh?'

'It's a little complicated.'

He pursed his lips. 'Take your time.'

'Well, Inspector. If I may explain? You may recall, that twenty-one years ago, a nurse was killed by a patient at that hospital in Pontylliath. The authorities naturally wanted to play it down, but the national newspapers made it front page news, with photographs of the hospital, the murdered nurse and the patient who killed him splashed across the front pages. They ran the most sensational headlines.'

Angel looked up from his writing and rubbed his hand slowly across his mouth. 'Twenty-one years ago? That's a long time. Mmm. Maybe I do remember it. I'm not sure. Please go on.'

'Well, the staff nurse in charge of that ward was accused, in her absence, of withholding medication, not only to the patient who killed the nurse, but also to the fifty other patients in the two wards which were her responsibility. She was working regular nights at the time and was not subject to the more careful supervision that she would be today. Anyway, the reduction in the dose of the sedative that should have been administered to that particular patient resulted in him being unstable and enabled him to kill the nurse. It was judged by the patients' consultant psychiatrist at the time that the staff nurse was responsible for the death. The victim's name was Derri Evans.' She paused, looked down for a second and then up to the policeman and said, 'I was to have married Derri in the June following his death on 13 May 1981.'

Angel nodded his understanding, 'I see. Tell me, why did the staff nurse withhold medication from the patients?'

'For money and for favours. She sold the drugs, the pills, the bandages, the plasters, the syringes, you name it. She stole everything she could lay her hands on and then sold the items. The drugs brought in the greatest sums, of course. When she was on duty, she held the key to the ward pharmacy and she had a free rein. And there was no end to her greed.'

'Uh huh.'

'Anyway, that nurse disappeared off the face of the earth. Everybody was looking for her: the hospital authorities; the North Wales police; the newspapers; Derri Evans' parents. Even her own parents didn't know where she had disappeared to.'

Angel looked up. 'I think I remember. There was a campaign run by one of the Sunday papers, wasn't there? "Have you seen this woman?"'

Miriam Thomas' eyes brightened. 'That's it, Inspector. That's it. Well, she has not been seen from that day, until my sister, Fiona, who came to Bromersley yesterday for the first time in her life, believed that she saw that woman here. Her name is Violet Rae. Staff Nurse Violet Rae. Fiona phoned me to tell me that she believed she had bumped into her. Unfortunately, I was out. So she left a message on the answerphone to say that she thought she had met her, here in Bromersley and suggested that I come immediately. I suppose she thought that the two of us would be better able to confirm her identity, jointly confront her and report her whereabouts to the police. I phoned my sister on her mobile phone, but there was no reply. Anyway, I caught the first train I could. When I arrived in Bromersley this morning, I went straight to the place where Fiona was staying, and asked for her. The man said that she had left this morning. He said that she had not left a message and he thought that she had said she intended returning home. I must say, Inspector, I would be very surprised if my sister would do that without either waiting for me or leaving a message.'

Angel looked up and pursed his lips. 'I see. Now what would you like the police to do?'

'Well, obviously, Inspector, I want you to find that woman.'

'Understandably, but your sister is not here to tell us her suspicions herself.'

'I want you to find my sister as well,' she added urgently.

'Of course. But if your sister had decided she was mistaken, and that the person she saw was *not* this Violet Rae, then I expect she would have tried to contact you, was unable to, and is now — at this very moment probably making her way home to prevent you making a fruitless journey.'

The woman shook her head. 'But she asked me to come, Inspector. She left a message on the answerphone *urging* me to come.'

Angel looked straight into the woman's eyes. 'But she didn't give you the slightest hint as to where this Violet Rae could be located?'

'No,' she replied thoughtfully. 'I'm sure she would have if she had spoken to me. In fact, I would have asked her. My curiosity would have had to be satisfied. But no, it was only a message on a tape.'

'Aye, well, perhaps things changed. Maybe she was mistaken and she decided to return home. And as *she* was leaving Bromersley, *you* were arriving here; you simply missed each other. It is easy to do. You weren't able to tell her you were coming, were you?'

'Well, no, Inspector. But she knew that I would come!'

'I expect it was a mistake and she has returned home. She'll be waiting for you in Wales.'

'Do you really think so?'

'I don't know.' Angel pushed back from the desk and rubbed his chin. Then he stared directly at the woman, 'But, look at it from my point of view, Miss Thomas. All this happened twenty-one years ago, in a different police authority area. There is nobody to corroborate your sister's possible sighting, and there seems to be room for some uncertainty as to whether this person really is Violet Rae. She isn't here to confirm anything and you have no supporting witnesses either. Looking at all the facts, there doesn't seem to be sufficient reason for me to mount an investigation, does there?'

Miriam Thomas' hand went to her face. She shook her head, her eyes closed.

Angel leaned back in the chair and looked at the ceiling briefly. 'She didn't give you the slightest hint where Violet Rae might be? No hint at all?'

'No, Inspector, I told you.'

Angel shrugged his shoulders and then stood up. 'Quite. I'll tell you what, Miss Thomas. If there is no message waiting for you when you get back, or circumstances have changed, and you are the slightest bit unhappy, phone me and I'll make some preliminary enquiries. How's that?'

Angel saw Miriam Thomas smile for the first time, it brightened her face. She shook his hand. 'Thank you, Inspector. Thank you very much.' At the door she turned back to him. 'I'll keep you to that promise, Inspector.'

'I would want you to,' he smiled and nodded. Then he turned to Ahmed, 'See Miss Thomas to the front door, lad.'

Ahmed came forward, opened the door and led the woman out of the room.

Angel settled down to reducing the pile of papers he had stuffed into the desk drawer. He pulled them out and began labouring through them. He hadn't made much progress when the phone rang.

'Angel.'

The switchboard operator said, 'Inspector Angel, it's your wife on the phone for you, sir.'

'Right. Put her through.' There was a click.

'Is that you, Michael?'

'Yes, love. What's the matter?'

'I've had a call from my mother. She's to go into hospital.'

'When? What's the matter with her?'

'It's her heart. Today. There's an ambulance coming for her. Taking her to the City Hospital.'

'Her heart? Oh. Well, what do you want to do about it, love?'

'I thought I would go down to her. I can stay in her house. Visit her in hospital and keep an eye on her.'

'Well, aye. Do that then. Do you want me to run you to the station?'

'No. I'll get a taxi, if that's all right.'

'Of course it's all right. Have you got plenty of money?'

'Yes. If I'm quick I can get a train at eleven o'clock. There's a connection at Sheffield for Derby. I don't like leaving you on your own, but it's only for a day or two. There's plenty of food in the freezer. Eat that turkey up. And there's some salad already washed. You'll want some more milk, and don't forget to feed the cats. It's only for a day or two. Do you think you can manage? I'll phone you tonight.'

'I don't like you going down there on your own, but I suppose it's the right thing to do. Of course I can manage. I expect you'll find she's all right, when you get there. You can get me on my mobile if I'm out of the office. Or leave a message. You're to let me know, do you hear?'

'Look at the time. Got to go, love. I must fly.'

'All right. Bye.'

Angel put the phone back on its cradle. He pulled a face. That news was not at all welcome. His wife had hardly ever been away in all the twenty years they had been married and he wasn't looking forward to being in the bungalow on his own. The place was all right but it could get so lonely with only the cats and the television for company. He fingered the papers in front of him, he could not concentrate on the paperwork now. He wondered how she was coping with this unexpected news. He grunted. He didn't like it at all, his mother-in-law had looked strong enough last time he had seen her. He had always thought she was as strong as a horse. But he had to be realistic, heart trouble could be serious. He hoped everything would be all right for his wife's sake; she would be dreadfully upset if anything happened to her mother and he wouldn't like to see that. His mind wandered down to his domestic arrangements. Turkey salad for tea sounded all right. He must remember to get some milk for the cats on the way home.

There was a knock at the door.

'Come in.'

It was Detective Sergeant Crisp looking pleased with himself. He was very smartly turned out — he had shaved, removed the earring and changed his clothes. It was a transformation, he looked like a model straight off the page of a Grattan's catalogue. Angel looked the man up and down. He approved of the turnout.

'Come in, lad. Come in. Don't stand there.'

Crisp looked at Angel uncertainly as he closed the door.

'Sit down. Sit down.' With a nod of his head, he indicated the seat next to the desk. DS Crisp settled down in the chair.

'Now then, lad,' Angel began, 'have you read today's round robin from the Chief Constable?'

'No, sir. Not yet.'

Angel raised his thick eyebrows. 'Oh? Well, let me give you the gist of it. From memory. I am sure you know that Superintendent Harker — my boss and indirectly your ex-boss — instructed the drugs squad to turn over the drum of a man suspected of dealing in drugs. He was acting on information received, but as it turned out to be the mayor of Bromersley, the information received was obviously duff! Of course, it should have been very carefully checked out, or it should have been verified by confirmation from another source. Well, apparently, it wasn't. And all hell broke loose. But before it could be hushed up, the local rag and several national daily newspapers got hold of the story and wrapped it well and truly round the Chief Constable's head.'

'I heard, sir,' he said looking down.

Angel raised his eyebrows again and leaned back in his chair and smiled. 'Not only did you hear, but you were one of the officers who turned the drum over!'

'Well, yes,' he replied in a low voice. 'I was acting under orders, sir.'

'Aye, lad. Oh yes. That's what Heinrich Himmler said!'

Crisp's jaw tightened.

Angel continued. 'Well, did you see what the papers made of it?'

'Yes, sir.'

'The nationals, the locals, the Sundays?'

'Yes.'

'Well, this bit you haven't heard, Sergeant. This is the best part. The upshot of that fiasco is that until further notice, we have to go through the Chief Constable if we want a search warrant. That's great, isn't it? And he says — and these are his own words — he says he is more likely to *refuse* a search warrant than to grant one, until all this newspaper interest goes away! Have you got that?'

Crisp pursed his lips. He said nothing.

Angel went on. 'So, not only do we have Judges' Rules to try to work round, we've now got Chief Constable's rules as well! I don't know why they don't make it a rule to employ only blind, deaf and one-legged men on the force. *That* would make it a bit more difficult for us. They could use the argument that it was for charity. Keeping the sick and disabled off the street and out of the dole office! They could make it a law that only blind and deaf men over eighty are eligible to be coppers. Or dwarves, little people they call them now. Yes. That's a good idea. The required height of an enrolling policeman has to be less than two foot nine. How about that? Eventually there would be so many stupid restrictions that we'd never catch any criminals at all! We'd just be here for decoration. The crooks would have a field day. They would take over the town. They would send out a round robin, "All policemen are to dress like fairies and look pretty for the annual inspection by Jack the Ripper on the village green on May Day!"'

The phone rang. He snatched it up. 'Hello. Angel speaking,' he growled.

It was the Chief Constable.

He changed his tone. Sweet reasonableness returned. 'What's that, sir?' He stood up. His eyes looked down at the Sergeant. 'Yes sir.' His jaw stiffened, 'I will, sir.'

He banged down the phone and turned to DS Crisp. 'There's been an armed robbery at that big petrol station at Bardsley. Come on.'

As Angel crossed the room, there was a knock at the door. Angel opened it and found a startled Cadet Ahmed Ahaz on the other side.

'Out of the way, lad!' Angel brushed past him and strode briskly out of the office. Crisp followed.

'Sir! Sir!' Ahmed called, running behind and waving a piece of paper. He followed the Detective Inspector up the corridor

'Got to go, lad. Got to go.'

Ahmed said, 'It's a burglary, sir. At Pettigrew and Shaw's.'

Angel turned and snatched the message from him. He read it quickly then shoved it into DS Crisp's hand. 'You deal with this. I'll do the petrol station.'

CHAPTER 2

Angel drove up to the Bardsley Service Station, a large self-service petrol station with eight bays of pumps set back at the crossroads where the roads to Bromersley, Barnsley, Doncaster and Sheffield met.

Two marked police Range Rovers and an ambulance were already on the forecourt, their lights rotating madly. A couple of policemen were putting up 'Closed' signs and red cones at the station entrance as Angel drove up. They recognised him and let him pass.

Two ambulance men in bright orange and green came out of the pay office carrying a small, young woman wrapped in a blanket and strapped in a chair. She had a shock of long ginger hair round her white face and her eyes were closed. She was holding a bloody cotton wool pad to her mouth. They carried her to the back of the ambulance.

Angel went up to the ambulance men, 'Is she badly hurt?'

One of them hesitated, he glanced at the girl as he unfolded a blanket and quietly said, 'I don't know, yet.'

Angel nodded. 'What happened?

'She was hit in the mouth.'

Angel screwed up his eyes, 'She's only a kid.' He looked around at the pay office. 'Are there any other casualties?'

'No.' The medics lifted the girl into the back of the ambulance and began to unfasten the strap.

'Did you see who did it, love?' he asked.

'Yes.'

He leaned into the back of the ambulance, took out his Warrant Card, and held it up to the two men. 'I'm Detective Inspector Angel. I need to interview the young lady. I want to come to the hospital with you.'

'Sorry, Inspector. You know it's not allowed,' one of them said as he wrapped her in a thick cream-coloured blanket.

The young woman opened her eyes, pulled the pad from her face and said, 'Please let him come.'

Angel looked at the two ambulance men.

The medics looked at each other, then one of them said, 'All right, Inspector. But don't get in the way.'

'Is there anything else wrong with her?'

'Her wrists and ankles are cut,' one of the men said quietly. 'She was tied up with wire. Maybe trauma as well. I don't know.'

'Tied up with wire?' Angel frowned.

The ambulance man stared at him meaningfully, Angel nodded his understanding. Then his eye caught something. 'Won't keep you.'

He turned round and reached out for the back of the yellow dayglo jacket of a passing policeman. 'Constable.'

'Yes, sir?'

Angel pointed upwards to a video camera pointed towards the forecourt. 'There'll be a tape in the pay office. When Scenes of Crime has finished, will you grab it and see that it gets to my office as soon as you can?'

'Yes. Right, sir.'

The two men ushered Angel into the back of the ambulance. 'Take it easy with her,' one of them whispered as Angel mounted the step.

Angel nodded and climbed inside.

The doors closed and the driver and his mate climbed into the cab. The ambulance pulled into the main road, switched on the wailing siren and sailed down the hill to Bromersley Hospital all lights flashing.

Angel took up a sitting position perched on the edge of the empty bed close to the young woman's head. He swayed slightly from side to side as the vehicle turned corners. He looked down at her, her eyes were closed. 'Are you all right?'

'Yes,' she spoke as if her nose was blocked.

'Do you want to sleep?'

'No.'

'What's your name?'

'Jane.'

'Well, Jane, can you tell me what happened?'

She opened her eyes and pulled the blood-covered pad from her mouth. He noticed the side of her face was blue and swollen.

'The usual.'

Angel shook his head. 'Go on.'

She closed her eyes and spoke a few words at a time, swallowing between each phrase. 'Two men came in a car. It was busy. And then suddenly it went quiet. I looked up. I was on my own. And there they were. Coming through the office door, screaming and swearing. There was nobody else around. They had balaclavas pulled down over their faces. They frightened me. One of them was waving a gun. They pulled out the till drawer. I hung on to it and yelled at them, so they hit me in the mouth with the gun and tied me up. I think he's broken a tooth.' She winced at a sudden shaft of pain.

'Did they take anything else?'

'Some cigarettes.'

'Do you know them? Have they been before?'

'I don't think *they* have. But there's been others.'

'What can you remember about them?'

'One was very tall and the other was short.'

'What were they wearing?'

She swallowed again. 'I don't know. I didn't notice. Balaclavas and woollen gloves.'

Angel leaned towards the cab as the driver braked. 'What were the balaclavas like?'

'Black.'

'Wool?'

'Yes.'

'Were they wearing coats?'

She didn't reply. She put the bloody pad back to her mouth, unravelled a hand from under the blanket and gripped Angel's coat sleeve.

'One of them, the little one — he was nasty he was wearing a big ring with a red stone in the middle of it. There was, like, writing round the stone. He was wearing gloves but he couldn't get the drawer out of the till, so he had to take a glove off. That's when I saw it. A big ring it was.'

'Which hand, Jane?'

She thought about it a second, 'The right hand.'

Angel smiled. 'That's good, Jane. That's great. It gives us something to go on.'

She closed her eyes.

Angel said quietly, 'What were the gloves like? Leather?'

'No. Wool. Dark colour. Navy blue, I think. Yes. Navy blue.'

'Navy blue wool.'

The ambulance lurched again. Angel peered out of a little rectangle of clear glass at the top of the window. They were coming up to the hospital.

'What's your full name, Jane?'

'Jane Mulholland.'

'Who can I tell that you're here?'

'My mum and dad. They're at the farm on the opposite side of the road to the service station.'

The ambulance rear door opened.

'I'll see to it, Jane. Don't worry. And I'll see you later.'

She tried to smile. She pulled him back by his coat sleeve. 'Careful how you tell my dad? He's not very well. All this foot and mouth has made him depressed.'

Angel forced a smile, 'It'll be all right. Don't worry.'

18

The ambulance man called out, 'Come on, Inspector.'

Angel bounded out of the back. He gave Jane a wave.

He stepped onto the pavement outside the hospital and watched the ambulance men slide the stretcher out. He saw Jane's swollen pale face and red hair. It was a sight he could not easily erase from his mind.

The automatic double doors opened and closed as the party disappeared into the hospital.

Angel kicked his way thoughtfully down the path at the side of the hospital as he reflected on the state of Jane Mulholland, and what he would like to do about it. As he poked down into his pocket for his mobile phone, his weather-beaten face changed from blood red to arctic white. He managed to stab in a number, but as the ringing tone started, a hot ball of fire rumbled in the pit of his stomach and spread outwards and upwards across his chest and then down his arms. He clenched his hands, digging his nails into his palms. His bright blue eyes darkened as he found himself looking through a red haze. He could feel his heart beating against his chest and hear the pulse roaring in his ears. The rage lasted a few seconds and then subsided, just as the phone was answered and a familiar voice said, 'Bromersley Police. Traffic Division. Give your number.'

'This is Mike Angel. Is that Alan?'

'Hello, Mike. What do you want?'

'Transport — anything will do, Alan — to take me to Bardsley. I'm outside the General Hospital.'

'When?'

'Now! It's urgent.'

'Hold on.'

The line went dead for ten seconds, then, preceded by crackling, the voice returned. 'On its way, Mike.'

'Thanks.'

'I hear your missus is away.'

Angel gripped the phone hard. 'Is she all right? What's happened to her? What have you heard?'

'Only that she's away, that's all. Steady on, Mike. Are you all right?'

Angel let out a long loud sigh. 'Sorry, Alan. Yes. Yes, I'm fine. Her mother's gone into hospital in Derby. How did you know? I only knew myself an hour ago.'

'You're to come round for a meal while she's away.'

'That's very kind of you, lad. I'll see how it goes. Thanks ever so much.'

'Anytime. Let me know. Bye.'

Angel slowly put the phone back in his pocket and looked across the hospital car park and beyond. He felt the hot summer sun on his face, noticed the leaves on the trees shimmering in the gentle breeze and considered the kindness of his old friend in the Traffic Division. His jaw relaxed. The heat and pain in his chest had gone and the banging in his ears had stopped. His watch showed ten past four and life was going on as before: an ambulance came up to the door at the side of him; a red bus passed on the road outside the car park; and a young couple, arm in arm, passed him, giggling. The world continued to go round. The telly would still go on pouring out bad news, corny comedies and plays without plots. And he knew he was going to be like a boil on a bus driver's bum until the two men who had cruelly assaulted Jane Mulholland were behind bars.

A marked Police Range Rover turned off the main road into the hospital drive. He waved across the car park. The uniformed police driver saw him.

'Thank you, lad. Bardsley Service Station quickly please.'

The Traffic Police Constable delivered him safely on the forecourt in six minutes. Angel went into the pay office. It was a well-lit, yellow tiled, compact shop with displays of newspapers, cigarettes and sweets on shelves near the counter at the far end of the room. A few packets of cigarettes and chocolate bars were scattered on the floor. Most of the fittings were dappled with patches of silver powder.

The two uniformed policemen were in a corner writing up their notes while Dr Mac, the forensic pathologist, was taking off his cumbersome overalls. The detective had recovered the till drawer from the floor and was dusting it with aluminium powder.

Angel went up to him, 'There should be something on that. One of the robbers had to take his glove off to get the drawer out.'

The young detective looked up at him shaking his head, 'There's nothing to copy on it, sir.'

Angel groaned. 'Are you sure?' he bellowed.

'Positive.'

He wrinkled up his nose and turned to the two policemen, who were standing in a corner. 'I'll take that videotape,' he said, holding out his hand.

'The robbers took it, sir. They must have opened the front of the monitor and helped themselves.'

Angel grunted, 'Have you found anything?' They shook their heads.

He turned to the fingerprint man, 'Have a good run over the front of the telly.'

'I've been over it. There's nothing there, sir. These robbers knew what they were doing.'

Dr Mac was crossing to the door with a black bag. He was a small, white-haired Scotsman in his fifties. Angel looked across at him. 'What have you got, Mac?'

'Nothing, Mike. Nothing. They left a clean sweep.'

He looked round at all the blank faces. 'Has anybody got anything at all? Aren't there even any witnesses?' He bawled.

The four men looked back at him, their faces blank.

Obviously nobody had uncovered any clue or information that was going to help to find and arrest the robbers. Angel shook his head. The corner of his mouth turned down. 'I don't know,' he grumbled, 'Dorothy had the Munchkins, and I've got you lot!'

The kiosk door opened noisily and a small, round woman burst in. Her face was white and her eyes stared round the gathering. 'What's going on? Another robbery? Where's my daughter?' She looked at the PC dusting the edges of the counter with a short thick brush.

Angel stepped forward, 'Is your daughter Jane Mulholland?'

'Yes.'

'She's going to be all right, don't worry. She's been taken to Bromersley Hospital. I went with her.'

The woman's eyes flashed. Her arms were raised, her lips trembling. 'What have they done to her? What do you mean she's going to be all right?'

Angel moved closer to her. 'Just a precaution, nothing more, Mrs Mulholland,' he lied.

'I'm her mother. I must see her.'

'Yes. Yes. And I'm sure she'll want to see you. I'll take you to her straightaway. We can go in my car. Come along now.'

＊ ＊ ＊

Jane's mother came out of the hospital subdued. She had found out that her daughter was badly bruised and would have to have a back tooth extracted. One side of her face was swollen and blue. The cuts on her wrists and ankles were superficial and would heal without assistance. Her psychological health, however, was uncertain.

Angel comforted her as he drove her back to her husband and the farm. On the journey he found out quite a lot. The Mulhollands had money troubles. They had lost their flock of sheep recently to an outbreak of foot and mouth disease, and with the repeated robberies from the service station, their income was almost non-existent. They were living hand to mouth and because they owned the farmland they didn't qualify for state hand-outs. She said that her husband was withdrawn and depressed and was being treated by their doctor. Mr Mulholland had said that if they had another robbery at the service station he would either have to try to sell it or close it down. His wife had been more hopeful and expected that between the three of them they would be able to run the service station if only the robberies would stop. Angel made sympathetic noises and meeting Jane's mother made him all the more determined to apprehend the robbers.

He was soon at the entrance to the farm, which was up a dirt track opposite the service station. Mrs Mulholland insisted that Angel leave her at the end of the drive.

The Inspector dropped her off and returned to Bromersley Police Station. He went straight to his office and picked up the phone.

'Inspector Angel. Tell Cadet Ahaz I want him.'

He noticed how stuffy his office was, it was one of those summer days that reminded him of his childhood. Days long gone by, when summers were summers. Now summer seemed to last ten days and then it was all over. He crossed to the radiators to see if they were warm, they were stone cold. He took out a handkerchief and wiped his forehead and cheeks and then opened a window. 'That's better,' he muttered, as he sat down at his desk.

He opened a drawer and pulled out a telephone directory. He quickly found what he wanted, and tapped the number into his phone.

A man with a bored, London accent answered. 'Yeah?'

Angel went straight into the enquiry. Time was precious. 'I'm looking to buy a large man's ring with a big red stone in the middle and lettering all the way round. Do you have such a ring in stock?'

'I think you mean a class ring, mate?'

Angel shrugged and then said, 'Do I? Well, yes then.'

'Hold on.' The earpiece banged noisily in the Inspector's ear. He jerked his head back and pulled a face. He waited a minute or so. Then he heard the man pick up the phone. 'Hello. What date did you want? I've got 1988, 1997 and 1999. Or did you want all three?'

'I'd like to have a look. Have they got lettering on the top of the ring?'

'Course they have. I told you they're class rings with the name of the school, the year and the class cast into the head of the ring. American class rings. That's what you're looking for, isn't it? Ten carat gold rings that jewellers sell to the rich American kids when they're at school?'

Angel smiled. 'Yes. Yes. That sounds like what I am looking for.'

The voice suddenly said, 'Who is this? I think I recognise you.'

'Yes, you do. It's me, Barney. Detective Inspector Angel.'

Barney had a small second-hand and antique jewellery shop in the town and was a long-time acquaintance of Angel. His shop had been the scene of an armed robbery several years ago. He had been slightly injured as he put up a violent struggle with an armed man. He was much admired for his bravery and was well respected by Inspector Angel.

Barney's voice softened. He laughed. 'Hi there. You're not interested in buying this rubbish, Inspector. I know *you*. It's some info you're wanting, isn't it?'

'It is, Barney, it is. And I'm pressed for time. I'm looking for a short man in his twenties or older, he was wearing one of those rings and he may have bought it from you. He held up a petrol station today. He's dangerous; he hit a young girl with a gun.'

Barney replied straightaway, 'About five foot two. Bottle-bottom glasses. Thin tight lips. Shouts when he talks. Yes, I know him, Inspector. I don't know his name. But I know who you mean.'

Angel froze in the chair; it was not the reply he was expecting. He stared transfixed at the plain wall in front of him momentarily, without seeing it, then snatched at a pen and grabbed the back of an envelope. 'Tell me all you know, Barney. This is very important.'

'He came into the shop to buy one of those rings. He's not very tall and he talks in short spurts, he doesn't seem able to talk ordinary. He swaggers when he walks. He's got thin lips and speaks in a clipped way, very distinct. He's well-dressed, black hair. He paid cash from a big roll. Cocky little devil, if you know what I mean.'

Angel scribbled fast. 'When was this?'

'Erm. About ten days ago.'

'Did you fit that CCTV our crime prevention people suggested?'

'Yes. But if you're thinking of looking at the tape, forget it. I only keep them for five days. He won't be on the ones I have.'

Angel growled.

'Sorry, Inspector.'

'Is there anything else you can tell me? Anything at all? Did he come in with anybody?'

'Yes, he did. A tall, lanky chap. He kept himself well back. I didn't see much of him.'

Angel screwed up his face. He was thinking hard and fast. 'Anything at all, Barney? Anything? Did he have a beard or a 'tache? Was he wearing a suit? A tie? Boots or shoes or trainers or Doc Martens? Was he smoking? Any tattoos?'

'No. Nothing comes to mind, Inspector. As I said, he kept himself well back.'

'Was he young or old?'

'Oh I'd say about thirty or so.'

'Thank you, Barney. If you think of anything, however small, get in touch, will you?'

'I'll be on the phone right away.'

'Good. Incidentally, you realise they might have been casing your shop?'

'I'm ready for 'em, if they try it.'

'You'd have to be careful. The little one is armed.'

'Don't worry about me, Inspector. I'd like to get the one that knocks girls around.'

'One more thing. I'd like to see one of those rings. Very urgently. I'd like to borrow one.'

'Certainly. Anything, Inspector. I'll send a lad up with it right away. I've got a personal interest in seeing them put away now.'

'Thanks, Barney.'

'Good luck, Inspector.' Angel put the phone back in its cradle.

There was a knock at the door.

'Come in.'

It was Ahmed Ahaz. He came in smiling, his white, even teeth shone in contrast with his smooth brown skin. 'You wanted me, sir?'

'Yes, lad. Have you got your notebook?'

'Yes, sir.'

He dived enthusiastically into his jacket pocket. He had trouble extracting it: the book was large and the pocket was small.

'I want you to feed this into the database of that computer you've got. Can you do that?'

'Oh yes, sir,' Ahmed's eyes shone with delight.

'I am looking for a male. White. Height range, five-foot-nine inches to six-foot-two inches. Age, twenty to thirty. Armed robbery. North of England. Petrol Station. Black knitted balaclava. Got it?'

'Yes, sir. How do you spell balaclava, sir?'

'Ask the computer. It's supposed to be smart, isn't it?' he growled. 'Now I want you to do the same again. A different man. White. Four-foot-ten inches to five-foot-five inches. Bottle-bottom glasses. Thin lips. And add, under jewellery, large finger ring. Carries a handgun. Idiosyncrasies, speaks sharply, also loudly. Got that? The two men worked together on this job. See if they have any associates. That should throw up something interesting.'

He wrote slowly, and his writing was neat and accurate. 'Yes, sir.'

'Let me know straightaway what you get, lad.'

Ahmed nodded and turned to the door. Angel added, 'And tell DS Crisp to come in here.'

'Yes, sir.' Ahmed was glad to have something different to do. He was fed up with filing and updating the computer database.

The phone rang.

'Angel?'

It was the woman on the station switchboard. 'There's your wife on the line, sir.'

'Put her through, Miss. Hello, love. Everything OK?'

'Mum's not so good, Michael. I am spending tonight in the hospital.'

'Oh? Is it as bad as that?'

'I don't know. Just being careful. Are you all right?'

'Very busy, otherwise fine. When are you coming home?'

'I don't know. Don't forget to pick up some milk on your way home. For the cats.'

'Oh? Yes. Right.'

'The money's running out. I'll have to go.' There was a click and the line went dead. He banged the phone down. 'Those two cats are more important than I am,' he muttered but he knew it wasn't so.

There was a knock at the door.

'Come in.'

It was DS Crisp. He looked across at Angel. 'Ah, yes,' the Inspector said and pointed to the chair. 'What have you got then?'

Crisp sat down, yanked out his notebook, coughed lightly into his closed fist and said, 'Well, sir, you know that Pettigrew and Shaw is a solicitors' practice on the corner of Bradford Road?'

Angel nodded impatiently. 'Course I do.'

'Well, I interviewed a man called Wexell, Peter Wexell. He's the boss — the senior partner — and he showed me round. It's a suite of offices on three floors. It's quite big.'

Angel screwed up his face in imaginary pain. 'I know all that,' he wailed. 'Now tell me something I don't know. What's the offence, if any?'

'Burglary, sir. Not the sort of place you'd expect to get burgled. Access was made through a downstairs rear window: a glass pane broken, window catch opened. It must have been dead easy. There is no burglar alarm, no nothing. They're only offices, but they are very posh for solicitors' offices. The reception area's a bit like a West End antique dealer's showroom. Furnished with old, and what looked to me, valuable furniture.'

Angel shook his head and pulled a face.

'Don't drag it out, lad. You're not auditioning for *Four Weddings and a Funeral*. What was taken?'

Crisp's jaw tightened, but he continued at a faster pace. 'There was a small private safe behind a picture — an Elliott 413. You know the sort of thing. Well, that was pulled out of the wall and opened on the office floor and the contents taken.'

'And what was in the safe?'

'Nothing of great value, I would have thought. Wexell said a videotape. A personal thing, he said. Film of his family and himself as a record of their development over the years.'

'Gripping stuff!' Angel sighed loudly, pulled a face and wiped his hand across his mouth. 'Anything else? Computers, drugs, cash, silver, gold, frankincense, myrrh?'

'No, sir. There was no money on the premises.'

'Well, who would want to steal a videotape?' Angel muttered.

'Perhaps they thought that it being in a safe meant that it must be something special. And they wanted some reward for the time and effort taken breaking into the place.'

'Maybe.'

'There was damage in Wexell's office; a big hole in the wall. Every other office had been entered. Most of them had been left unlocked and those that had been locked were forced with a jemmy.'

'Sounds like a job executed by Flopsy, Mopsy and Cottontail. Any witnesses? Anything from the night duty patrol?'

'I don't know, sir.'

Angel grunted his annoyance.

'I haven't had a chance to check up on that, sir.'

'Well, you'd better get on with it. Anything from forensic?'

'I haven't heard anything from them, either.'

Angel stared hard at him, 'Well, you'd better chase them, lad. You don't get anywhere in this world leaving them to come to you. He who shouts loudest gets most attention. See to it.'

There was a knock at the door. Crisp was glad of the interruption.

'Come in!'

It was Cadet Ahmed Ahaz. He was carrying a small bulging brown envelope. 'Young man has just handed this in at reception, sir. Said it was for you and very urgent.'

'Oh? Ta.' Angel grabbed at it eagerly and tore open the little package. 'That was quick. Good old Barney.'

Ahmed went out quickly and closed the door.

The envelope contained a thick, heavy yellow ring with a big red translucent stone in the centre with moulded letters around it. Angel read the letters aloud, 'St Luke's High. Iowa. 1988.' He put the ring on a finger and looked at it again. He sniffed and then said, 'Mmm. I see what he means.' He took the ring off and passed it over to DS Crisp.

'Right. Take that up to the hospital, now. See a patient admitted today, Jane Mulholland, tell her I sent you. Show her this ring. I want to know if this ring is similar to the one worn by the man who assaulted her at the petrol station this morning. See what her reaction is. Then phone me here and let me know. It's urgent. Off you go.'

Crisp stood up.

Angel said, 'And when you get back, check on the night book and the patrol and let me know what you find out. Then see if you can find out anything from a door-to-door. And chase up forensic. And keep me posted.'

'Right, sir.'

Angel watched him turn to the door and exit. He shook his head and leaned back in his chair; he was a disappointed man and he resented DS Crisp being pushed onto him at no notice so that the Chief could send Ron Gawber on a course. Crisp was slow and disinterested, he really didn't care whether he caught criminals or not. He was not a patch on DS Gawber, who would have had all the interviews completed, the night patrol consulted, a door-to-door executed, and would now be chasing Dr Mac to speed up any forensic evidence that might be forthcoming. When he returned from his profiling course in one week's time, he would return with a good report, of that Angel had no doubt. He'd likely be promoted to Inspector leaving Angel compelled to put fire in the belly of Sergeant Crisp, and that would be very hard work.

There was a knock at the door. 'Come in.'

It was Cadet Ahmed Ahaz again. He was carrying a bundle of papers. His face was long. 'I'm afraid there are no matches from the database, sir.'

'What? Nothing?'

Ahmed sucked in a deep breath. 'Nothing, sir.'

'Didn't that gold ring produce any names?'

'No, sir. There was nothing that fits *all* the criteria you gave me. I tried all the logical permutations of the same information I could think of, but I could not produce a shortlist.'

Angel sighed. 'Right, lad.'

Ahmed turned to leave.

'Oh Ahmed. Will you go to the corner shop and get me a bottle of milk?' He fumbled around in his trouser pocket. 'Here,' he said handing him a coin.

'They don't sell it in bottles now, sir. It's in different containers.'

'Oh?'

'And I'll need more than that,' he said, looking at the money. 'What sort of milk do you want, sir?'

Angel scowled, 'What do you mean?'

'Well, there's skimmed, semi-skimmed, organic, pasteurised, unpasteurised and full-cream. Then there's green top, yellow top, red top or gold top. You can get it in half-litre, one litre, four litre or six litre plastic containers, I think, sir.'

Angel's eyes popped out, his face went red. 'I just want some milk! White stuff! You know! From a cow! To put in a saucer! For cats! Milk lad! That's all!'

Ahmed's jaw dropped and his hands shook. 'You don't have to shout, sir. I just need to know what to bring. I would not like to bring you what you do not want.'

Angel closed his eyes momentarily, he breathed out loudly and then said, 'Those two cats will be the death of me.'

CHAPTER 3

Lola Spedding was a 24-year-old dark-haired beauty, and she knew it. Her hair was short and fitted round her doll-like face like the petals of a flower. Her skin was clear and white like a pot dog. She had a lot going for her. When she walked down the street, everybody turned and smiled. However, she didn't smile back much. She didn't think she had much to smile about; she was short on friends and short on family. She hated her mother because she was always telling her what to do. And Lola didn't like being told what to do; the nuns at school had always told her what to do. How she hated those nuns!

She'd had the marriage, and she'd got the divorce. She married when she was seventeen. He ran off after three months. She hated him running off. He married her for her money, but she didn't have any. And now Lola wanted what she had missed out on and more besides. And she intended getting it. She used to be a Daddy's girl. He had taught Lola all about investment, about stocks and shares. He'd taught her the principles of maximising returns on capital. That was his business and he knew his business. But that was *all* he taught her. She was pretty sick of Daddy now; he had left her mother when Lola was in her teens. Her mother brought her up on her own. Poor Lola. Poor mother!

She was dressed in a smoky black negligee, which showed off her lovely long legs. She was on the big bed smoking a cigarette, her smooth brown shoulders pressed against the pink plush bed head. She smoked too much, but she didn't care. She was wearing a pair of black horn rimmed spectacles and reading a hardback book called, *How to Get Rich Without Really Trying*.

She had been reading the book for an hour or so, when she heard the jingle of a bunch of keys followed by the noise of a key being pushed into the lock in the flat door. She tossed the book and spectacles across the bed, put the cigarette in the ashtray and swung her legs over the plush Chinese carpet.

The door opened and a smartly dressed man wearing the most expensive suit in Bromersley came in. He had a black moustache, black curly hair, crisp white shirt and a bit of handkerchief sticking out of his top pocket. He was carrying a box of chocolates and sporting a big smile. He stretched his arms out towards her. 'Darling!'

Lola stood up. She was an inch or so taller than he was. She angrily kicked off her shoes to make herself shorter and glared at him. 'Peter Wexell, where the hell have you been? Look at the time.'

He leaned over to kiss her. She turned away. Nevertheless he grabbed her by the arm, gave her a peck on the cheek, and then pushed the box into her hands. 'Chocolates.'

She switched a smile on and then off. 'Thank you.' She threw the box of chocolates on the bed and then launched into the attack. 'Do you realise I've been here on my own *all* day.'

'Well, Lola, darling. I know, I know. But I've a practice to run.' He opened his arms expansively and smiled toothily. 'I can't be here, and there as well, now can I?'

She softened. 'If I had money I could at least go out,' she sniffed. 'Meeting like this in this rat trap…It can't go on.'

'It's a nice rat trap, isn't it?' he said, still smiling and looking round. He unbuttoned his coat. 'It's costing me enough, Lola darling. But if you don't like this rat trap, I'll look for another rat trap.'

She turned towards the bed and then turned back. 'You know I don't mean *that*. I need money.'

Peter Wexell dug into his inside pocket and pulled out a small bundle of notes. He waved it in the air. 'Fifty pounds, Lola. How about that?'

She reached up for it. He held it away from her, and smiled. 'What do I get for it?'

She smiled then and, like a small child, wrapped her arms around his neck and gave him a smacking kiss on the cheek. As she did so, he lifted her up. A lock of her hair brushed against his cheek. Peter Wexell closed his eyes. She smelled like a garden in Paradise.

'Put me down. Put me down,' she protested giggling, and as he lowered her, she took the wad and stuffed it deftly under the pillow. She turned back excitedly and said, 'Come on. Come on. Did you bring it? Did you bring it?'

'Bring what?' He added showing an even set of white teeth and a twinkle in his eye.

'You know damned well what,' she replied refusing to be teased. She looked into his smiling, tanned face and held out her hand. Her anger had now vanished completely.

Like a magician, he produced something from inside his coat with a flourish. It was the *Financial Times*. '*Voila!*'

'Oh,' she whooped excitedly. She grabbed it from him and turned away.

'I want to see a price.' She opened the paper quickly at a page with long columns of figures on it. Sitting down on the edge of the bed she reached for the black-rimmed spectacles and ran her perfectly manicured fingers down a list of figures and across a column. A smile developed and her eyes lit up as she cried out, 'They're down!'

Peter Wexell stood in the middle of the bedroom, pleased to see her looking so happy. 'Is that good?'

'If you're buying it's good. And I'm looking to buy.' She threw the paper across the bed and took a pull at the still-smoking cigarette. She looked thoughtfully into the smoke as she slowly exhaled. and then across at him. 'It's no good, Peter, we can't go on like this. You'll have to think of a way.'

'*I'll* have to think of a way?' he repeated with a forced smile. He leaned over her, 'What am I supposed to do? Put her in a rocket and send her to outer space?'

'You could do something.'

'What?'

Her eyes flashed and the corners of her mouth turned down. 'Leave her,' she said intently. 'I can give you a lot better time than she ever could.'

'I'm sure you can, honeybunch. I'm sure you can. But you are forgetting one important fact. She owns the practice, and she holds the purse strings. If I leave her, I leave the money as well.'

'You're a qualified solicitor, aren't you? You could get a job with another practice couldn't you?'

'Not on these terms, sweetheart. Remember, I'm the senior partner. I'm the boss and I get the biggest screw and a percentage of the take. If I went anywhere else I'd have to start from scratch. Besides, I've worked damned hard to get Pettigrew and Shaw to the position it is in today.'

She took a short sharp suck at the cigarette then stubbed it out viciously in the ashtray. 'There *is* a way, Peter,' she said, deliberately and quietly. 'There has to be. I can't — I *won't* wait forever!' She looked straight at him. His eyes looked unsteady for a moment. Then he looked briefly at her and turned away.

'Maybe. I'll think of something,' he said quietly.

'I'm sure you'll think of *something,*' she said meaningfully. She crossed her legs and then rocked them both on the edge of the bed, while smiling and looking up at him. Suddenly she said, 'Come here.'

He took a step towards her. She reached out and pulled him down by his tie close to her face and then onto the bed. The smell of a thousand lavender buds reached his nostrils, and, gently holding his head in her arms, their lips met.

She gave him a kiss that made him forget all reason. Then she leaned back on the pillows and pulled him close to her bosom. His lips gently slid off her warm moist mouth down the curve of her neck.

* * *

The phone rang. Angel put the letter down and reached across the desk, 'Angel.'

It was DS Crisp. 'I'm ringing from the hospital, sir. About that ring you sent me to show the witness, Jane Mulholland.'

'Yes, Sergeant. What about it?'

'She confirms that the ring is just like the ring she saw on the man's hand, sir.'

'Right. That's great. Now come back here, give the ring to Cadet Ahaz and get onto that door-to-door before Joe Public forgets what day it is!'

'Right, sir.'

'And Sergeant,' he said quickly. 'How is the girl?'

'Not so bad. The Sister said she might be discharged tomorrow, sir.'

He nodded and smiled. 'Right.'

He banged a finger on the cradle to cancel the call, then dialled a number.

A voice answered, 'CID.'

'Send Cadet Ahaz in to me.'

'Right, sir.'

A few moments later Ahmed's beaming face peered round Angel's office door.

'Come in, lad. Come in. You're harder to find than the meat in a Cornish pasty!'

The smile left Ahmed, he gave a little sigh and shook his head. 'I came straightaway, sir,' he replied earnestly.

'I have instructed DS Crisp to give you a gent's finger ring. It has been identified as a ring similar to one worn by one of the two lumps that attacked that young girl at Bardsley

Service Station this afternoon. Get it photographed and copies circulated to all officers at this station, and Sheffield and Barnsley and Rotherham. You already have a description of the two men we are looking for, haven't you?'

Ahmed nodded.

'Print those descriptions with the photograph. Put it out as a "Wanted" poster. All right?'

'It's not much to go on, sir.'

Angel shook his head. 'I know it isn't, lad. I know it isn't. But at the moment, it's all we've got. Now off you go, chop-chop.'

'Yes, sir.' Ahmed turned to go.

Angel stood up. 'And if anyone wants me, I'll be at home,' he said leaning over to pick up the plastic bottle of milk that had been sitting on the windowsill.

He drove out of the police yard with the car windows all the way down to disperse the smell of the plastic trim and upholstery, which the powerful sun had caused to be more pungent than usual.

Detective Inspector Michael Angel lived in a modern semi-detached bungalow on a small estate on the edge of town. Despite the heavy five o'clock traffic through Bromersley, he was there in six minutes. He drove straight into the garage, lowered the up and over door and locked it. He let himself in through the side door and crossed the kitchen to the pantry to cancel the burglar alarm. He loosened his tie and unfastened the top button of his shirt, even the kitchen was hot. The sun had been beating down on it all afternoon and the house had been locked up since the morning making it unbearable. He opened a window and switched on the expelair. He put the plastic container of milk into the fridge and took out a bottle of German beer. Kicking off his shoes, he shuffled into the sitting room, switched on the television and flopped into a chair. A black cat with white markings appeared from nowhere. It cried and then climbed lazily onto his stomach.

'Hello, Sundance. Nice to have someone to welcome me. Don't worry. I've got some milk for you.' He tickled him behind the ear and the cat purred. Angel smiled, 'You're a softy, aren't you? Where's Butch?'

A second cat ambled into the room, he was ginger with a white stomach. He stopped after a few strides, lay down and scratched the side of his neck, then stood up and looked at Angel and Sundance.

'Come here then, Butch. Don't act daft.'

Angel stroked the two cats. They wound themselves around his stomach and lap and eventually settled, contented, next to each other while he drank the beer and watched the news on television. The cats' tails waved around occasionally jerking to one side and then back again until they came to rest along the crease of Angel's trousers. Their eyes soon closed and their bodies became still.

It was a warm, pleasant summer's evening. Angel finished the beer and put the glass on a coaster. The television was boring; there was nothing interesting in the news. The cats were utterly relaxed and motionless in a deep happy sleep, Angel looked at them fondly and smiled. 'You're just like two dead uns,' he muttered. Then he closed his eyes. The sound from the television became very faint, just a mumble, as Angel yawned, smiled, put his hands on his chest and fell asleep.

The telephone rang stridently, piercing into the silence.

Angel slowly became aware of the noise. Gradually he opened his eyes; the sitting room was dark and the moon was shining in through the window. He wondered how long it had been ringing. He fumbled around for the lamp on the table beside him and switched it on. The sitting room burst into bright illumination showing off the new beige carpet and floral patterned wallpaper, he screwed up his eyes. The sudden movement of his legs sent the two cats scurrying. He reached out for the telephone, hoping it was his wife to tell him how her mother was progressing.

'Hello,' he muttered into the mouthpiece while squinting at the clock on the mantelpiece; it was 11.45. He found the remote control and switched the television off.

'Is that Michael Angel?'

He recognised the voice of Superintendent Harker. 'Yes, John. What's up?'

'A report of a body being found in Jubilee Park has come in. I've sent a PC down. He's made contact with a witness. I've got Mac attending and Scenes of Crime are on their way. I want you to deal with it, Mike. Everybody else is busy. And I've managed to get hold of Crisp.'

'Right.'

'I've told them to rendezvous with you at the bandstand.'

'Right, John.'

The phone went dead.

Angel pushed the footstool away and got to his feet. He realised he hadn't had his tea, nor fed the cats. He swallowed, his tongue felt like a piece of an old lag's bicycle saddle. He made his way to the kitchen and tripped over his shoes; he put them on in front of the sink and rinsed his hands and face and had a slurp of water. He looked round for the cats, but they had disappeared. He looked in the mirror over the sink, and blinked at the brightness of the reflection and then pulled a face, 'What a mess!' He set the alarm, switched off the lights, locked the door and went out to the garage, fastening his top shirt button and pulling his tie up on the way.

Although nearly midnight, it was still warm and the moonlight shone brightly in a clear summer's sky as he drove through the big black iron gates of Jubilee Park and along the narrow track to the bandstand. He knew exactly where it was; his mother had taken him to hear bands play on Sunday afternoons when he was a boy. Not many bands had played there recently but at one time it had been a regular place of entertainment. The bandstand was in a flat open turf covered area of the park quite close to a rear pedestrian exit, away from the trees and bushes.

There was already a gathering of police service vehicles. He could see several people standing together, illuminated in the vehicles' sidelights. There was Dr Mac's car, the mortuary van, Scenes of Crime van, and a Panda car. A hospital ambulance was driving away, rocking dangerously as it crossed over the uneven grass and onto the narrow track. Angel parked where the ambulance had been.

Leaping out of the car and flashing a torch, he called across to a PC, 'Where's that ambulance going to?'

'It's empty. He couldn't do anything for the victim, sir. He's going back. Dr Mac said it was all right.'

Angel straightened his tie and passed a hand through his hair. 'Right. Where is Dr Mac?'

The young PC left the small huddle of people he was with and came up to the Inspector. He pointed to the nearest clump of bushes. 'He's over there, that's where the body is, sir.'

'Have you got a witness?'

'That's me,' a man from the dark stepped forward.

'And me,' a young woman added, clasping the man's hand.

Angel flashed the torch briefly into the faces of a man and a woman in their twenties. He was a pleasant clean-shaven young man, nicely spoken and well dressed in a suit, shirt and tie. She was in a brightly coloured flowered dress and cardigan.

'Good. I'm Inspector Angel. Can you tell me what you saw?'

'Well, Inspector,' the man began, 'we were walking up here for what we thought would be a quiet, pleasant stroll to cool off after a hot day.'

'I know what you mean. What did you see?'

'When we reached the top of this rise, we stopped by that bush to look at the lights of the town. You can see the town hall and the hospital and St Barnabas' Church. They're all lit up. As we were picking places out, we heard the footsteps and breathing of a man rushing quickly past and down the track towards the main entrance. He was carrying what we now know to be a dead woman over his shoulder like a roll of carpet. He didn't see us at first. I called out, 'Good night,' so as not to startle him. He stopped, turned to look at us, hesitated, and then threw the — er —dead body at us. It pushed us over.'

'Are you hurt?' Angel asked.

'No,' the young lady said.

'She screamed,' he said accusingly.

'I did,' she confirmed. 'I was scared.'

'Anyway, he turned back and ran off in the direction he had come from,' the young man continued. 'Well, of course, by then we could see what it was and that she was dead. I checked that my girlfriend was all right and then ran after him up there towards the back entrance. He had a good start on me, but it isn't far. I made good time and I followed him to a door in the wall that leads to the gardens of two houses. I opened the door and just stood there and looked and listened for a while, but he had disappeared. I don't know where he went from there. I didn't fancy going in, and I didn't want to be accused of trespassing.'

'You didn't see or hear him enter either of the two houses?'

'No. It's pitch black in those gardens. The high garden walls and the houses themselves keep the moonlight out. I didn't hear anything. It was as quiet as a grave.'

'But do you think he went into either of those two houses?'

'Well, I *think* so. But if he did, I wouldn't know which one. He may have gone around the side of either house through the back garden and away. But I didn't hear or see anything after I opened the door in the wall.'

'Which suggests he had by that time entered one of the houses, would you say?'

'Well, er — yes.'

Angel nodded approvingly. 'What was the man like? Can you describe him?'

The young man scratched his ear. 'Average, I would say, Inspector. My height. Say five foot ten. Average weight.'

'Was he fat or thin?'

'Average.'

'What was he wearing?'

'I couldn't see in this light. Something dark. A dark suit or coat.'

'Did he have a 'tache or a beard or anything? Was he bald or was he wearing a hat?'

'No, I don't think so. He wasn't wearing a hat.'

'Would you recognise him in a good light?'

'No, I don't think I would be able to.'

Detective Sergeant Crisp came bustling up to the Inspector. 'Sir.'

Angel turned and glared at him. 'About time!' He turned back to the young man.

'Hang on a minute, sir.'

'Come here,' Angel snapped and he walked up the field with Crisp following until they were out of earshot. 'Where the hell have you been? I've been here on my own a good ten minutes. The Super said he had let *you* know before he phoned *me*!'

Crisp groaned, 'I was in bed. I had to get dressed.'

'Look, lad. This is no good. You're about as much use to me as a one-legged man in an arse kicking contest. There's been a murder, and for once in our lives we've got a live, articulate, human witness who's seen a man actually carrying the dead body. Now if we can get an ID, this case would be a walkover. But we've got to jump on it now and quick! I want you to get a full written statement from that man and woman of all they've seen; a description of the man they saw; their names and addresses; and anything else that might be useful. All right?'

'Yes, sir.'

'Now I'm going to knock on the doors of those two houses on the edge of the park to see what I can find out. There's no time to waste, so crack on with it.'

Angel turned away and walked quickly up towards the back exit of the park. He reached a farm style gate and flashed his torch at it. It was closed, but when open would just about give enough room for a tractor and trailer to pass through. Alongside was the beginning of an alley four feet wide and approximately two hundred yards long. The low wall on the left side of the long ginnel marked the perimeter of Jubilee Park, and the wall on the right was eight feet high and led directly down the outside of the grounds and gardens of Sycamore Grove to a main road that connected Sheffield to Bromersley town centre. A freshly painted door was built into the nearest end of the high wall. Overhanging large and thickly leaved trees blocked out the moon and kept the area dark. He flashed his torch up to the neat, white painted writing on the door. It read, 'Nos 1 and 2 Sycamore Grove only'. He lifted the latch in the green painted door and pushed it. It opened easily. He shone the torch on the ground; there were three wide stone steps down to a gravel path. He entered and closed the door behind him. He could see the outline of the two identical tall detached houses with plain neat lawns in front of each and a low laurel hedge dividing the garden area into two. Even by torchlight, Angel could see the houses appeared to be well maintained, early Georgian buildings with cream stucco walls, stone pillared entrances and wide steps leading up to big dark painted front doors and window frames. No lights shone from the windows. No one appeared to be around at that late hour. It was still, quiet and dark.

Angel sighed. He made his way along the gravel path, noting the unavoidable noise his shoes made. He went up the steps to the nearest door and pressed the bell. He waited. He shone his torch on his wristwatch, it was 12.15 a.m. He pressed the bell again and kept his finger on the button for half a minute. Then he turned and came back down the stone steps and walked around the side of the house looking for the back door. This route took him between the house wall and an outbuilding. He descended a dozen steps and walked on a few paces. The torch picked out an iron grate at ground level in the wall of the house. It was set on a hinge and was wide open. He shone the light through the opening onto a chute. It was for the delivery of coal or coke to the cellar. No one could have squeezed through it. Strange that it was open, someone could have tripped up over it. He lifted it and closed it, it clattered loudly in the still night.

He heard a woman's voice cry out, 'Who's there?'

It was behind him. He turned round. 'It's the police, Madam. The police,' he called as he strode up the steps and round the corner to the front door. It was open wide and the silhouettes of a man and a woman wearing dressing gowns were standing framed in the doorway. White light streamed out behind them onto the steps and the garden.

'The police, did you say? Whatever do you want at this time of night? What's wrong?' The woman said sternly.

'Ah, yes.' Angel said as he reached the top step panting and with the hall light in his eyes. 'There's been an incident in the park, Madam. I wondered if you had heard or seen anything in the past few minutes.'

'An incident? What sort of an incident? No we've heard nothing have we, Tal,' she said looking at the big man at the side of her who was yawning and scratching his head.

'Are you sure? Is there any way a man could have gained access to your house. He could be dangerous. A witness has said he saw a man come this way?'

The woman's jaw dropped. 'Dangerous? What sort of dangerous?' She turned to her husband. 'Oh. Now then, Tal, nip down and check the back door. And the kitchen window.'

The man who was in his fifties protested. 'It's all right. I locked it earlier on.' Then he turned and went out of sight, shaking his head and scratching his stomach.

'Well, make sure,' she called after him. Then she turned to the Inspector and taking a step backward said, 'Do you want to come in? What's your name? What sort of an incident, did you say?'

'No. I won't come in, thank you. If you're sure you haven't had an intruder, I must press on.' He pulled a business card from out of his inside pocket. 'Inspector Angel. And your name?'

'Lowbridge, Mrs Lowbridge.'

'Thank you, Mrs Lowbridge. I'll be in touch tomorrow.' He turned to go, and then he turned back, 'Do you happen to know if there is anybody in next door?'

'As far as I know, they are not away, Inspector. I don't know them very well.'

The man returned and shuffled into the light behind his wife. 'I told you it would be all right,' he moaned.

'Do you know the name, Mrs Lowbridge?'

'Oh yes. He's the boss of the solicitors, Pettigrew and Shaw, you know. He lives there with his wife. He's called Peter Wexell.'

CHAPTER 4

The residents at number 2 Sycamore Grove were easier to rouse. Peter Wexell came to the door in a Chinese patterned silk dressing gown over light blue cotton pyjamas, appropriate for a warm night.

'No, Inspector. We've heard nothing, and I'm sure we would have heard if anyone had tried to break in. My wife is a very light sleeper.'

'Well, perhaps you'll have a look round, sir, before you return to your bed. A person was reported to have entered your garden from the park. Make sure everything is locked and secure. I'll have a quick look round out here before I go.'

'Certainly will, Inspector. Dammit, I'm getting used to break-ins. My own office was broken into last night. This town has become a haven for thieves.'

'Oh, we hope to be finding the person who broke into your office, sir. Enquiries are proceeding as we speak.'

'I'm glad to hear it.'

Angel nodded. 'Well, I'll say goodnight, sir.'

'Goodnight, Inspector.'

Angel came down the steps as the door closed. He turned left and made his way along the gravel path to the side of the house and down the steps towards the back door.

Numbers one and two Sycamore Grove were carbon copies of each other. He descended the steps and walked on a pace or two. He flashed the torch low down on the wall in the same place where he had discovered the open coal chute on the house next door. There was a grate there as he expected. It was closed. He leaned down, lifted it open and shone the torch onto the chute. It was exactly the same as next door: simply a chute for the delivery of coal into the cellar. The house was probably heated by means other than coal these days, but coal was inexpensive in the twentieth century. He closed it, and had a lingering look round the back door area and the long garden. Everything was quiet. There appeared to be nothing out of the ordinary. He shook his head and then walked up the stone steps, across the noisy gravel path, through the door in the wall and back into Jubilee Park.

The area by the bandstand was a blaze of white artificial light and activity. Two arc lights on tripods had been set up and were focussed on the grass. The grey haired, Scottish pathologist was on his knees with two assistants in whites pawing the ground. A uniformed policeman was tying the ends of the 'Do Not Cross' tape to iron stakes screwed into the turf. Two men were loading the body covered by a sheet on a stretcher into the mortuary van. DS Crisp was chatting with the young couple who had disturbed the man carrying the body.

Angel lifted the white and blue tape and walked over to the pathologist as he closed his bag and was rising to his feet.

'Hello Mac. What have you got?'

The Scotsman peeled off the rubber gloves, pulled back the white plastic head cover and wiped his forehead with a piece of pink lint. 'Phew. It's you Mike.'

'What's the matter? Got a sweat on?'

The doctor nodded. 'Aye. It's hot under this plastic.'

Angel smiled at him. 'It's all that formaldehyde and alcohol in your bloodstream. You're running on too strong a mixture.'

Mac ignored the comment. 'What a time to find a corpse. Why can they no find a body at a reasonable time?'

'Oh dear me, do stop moaning. That's all I hear. Moaning, moaning, moaning. You've your pension coming up soon. You'll know how to moan then!'

'It can't come too soon, I can tell ye.'

'Then you'll be at home all day with your wife. Think of that. How are you going to spend your time? It's well known you two don't get on. The only thing you've got in common is that you got married on the same day.'

Dr Mac smiled wryly, 'You've been reading the jokes in those Co-op Christmas crackers again?'

Angel wrinkled up his nose. 'Got to say something to keep cheerful.'

The doctor pulled down the zip from his chin down his front and opened up the overall. 'Och. I heard your wife's mother's not so well. Sorry to hear that.'

'How did you know that? Yes she's away in Derby so she can keep an eye on her in hospital. She doesn't want to let any haggis-eating doctors give her the wrong jollop while they are in their cups.'

'You're still sniping, Mike.'

'Aye, I know. I can't break the habit. You're such an easy target.'

'Don't you want to know about the corpse?'

'Of course. Whenever you're ready,' he said, pulling out his notebook and clicking his pen.

'Well, it's a woman about forty or fifty. Brown hair. Brown eyes. Slim build. Weight around a hundred pounds. Can't tell what she died of yet. No bruises or contusions detected in situ.'

'Time of death?'

'Mmm. Well, she's stiff. And she's cold. In this weather, I'd say about twenty-four hours. That's only a guess. It depends where she's been kept.'

'Any ID?'

'I don't know. Tell you tomorrow.'

'Today, I hope. Handbag, purse? Anything in her pockets?'

'No. No. Look at the time. I want to get to bed.'

'We *all* want to get to bed, Mac.'

* * *

There was a knock on the door.

'Come in,' Angel called.

It was DS Crisp. 'You wanted me, sir?'

'Aye. Shut the door. Sit down. There were some outstanding matters from that inquiry into the robbery at Pettigrew and Shaw's. What have you done about them?'

'I did them first thing this morning.'

Angel looked up, his mouth open. 'Oh?'

'I did the door-to-door. There wasn't much to do because the buildings around Pettigrew and Shaw's are mostly offices and shops, which, of course, weren't occupied when the break-in occurred. There are three flats above the East Riding Building Society. I have spoken to the occupants: nobody saw or heard anything.'

'Oh.'

'The next thing was the night shift. I looked in the book and there's nothing. Sergeant Yates was on duty that night. I saw him this morning before he went off. I asked him if there were any verbal reports about any disturbance in or near Pettigrew and Shaw's offices. He said that nothing was reported.'

'Oh.'

'And lastly, forensic. I phoned Dr Mac's office. The report's in transit but his assistant told me that one of the intruders was probably wearing navy blue woollen gloves. There were fibres caught on a screw on a doorknob. The fresh prints they found on vital places, safe dial, handles and so on were smudged knitted wool marks. That's it, sir.'

Angel blinked. 'Oh? Navy blue woollen gloves?' His pulse raced up to 180. He reached over to the phone and dialled a number.

A voice answered, 'Pathology.'

49

'Dr Mac, please. Inspector Angel.'

'Hold on.'

'Hello. Mac here.'

'Mac, you found fibres of blue woollen gloves on a doorknob at Pettigrew and Shaws, didn't you?'

'Yes.'

'Did you find any similar fibres at Bardsley Service Station?'

'No, Mike, we didn't.'

Angel looked down. He breathed a long sigh, his pulse stopped racing. 'Thanks, Mac.'

'Sorry, Mike.'

He returned the phone to its cradle and looked across at Crisp. 'No fibres at the scene. But the general description of the men and the gloves they were wearing all fit.'

The phone rang before he could take his hand off the handset.

'Angel,' he grunted down the phone.

The girl on the station switchboard said,

'There's a man who says his name is Barney to speak to you, sir. Says it's very urgent.'

He sat up in the chair, 'Put him through.'

'Is that Inspector Angel?'

'Yes Barney.'

He spoke very quickly as if he was short of breath. 'I spotted them looking in my shop window five minutes ago. I left my shop in charge of the boy and followed them back to a car parked in Sheffield Road car park. They got in it and drove off. I followed them in my car, which was parked near theirs. They went on Sheffield Road, then branched off onto Sebastopol Terrace and pulled up by the old bakehouse there. They got out and went the back way into a house on Sheffield Road. If you are quick, they might still be there.'

'What colour is the car?'

'Grey. A silver grey Volkswagen Passat.'

'Did you get the licence number?'

'No, it was covered in mud. But you can't mistake it. It's a big, powerful job.'

'Right, Barney.'

He slammed the handset down. 'Come on,' he called across at Crisp.

They ran up the olive green corridor, through the security door and then through the main door. 'Do you know where Sebastopol Terrace is, lad?'

'Yes, sir.'

'Take your car. Make for there. Come down it from the far end. I'll speak to you on your mobile.'

'Right.'

They each made for their cars, negotiated themselves out of the yard through the parked police cars and sundry other traffic, then round the island and down Bromersley High Street.

Angel was at the bottom end of Sebastopol Terrace first. It was a straight street. He picked his way over the potholes, passing a dozen or so of the endless row of 1920s terraced redbrick houses on his right, and the end walls of outbuildings or boundary walls of the back gardens of the Victorian houses on his left. He stared straight ahead, looking for the grey car. It was there sure enough. That familiar regular thumping in the chest started, and he felt heat rising from his solar plexus to his face. The car was 200 yards away. Parked half on the pavement and half off. As soon as he saw it he stopped, pulled on the handbrake, dug out his mobile from the bottom of his pocket and dialled a number.

Eventually Crisp answered. 'Hello.'

'Where are you?'

'Just turning into Sebastopol, sir.'

'Ah yes. I can see you. Stop there, where you are. It's near enough. I'll send for back-up.'

Ten minutes later, two unmarked police cars arrived. Angel got out of his car and went round to them.

Each car contained four burly uniformed men, one of whom was armed and appropriately clad in navy blue flak jacket and body armour. The armed man was holding a rifle, its butt resting on the floor and the muzzle covered with a police issue flat cap to help conceal it. There was also a yellow battering ram on the car floor under the men's feet. Angel instructed one car to park behind him. He despatched the other to join Crisp via the long way round.

Then Barney arrived. He was a small, active young man in his thirties, with fair hair and an open face. He was wearing a blue short-sleeved shirt and denims.

Angel put his head through the window into the police car. 'Look here. This is Barney. He's the only one who can identify these two villains, so look after him.'

'He'll be all right with us, sir.'

Barney smiled at them weakly. He looked flushed and awkward among all the policemen.

Angel added, 'Aye. I hope so.' Then he withdrew his head, turned to Barney on the pavement and said, 'Right lad, which house is it?'

'It's number seventy-one, Mr Angel. It's the one with the little bakehouse in the garden.'

'Right, Barney. Wait here.' Then he called to the men in the car. 'I'm going up to rekky the place.'

Angel set off determinedly on the broken and uneven flagstoned pavement of Sebastopol Terrace and noted the worn condition of the road. Little wonder there was hardly any motor traffic. A woman with a pram passed him, barely giving him a glance. Two small girls in summer dresses were bouncing a ball against a house wall and screaming excitedly in the bright sunshine. Otherwise the street was quiet.

Angel checked off the numbers of the Victorian houses on his left. Some were marked on the tumbledown wooden gates, which were in need of a coat of paint; some were numbered in chalk on the wall; some weren't numbered at all. He saw the number sixty-seven on a gate and he slowed down. The big grey Volkswagen was close by. It was parked outside a small brick building with big windows and a blue-tiled roof. Its door opened onto the pavement and a sign above it read: 'Sebastopol Bakery'. There were no signs of any activity in the building; it looked deserted. A gate along the side of the bakehouse was painted green and had the figure seventy-one screwed onto the middle of it. Glancing over the gate, Angel saw an overfull grey dustbin with its lid on the pathway. Empty pizza boxes were visible at the top of the open bin and several more were strewn messily on the path, which led to the back door of the big old house. He sniffed and continued towards Crisp and the other car of policemen at the top of the street.

As the DS saw him approaching, he got out of his car and walked towards him, 'Are we going in now, sir?'

'No.'

'They might come out at any minute.'

'I know, lad. I know,' Angel said tetchily. 'And one of them is armed. I don't know their style and we're not going to take unnecessary risks. We don't even know if they're still there. And I don't want any of you to get hurt. More importantly, *I* don't want to get hurt!'

He pulled a handkerchief out of his pocket and wiped his forehead. He breathed out a long sigh. 'Get the station on the line.'

Crisp leaned into the car and grabbed his mobile phone. 'Do we need reinforcements?'

'Yes,' Angel snapped.

Crisp's jaw dropped and his eyes flashed. 'There's *ten* of us, sir!'

'I know. I know. I want one more. I want Cadet Ahaz.'

'Ahmed?' he said incredulously as he dialled the number. 'He won't be much use in a punch up,' he muttered.

Angel glared at him.

'It's ringing out, sir.'

The Inspector snatched the phone from him. A woman's voice answered. 'Bromersley Police.'

'I want CID very urgently,' he snapped. He turned away and walked up the road out of earshot. He spoke animatedly on the telephone for a minute, then came back and, without a word, handed the mobile back to the sergeant. Sticking his hands in his pockets, he began to traverse a fifteen-yard length of the pavement. Crisp could hear him turning coins over in his trouser pocket. After a minute or two, Angel rubbed his jaw with his hand and came up to Crisp. 'Where is the nearest pizza place?'

Crisp stared at him, 'Pizza place?'

Angel opened his wallet and pulled out a ten pound note. 'Well, fetch two, quick. And make sure they're piping hot!' He pointed down the street. 'I'm going back down the road to my car. Bring them to me down there.'

* * *

It was only twelve minutes later when another unmarked police car dropped an untidily dressed Cadet Ahmed Ahaz at the bottom of Sebastopol Terrace. He was in scruffy denims, trainers and a baseball cap turned round the wrong way.

Ahmed looked self-conscious as he got out of the car. He kept his eyes down looking at the pavement, anxious not to catch the eyes of the other policemen.

Angel greeted him breezily and looked the young man up and down. 'That's great. Just what I wanted, lad. Make a good job of this and I'll have a word with my friend Steven Spielberg. He'll make you an Oscar winner!'

Ahmed still looked down at his feet. 'I didn't want to get dressed up, sir. I don't want to be an actor, sir. All I want to be is a policeman.'

'Aye, lad. And so you will be, and a damned good one at that. In this business you've got to be adaptable. Sometimes you've got to be all things to all people.' Angel turned round and went over to the car parked behind him with the four policemen sweltering in the heat.

'Are we going in, sir?' One of them asked.

'I'm just waiting for DS Crisp to get back.'

'He's here now, sir.'

Barney came up to the Inspector. 'I ought to be getting back to my shop, Mr Angel.'

'Yes, Barney. We're going in now.'

Crisp jumped out of his car with two boxes of hot pizzas in his hands. 'You didn't say what kind you wanted. I don't like olives, so I got both without olives.'

Angel took the pizzas from the Sergeant and gave them to Ahmed. 'Ta. There you are, lad.'

Ahmed looked at the boxes and then back at Angel.

'You'll be all right, lad. When the time comes, just do what I told you. The lads, DS Crisp and I will only be inches away from you.'

Ahmed's big eyes opened even wider. 'I'm not afraid of being hurt, sir. I'm just afraid of getting it wrong!'

'You won't, lad. You won't. Don't worry.' Angel said as he put his arm round the young man's bony back and squeezed his shoulder.

He then turned to Crisp and with a jerk of the head summoned him over. They walked a little way up the street while he explained the plan in detail. Crisp nodded.

Angel phoned the police driver in the car at the other end of the street and said, 'Right lads. Off you go. Let me know when you're in position.'

'Right, sir,' a voice replied enthusiastically, glad to be on the move. The car made a three point turn and disappeared round the top of the street.

Angel turned to the other car and stuck his head through the window, 'Right lads. Very quietly now. You know what to do. At least one of them is known to have a handgun. I don't want anybody hurt.'

The policemen got out of the hot car into the sunlight. The armed man put on a black helmet with the word, 'Police' stencilled across it and pulled the strap under his chin. Angel assembled the procession in order: he led, followed by Crisp, the man with the rifle, Barney, Ahmed, and the three PCs brought up the rear.

From the other side of the road a man in shorts and a sun hat carrying plastic carrier bags of shopping stopped. He stared at the gathering in wonderment for a few seconds and then walked on, looking back at them occasionally.

Angel's mobile phone rang out.

'Yep? Right.' He switched off the phone and dropped it into his pocket. 'That's it, lads. They're in position. Let's go.'

The assembly made their way up the street to the bakehouse. Angel opened the back gate of number seventy-one and then stealthily led the way up the path to the door. Ahmed went up to the door holding the two pizza boxes in front of him. Crisp stood at one side of the door; Angel at the other; the policemen and Barney behind Angel. They pressed themselves hard against the house wall.

Angel looked at Ahmed with raised eyebrows. Ahmed licked his lips, swallowed and then nodded.

Angel rapped hard on the door and then pulled back to the wall. He could feel his heart thumping and hear the drumming in his ears. The skin on the back of his hands tightened. They all froze and waited. Nothing happened, the house was as still as a grave.

Angel waited a few seconds then knocked again. Silence. He pulled a face. Supposing this Christmas party had been set up for nothing? He looked across at Crisp, the young man stared back, his jaw set square.

Ahmed's perspiring nose twitched as a fly came buzzing round the top of the pizza boxes. He waved a hand to chase it away and then tugged at the collar of his t-shirt to loosen it.

Suddenly there was a noise from behind the locked door.

'Who is it?' a muffled voice called.

Angel looked at Ahmed and nodded.

Ahmed began, 'Did you...' He broke off. Angel held his breath.

Ahmed coughed and then said loudly, 'Did you order two pizzas?'

'What?' the voice came through the door.

'Did you order two pizzas?' Ahmed said louder. 'They're paid for.'

There was a pause, and then the voice said, 'Just a minute.' There was a rattle of keys and the door opened three inches.

The voice speaking through the gap said, 'Did you say they were paid for?'

'Yes.'

The door closed. A chain rattled and the door opened wide. A pair of long, white arms reached out for the boxes. Ahmed deliberately stepped backwards to evade them. The hands came out further and with the speed of light, Angel grabbed one hand and Crisp took the other and the man was yanked into the backyard like a pebble in a catapult. Then, using the momentum, they brought his wrists together behind his back and upwards and Crisp had handcuffs on him before he had time to say 'Lily Savage'. At the same moment, the other policemen charged through the open door into the house.

The owner of the hands was a tall, thin young man. He was wearing a blue shirt with the sleeves turned up, navy-blue suit trousers and black leather shoes. His long hair fell about his sloppy red mouth and white face as he yelled alternately at Angel and then at Crisp, "Ere, what's all this? Leggo! Leggo! Leggo!"

Angel put his hand on the young man's shoulder, squeezed it hard and said quietly, 'We're police officers. Settle down, lad. Settle down. And you won't get hurt.'

'Leggo! Leggo! You can't do this to me!'

Angel looked at Barney and said, 'Is this one of them?'

Barney nodded.

He turned to Crisp. 'Search him, caution him and book him.'

'Yes, sir.' Crisp pushed the protesting young man up the garden path.

Angel turned to Ahmed. He pointed to the pizza boxes and said, 'Get rid of them and assist DS Crisp with the prisoner back to the station.'

Ahmed turned to Barney holding out the pizzas. Barney shrugged and turned away. Then to the Inspector, Ahmed called, 'What shall I do with these, sir?'

Angel turned back from the house doorway, his face red, 'Eat 'em, lad. Eat 'em!' he bellowed. Then he turned and hurried into the building. He went straight through the small kitchen along the hallway to the front door and unlocked the door to admit the policemen who had been waiting at the front of the house. They rushed in and clattered their way up the uncarpeted steps facing them to the bedrooms. The others were looking in the living room and dining room.

There was very little furniture in the house. The living room had two bunk-type beds, two chairs, a table and a television and video and the upstairs was unfurnished.

Several minutes later the squad grouped in the hall round the Inspector to report the house was safe and unoccupied. All the fitted cupboards, fitted wardrobes and the like had been opened; a man had searched the loft with a torch; and others had explored the cellar. Also all windows had been checked and it was established that every one had been locked from the inside.

'Well thanks lads. I expected to find two of them, but there you are.' He checked his watch. 'The time is 17.30 hours. Stand down and return to the station.'

The squad made their exits from the front and the back doors and Angel found himself alone in the hall. After the surge of activity, the house was suddenly very quiet. He went to the front door, turned the key and put it in his pocket and made for the back door. On his way through the hall, he slapped his pockets searching for cigarettes, and then remembered he had given up smoking earlier in the year. It was at times like this he would have enjoyed a drag. He wiped his forehead with a handkerchief and as he reached the door, he saw Barney standing on the back step.

'Have you done with me, Mr Angel?'

'Oh. I'm sorry, lad. I'd forgotten about you.'

'I need to be getting back to the shop.'

'Course you do. There's no sign of the other one. He must have slipped out before we got here. Anyway, you get off. If you'll pop into the station sometime to make a statement — tomorrow will be soon enough?'

'Righto.'

'Thanks lad. Bye for now.'

Angel closed the back door, locked it and returned to the living room. He went across the bare-boarded floor to the television set in the corner with the video player beneath it. On the floor beside the television were three videotapes in cardboard sleeves. He wondered if one of them was the security videotape taken from Bardsley Service Station.

CHAPTER 5

'Come in, lad. Sit down.' Angel nodded towards the chair at the side of his desk. 'You're harder to find than The Lost Chord.'

DS Crisp shook his head. 'I was only in the CID office, sir.'

'Yes lad,' he said dismissively and leaned forward across the desk, looking him straight in the eye. 'Now before anybody upstairs starts asking me whether I have a search warrant or not, I want you to go over that house like an alcoholic looking for a wine gum. I don't want you to miss anything. As well as the usual: drugs, arms, balaclavas, gloves, jelly, possible stolen goods and so on, I'm anxious to find the videotape taken in that raid on Bardsley Service Station. That is vital. I think that lump in the cell is one of the two candidates for the job.'

Crisp nodded.

'Start by informing Dr Mac at Forensic. And then get that car taken in. We might get a lead from the DVLA Swansea, if those plates are genuine. We'll get fingerprints if nothing else. And I want a guard posted on that house immediately. The other villain might return. Now you've got your work cut out. And I want you to move fast before 'im upstairs starts asking me about search warrants. Do you get my drift, lad?'

'Yes sir.' Crisp stood up to leave.

Angel waved him to sit down. 'Have you got that lad properly banged up?'

'Yes, sir.'

'And what's his name?'

'He won't give it. He won't talk.'

'Eh? Nothing in his pockets to give us a lead?'

'Nothing.'

Angel pursed his lips and eased back in the chair, thoughtfully. 'Have we got a professional here? A career criminal?'

'Hard to say, sir.'

The Inspector muttered something indistinguishable, looked up at the ceiling for a few seconds then across the desk at the Sergeant. 'Did you fingerprint him yourself?'

'Yes, sir.'

'Did you get the impression he'd been printed before? They usually know how to roll their fingers if they've been done before, you know.'

Crisp shook his head. 'No, sir. It seemed as if this was his first time.'

Angel raised his eyebrows, 'And yet he knows to keep his mouth shut? Mmm.' He made a decision, 'Right. Don't talk to him. Don't let *anybody* talk to him. And especially don't ask him any questions. Tell them in the custody suite what I say. We'll try *that* for twenty-four hours.' Angel drummed his fingers on the desk. 'He's had a cup of tea?'

'Yes, sir.'

'I'll have a go at him tomorrow.'

'Right, sir,' Crisp said, standing. 'I'll crack on.'

Angel nodded thoughtfully. 'Aye. Right, lad.'

Crisp went out and closed the door.

Angel gathered together the papers on his desk and put them in a drawer. He glanced outside at the brilliant sunshine and noticed a black cat high up on a decorative ledge on the Georgian stone house next door. It had one leg in the air and was industriously washing itself with its tongue. It was making a thorough job of it, when suddenly something apparently caught its eye and it stopped. It pulled the leg down, turned and stood up arching its back. A ginger cat had appeared on the ledge from around the corner. The two cats stood, motionless, staring at each other. The stone ridge was about six inches wide, three storeys high. Below them was the hard concrete drive to the police garage. If they only stared at each other and didn't get into a fight they would be safe. But so high up the building, if they fell, it could very well result in two dead cats.

Angel watched for another minute, curious and concerned for their welfare, and then chastised himself for wasting time. There was nothing he could do about it and cats had a habit of surviving short odds. He must press on. He turned away, and strode out of the office down the olive green corridor to a door at the end. On the brown door was painted in cream letters: 'Superintendent J. Harker.' Angel knocked.

'Come in.'

He pushed open the door, 'Have you a minute, John?'

A big man with a long face topped with white close-cropped hair looked up and smiled. 'It's you, Mike. Come on in. Sit down.'

Angel took the chair by the desk.

'Trouble?'

'No. No,' he lied.

'Is it that park murder? How are you getting on with it?' he said, closing a file of papers and putting it on the corner of the desk.

'Well, we've not got anywhere yet,' he said, pulling a face.

'Is that what you want to see me about?'

'Yes. In a way. I suppose. I am a bit bothered about this embargo on searches.'

The Superintendent pulled his chin into his chest and licked his lips. 'Well, er Mike, er, it's not exactly an embargo.'

Angel sniffed, 'Well, you know what I mean.'

Harker put his elbows on the desk and steepled his fingers for a moment. Then he unnecessarily straightened the blotter on his desk and returned his hands to their former position. 'Well, there's no problem is there?'

'Not for me, no. I just wanted to clarify the situation.'

'By all means, Mike. What's troubling you?'

'Well, the suspect was carrying a dead body through the park when he was disturbed by a courting couple. They startled him, he threw the body at them and ran like hell. The young man recovered quickly, found out what the suspect had been carrying and ran after him. He chased him out of the park and through the door in the wall leading to Sycamore Grove.'

'I know that door. There are two big houses behind it.'

'Aye, that's right. Well, he believes the suspect went into one of the two houses there.'

Superintendent Harker inhaled noisily, leaned back in his swivel chair and stared pointedly at Angel, 'Ah! *One* of the two houses?'

'Yes.'

He smiled across at Angel, 'Well, that's all right. I'll give you a search warrant to search the house. No problem.'

Angel shook his head. 'No John. You haven't quite got it. He doesn't know *which* house.'

Harker put his hands on the chair arms and pushed himself further back in the seat. 'You mean he is certain that the suspect went into *one* of the two houses but he doesn't know which one?'

Angel shook his head again. 'I wish life was so simple.'

'You mean he isn't even certain about *that?*'

He nodded slowly. 'He *thinks* the suspect went into number one or number two Sycamore Grove, but he is not certain. It's also possible he could have gone across number one's front garden, down some steps at the side of the house to the back garden and out through the back gate and away.'

'And is that all you've got? No other witnesses? No evidence?'

'That's all I've got.' Angel stood up, resigned to the outcome.

'Hmmm.' The Super waved his hand at Angel. 'Well,sit down a minute. We may still be able to get round this. Who lives there?'

'A couple called Lowbridge, live in number one, and Peter Wexell and his wife…'

'The solicitor chap? The man at Pettigrew and Shaw?' John Harker asked quickly, his black eyebrows raised.

'Yes.'

He shook his head decisively. 'Then there's no chance, Mike. I'm sorry.'

Angel glared at him. 'Why?'

The Superintendent smiled, 'Can you imagine our lads tramping up and down Peter Wexell's Chinese rugs and Ming vases? I know that chap. He has a taste for the expensive, the exotic. His offices are furnished like Buckingham Palace. And he's a tartar in court. I don't think he'd be sympathetic to us taking his house to pieces because of some vague suspicions of a witness. If we searched his house and didn't find evidence he was guilty of *something*, after that fiasco last week with the mayor, he'd take us to the cleaners.'

'Oh?' Angel bristled.

'And I don't want to make an enemy out of him either.'

'Are we suddenly afraid of solicitors then?'

'Of course not. I hope you know me better than that. But taking everything into account, Mike, I can't see that with such flimsy evidence I can OK a warrant to search the house of such a potentially troublesome and unlikely suspect as Peter Wexell, which means I can't OK a warrant to search Lowbridge's house either. If it got out that we were apprehensive about issuing a warrant to search Wexell's house and instead chose to search another house simply because the householder wouldn't cause trouble, we'd be the laughing stock of the media.'

Angel sighed a long sigh. He wiped his hand across his chin. 'And if it turns out that either Mr and Mrs Wexell or Mr and Mrs Lowbridge are murderers or harbouring a murderer, what then?'

The Superintendent's face tightened. 'I know! I know! But you'll have to find another way.'

'So no search warrant?'

'No search warrant.'

Angel came out of the office with a smile on his face. He had rattled the Superintendent's cage even if he hadn't got the search warrants he wanted. There was a certain satisfaction in testing the morality of your superiors in the force.

He returned to his office and found a folded piece of paper under a box of paperclips in the centre of his desk. He picked it up and opened it, it was in Ahmed's clear, spidery hand and it read:

'To Inspector Angel. Your wife phoned while you were out. Her mother is improving but she is going to stay another day or two until she comes out of hospital. She says she hope you are managing and please not to forget milk for the cats.'

He pulled a face and leaned over the desk to the phone and dialled a number. 'Find Cadet Ahaz and send him into me.'

He slumped down in the chair. He was fed up of his wife being away, fed up of thinking what he might have for tea. There was all the bother of deciding what he would like, then buying it, preparing it, and then washing up after it! The only part he enjoyed was the eating. There must be an easier way! Hell, was that the time? He reached over for the phone again and dialled. A voice answered, 'Mortuary.'

'Dr Mac, please.'

'Hold on.'

'Right.' Angel opened the leather-covered notebook from his inside pocket and pressed the top of his pen with his thumb.

There was an unmistakable cough as the Glaswegian doctor picked up the phone at the other end. 'Dr Mac speaking. Who is that?'

'It's Michael Angel. Have you got anything for me on that woman in the park, Mac?'

'Och, it's you, Mike. I was surprised I hadn't heard from you before now. You're always so quick off the mark. As a matter of fact I am examining her now. Not much to say, as yet.'

'Well, what you got so far?'

'Aye. Well, she's nobbut a slight woman in her forties, about five foot two, brown hair and brown eyes.'

'And what did she die of?'

'I am not sure, yet. There is some hypnotic residue in her stomach, but I don't think there was enough to kill her. I canna be sure of that yet.'

'What's that mean?'

'She took some sort of drug a few hours before she died. Of course, it may have been a properly prescribed medication.'

'What for?'

'Och it has various applications. To sedate her or slow down her metabolism.'

'You mean a sleeping pill?'

'It may have been.'

Angel puffed impatiently. 'Well, Mac, was she murdered or not?'

The doctor hesitated. 'All I'm saying is that she did not die from natural causes.'

'Does that mean she was *murdered*?'

'I don't know. You're always in too much of a hurry, Mike. Wait for the results of my tests.'

Angel knew the doctor very well and had come to like him and respect his work over the years. Mac was always supremely careful in what he reported; he never commented on forensic matters unless he was positive his observations could be proven. That made him an admirable expert witness in court.

He plodded on. 'Well, when did she die?'

'Late on Friday night or Saturday morning.'

'Any ideas on her identity. Do her clothes tell you anything? Any engraved jewellery, a locket or a ring? Anything in her pockets? Any tattoos. Is she British?'

'Hold on. Hold on. I should think she's British. Her clothes seem to be typically British. Maybe a wee bit old-fashioned. Incidentally, she was wearing stockings. And the right one was inside out and not fastened or adjusted properly.'

Angel rubbed his chin. 'Eh? What does that mean? Is it significant? What does it matter?'

'I don't know what it means. It would matter to her, I suppose. Just thought you'd want to know.'

'Aye. Well, I don't know what it signifies, Mac. Anything else?'

'No. And I don't know how I was able to tell you *that* much.'

Angel grinned. 'I'll have to get onto missing persons then. We've had no local reports. All right, Mac, you old war horse. Thanks ever so much.'

''Bye, Mike.'

As Angel returned the phone to the cradle, there was a knock at the door. 'Come in.'

It was Cadet Ahaz.

The Inspector smiled at him. 'Ah, Ahmed. Where've you been? You are harder to find than Lord Lucan.'

Before Ahmed had a chance to say anything, Angel said, 'You did all right this afternoon, lad. If you don't make it as an actor, you've a career as a pizza delivery boy waiting for you.'

'I only want to be a policeman, sir. My mother would never let me wear those denims and baseball cap as a regular thing.'

'Good for her, lad.'

'I put a note on your desk, sir. A phone message from Mrs Angel.'

'Yes, lad.' Angel's eyebrows shot up, 'Ah, that's what I wanted you for. Will you get me some milk, same as yesterday? And will you ring The Feathers and book me a table for one, for dinner tonight?'

* * *

It was another hot day.

The July sun shone strongly in this unusual spell of English weather and the forecasters were reporting more record temperatures. Angel went through the private door in the garden wall, along the noisy gravel path, up the six stone steps and under the portico to the big door of the first house in Sycamore Grove. The figure 1 was screwed on the door with brass screws, the brass bell push sparkled in the bright morning sun and contrasted with the glossy black paint.

The door was answered by a small lady in a blue smock coat and pink lipstick spread across an area of her face greater than that occupied by her mouth. Her hair was built up in the beehive style of the 1950s which gave the impression that she always walked with her head erect. She had a ready smile.

'Good morning, Inspector. I've been expecting you. Please come in.' She opened the big door more widely.

Angel smiled. Mrs Lowbridge seemed pleasant enough. Was this interview going to be easier than he had thought? He stepped into the large hall. 'Thank you.'

'You want to ask me some questions, I believe. We can talk in the study.' She closed the door. 'Please follow me.'

He observed the highly polished parquet flooring and the walls, which were panelled with dark oak all the way to the ceiling. There was a big window with coloured glass in it on the left, next to which stood a wide oak staircase leading upstairs, then there were three closed doors, and, through an open door, Angel saw a stone staircase going down to the basement. He noticed the strong smell of wax polish.

Mrs Lowbridge crossed to the door of a room at the far end of the hall. The head of hair bobbed up and down and she kept fiddling with it as she walked. She turned her finger through an undisciplined tiny curl and tried to tuck it in, that was followed by much patting and pushing of the beehive inwards with both hands.

They entered a small sitting room furnished with a three-piece suite, a standard lamp, a small bureau and a coffee table. A large bunch of yellow chrysanthemums overhung a vase on the hearth in front of a black tiled Victorian fireplace. A French window leading onto a small balcony stood open and the smell of freshly cut grass wafted through the window. The white chiffon curtain quivered in the slight breeze.

'Please sit down.'

Angel eased himself into a comfortable easy chair facing the window.

'You won't be in a draught over there, Inspector?'

'No. No. I'll enjoy any fresh air there may be. I don't really enjoy the heat, thank you.'

'And I can take all that the weatherman can throw at me.' She chose the settee so that she would be seated opposite him, and put a hand up to fiddle with a wisp of hair again.

They exchanged polite smiles, as he reached into his inside pocket and pulled out his notepad and pen.

'Well, now, Mrs Lowbridge, what can you tell me about your activities yesterday? Did you or your husband go out at all?'

'No,' she replied easily. 'We had no reason to, Inspector.'

'And do you and your husband live alone in this big house? Where is he, by the way? Is he out?'

'No. He's in the kitchen, preparing vegetables for dinner tonight. Did you want to see him?'

'Before I leave, I'd like a word.'

'Surely. Yes, we do live here on our own. We take paying guests, on a bed and breakfast or half board basis. We have no guests tonight, but casuals can arrive any time. We have some guests coming in next week. Twenty school teachers.'

'And have you had any guests in the past few days?'

'Yes. A woman telephoned and booked a room for the one night, Friday night,' she said patting her hair again and pushing a loose tuft into the mass.

'What was her name?'

'Thomas, I think her name was. Fiona Thomas. She was from somewhere in Wales. There's a visitor's book if you would like to see it. There's her name and address.'

Angel felt his pulse rate increase slightly. This information was confirming what he already suspected. He nodded but did not show any reaction. Fiona Thomas was the sister of the woman who came to see him, Miriam Thomas, and the one whose disappearance she was so worried about. 'Fiona Thomas,' he repeated slowly as he wrote the name in his notebook. He would have to make contact with Miriam as a matter of great urgency. It looked as if her life might be in grave danger.

'Thank you. Yes. I'd like to see the visitors' book. I'll take the address. And what can you tell me about her?'

'She was just a woman. She stayed the one night, had breakfast and left the following morning. There's not much to tell. Polite. Respectable. Pleasant enough.'

'Did she come in her own car?'

'No, I don't think so. I expect she came by taxi.'

'And how did she leave? Did she also leave by taxi?'

'I expect so, Inspector. I really didn't notice.'

'And did she make any phone calls?' he continued, trying to keep his concentration.

'Not from our telephone, she didn't. I would have known.' She put her head on her chest so that she could more easily reach some loose wisps of hair at the nape of her neck.

'And did you take any messages for her, from anybody?'

'Who? No.'

'Who did she meet while she was visiting Bromersley?' he asked hoping for a helpful reply.

'I really don't know,' she replied. She stared at him and stopped fiddling with her hair.

The answer didn't help. He continued unmoved. 'Have you any idea what brought her to the town?'

'No, Inspector. We barely spoke,' she replied shaking her head.

'Did you have an enquiry from her sister about her whereabouts?'

'Yes. That was on Saturday morning, I think. My husband dealt with it. She thought her sister was still staying here. What is all this about, Inspector? What happened in the park last night? All you told me was that there was an "incident". That could mean anything. And what has it to do with me?'

'You are entitled to know, Mrs Lowbridge. A man and his young lady were taking a midnight stroll in the park. As they were walking along a man came rushing out carrying what they now know to be a dead body — that of a woman. They startled him. He threw the body at them and ran in the direction of this house.'

Her jaw dropped. 'A dead body? And you think he might have run here?' Her voice went up an octave. 'Oh no. It makes my blood run cold to even think about it. How did she die?'

'We don't know that for certain yet.'

'Ooooh! He didn't come here, Inspector. He wouldn't have dared. My husband would have soon seen him off.'

'There's more to it than that, Mrs Lowbridge. It looks as if the murdered woman might have been none other than your guest of Friday night, Fiona Thomas.'

Her face turned suddenly severe. Her mouth opened, but no words were spoken. Eventually she said, 'Surely not. She was such a quiet woman. How can that be?'

Angel shook his head. 'It is imperative I find out who she met while she was in Bromersley. I have to find out where she was for those missing three days. Whoever it was would very likely be the murderer or lead us to the murderer. I was hoping you would be able to throw some light on it.'

'The woman left here on Saturday morning. I have no idea where she was staying between then and last night? I am sorry, Inspector.'

'Very well. I'll have a look at that visitor's book now, if you don't mind. I'll have a word with your husband, and then I'll have a look round the house.'

The last entry in the visitor's book was that of Fiona Thomas. The address was: Flat 2, Dragon House, Pontylliath, North Wales. He copied the address into his notebook.

'I'll lead the way, Inspector,' Mrs Lowbridge said, as she took hold of the black ironwork banister handrail and clattered down the stone steps. He observed how she carefully held the rail with one hand while still attempting to push a recalcitrant curl into the beehive hairdo with the other. She clattered across the noisy stone flags through a door behind the stairs to the kitchen. Angel followed her passing several doors to store rooms, a pantry, a cloakroom and a boiler room. As they entered the brightly lit, tiled kitchen, her husband turned away from the worktop where he was cutting up some carrots. A balding, round-faced man with a small moustache, he was wearing a white apron over a smart shirt, bow tie and grey flannel trousers. He was in his fifties, softly spoken and seemed happy to let his wife take the initiative. Angel asked the same questions he had asked in the sitting room. Tal Lowbridge looked across at her after answering each of the policeman's questions as if seeking confirmation that he had answered correctly. The answers were virtually the same as hers. He confirmed that he had spoken to Miriam Thomas on Saturday morning last and confirmed that she seemed surprised that her sister had left them, but she had only booked in for the one night. He was able to add that he had seen Fiona Thomas get into a taxi with her luggage at about ten o'clock on Saturday morning.

Angel closed his notebook and asked to look round the house.

He systematically checked all the basement window fasteners and found them to be working and in good condition. One of the windows near the back door was open at the top a few inches. When he spotted it, he turned to Mrs Lowbridge and asked, 'Is this window usually left unlocked?'

She looked at her husband and then said, 'Yes. I think it usually is in the summer, isn't it, Tal?'

Mr Lowbridge said, 'We usually open that one for a bit of fresh air. It has been exceptionally hot.'

Angel nodded. He went to lift the lower half of the window. It moved easily. He looked round at Mrs Lowbridge. 'I should keep that window securely locked at all times, if I were you. It's on ground level and it opens and closes very easily.'

She nodded. 'Very well. But the temperatures have been quite exceptional.'

The cellar where he had found the outside grate open the previous night was of particular interest. Several powerful rays of sunshine shone through the patterned holes in the grate into the windowless room, showing dust swirling in their path. A small amount of coke was loose on the flagged floor on one side and a small furnace stood opposite. For no apparent reason, Angel took hold of the wired handle of the furnace to open it. It was unexpectedly hot. He quickly released his hold and pulled his hand away.

Mrs Lowbridge said, 'Oh? I'm sorry, Inspector. I should have told you it had been fired this morning. We like to burn our catering waste daily in this hot weather. We can't do with it hanging about in these temperatures, odours and flies, you know.'

Angel nodded. 'You certainly keep everything beautifully spick and span.'

Mrs Lowbridge smiled.

They climbed the stone steps into the front entrance hall. The three doors from there led to a dining room with six tables to seat twenty-four guests, a lounge and a small TV room.

On the upper floors, as well as the Lowbridges comfortable personal living accommodation, there were fourteen guest bedrooms, which were plainly furnished with beds, dressing tables and bed lockers in stripped pine. Everywhere was spotlessly clean and well ordered. There was not a speck of dust in the house.

He asked to see the room where Fiona Thomas had stayed and enquired if the sheets had been laundered. They had. They were on a rack in the basement kitchen airing off. He asked if the rooms had been cleaned. They had. He looked in the wastepaper baskets. Each one was empty and fresh lining paper had been fitted. 'There's such a thing as being too damned efficient,' he said to himself.

Angel took his leave and stood on the portico, scratching his head and gazing across the lawn to the high garden wall partly covered with ivy. The hot sun warmed his face and he squinted to reduce the glare. Dragging a handkerchief out of his pocket, he wiped his forehead; this was not the weather for working. He could feel his shirt sticking to his back. If he had been on holiday at Scarborough, he could have taken off his shirt. He pulled out the notebook and fingered through the pages thoughtfully. The Lowbridges had answered all the questions he had put to them, but he would have liked the forensic team to have examined that house. For instance, they may have been able to determine whether the man carrying the body was or was not Tal Lowbridge.

Angel ran his fingers across his mouth. New questions now had to be addressed. Where was Miriam Thomas? Had she returned home to Wales? He would need to contact her promptly and ask her to identify the body formally. That was not a job he relished. As the body on the slab at the mortuary at Bromersley Hospital was almost certainly Fiona Thomas, Miriam may need some personal protection, unless she had already become a victim of Nurse Violet Rae. And where had Fiona been in Bromersley on Friday? Who had murdered her and where? Presumably Fiona had recognised the mysterious Staff Nurse Rae, whoever she was, and, as a result, been murdered to protect her identity. These were matters he would have to address urgently. But he must interview the

Wexells next. That was the priority, the Super could reach him on his mobile phone if anything urgent cropped up.

He returned the handkerchief to his pocket and walked down the steps onto the gravel path. He followed it round the front garden and up the next pathway to number 2 Sycamore Grove.

A slim, suntanned woman in a skimpy summer dress and a big straw hat answered the door. 'Yes, Inspector,' she said, taking off the mirror sunglasses.

Olga Wexell had a few wrinkles around her eyes and neck but was still a beautiful woman. Her teeth were even and very white. Her deep blue eyes were the colour of the Mediterranean, but they had no twinkle and she rarely smiled.

'My husband told me about your visit last night,' she replied in a superior nasal drawl. 'He said you would be calling in. He's at the office. He's the Senior Partner of Pettigrew and Shaw, the solicitors, you know. I was a Shaw before I was married,' she added unnecessarily. 'Shall we sit by the pool?'

Without waiting for a reply, she came outside and, closing the door behind her, made her way along the side of the house turning towards the back. The white flagstones and stucco reflected the bright sunshine and contrasted with her long brown legs and bare feet. Angel followed her to a rectangular area of blue water surrounded by orange coloured tiles and low white walls. Four sun chairs stood in front of an open French window. The pool was situated between the park wall and the side of the house, making it an excellent suntrap.

Angel tagged along, mopping his brow with his handkerchief.

She gestured towards the sun chairs.

'Thank you.'

She replaced the sunglasses, put a hand across her forehead and looked towards the blue sky. 'It's not often we get days like these, Inspector. It is good to take advantage of them, don't you think?' She climbed gracefully into a chair and began to display her face, arms and legs to the sun.

'Yes,' he said unconvincingly, thinking how lucky she was that she didn't have to work. He carefully lowered himself into a chair he had rearranged so that he was facing Mrs Wexell and not the glare.

'What happened last night then, Inspector?' She asked in her loud, nasal voice.

'A woman's body was found in the park. We believe she was murdered.'

'Oh?' She squawked. 'How awful.'

There was a short pause. She gazed pensively down the large green spread of lawn and trees at the other side of the pool and then said, 'What do you want to ask me, Inspector? I didn't do it, you know,' she smirked, removing the sunglasses and looking at the policeman.

He didn't reply. He was busy turning the pages over in his notebook. Without looking up, he said, 'I'll be with you in a minute.'

She replaced the sunglasses and returned to the sun.

At length, he sighed and said, 'Now then, Mrs Wexell who lives in this house apart from you and your husband?'

'Nobody. We have no children.'

'And did you or your husband notice anything unusual last night?'

'Apart from being woken at about midnight, no,' she smirked again and looked at him.

'Quite. You didn't see or hear anybody or anything unusual — the sound of footsteps for instance? The gravel does rather make a noise when you walk across it.'

'I didn't hear a thing. No.'

'Were there any signs of an attempted break-in?'

'No. Our sophisticated burglar alarm system would have made us aware of any intruder, Inspector.'

'I see. Yes.'

'We have a very expensive system, you see. As a matter of fact one of your men came and advised us. From your Crime Prevention Office, I think it was.'

'Oh, yes?'

'You see we collect antiques, Inspector.'

Angel nodded. 'The murderer was seen approaching this house or the house next door.'

She shook her head and held up her hands. 'As I said, Inspector, I saw and heard nothing.'

Angel closed the notebook and put it back in his pocket. That was short and sweet. 'I'll catch your husband at his office later.'

'You'll have to make an appointment,' she said.

Angel's jaw tightened for a second, then relaxed. He wasn't going to let Olga Wexell annoy him. Besides, he needed the maximum amount of diplomacy he could assemble to overcome the next tricky bit. He didn't hesitate, he went straight in. 'I'll have a look round the house now,' he announced and rose to his feet.

'Oh?' she looked at him in surprise and whipped off the sunglasses.

'Will you show me round?' he said, walking towards the French window. 'Just a formality.' He called back over his shoulder.

'Er yes. I suppose so,' she replied elegantly rising to her feet.

'Shall we go in this way? Oh, what a lovely room. Is this the drawing room?'

CHAPTER 6

The Wexell's house was the picture of Victorian (and Georgian) good taste, but without all the clutter. All the rooms were furnished with oak, mahogany and rosewood furniture, old paintings, copper and brass fireplace furniture, aspidistras in big Chinese pots, animal heads mounted on plaques and foreign and English pottery of every description. Even the bed was a four-poster with a tiled headboard depicting Greek slaves carrying jugs of water.

Clearly, the Wexells did not utilise all the rooms for domestic purposes. The top two floors of the house were used as store rooms but the contents were set out as near as possible to the way rooms might have looked years ago.

Angel moved through the house from room to room with Mrs Wexell immediately behind him chattering incessantly about how valuable everything was and how rare some of the pieces were. There were no signs of an intruder or where a trespasser might have gained access. He tried all the ground level windows and they were all fastened securely.

He looked in the cellar and found the furnace and the grate in the same place as next door.

Disappointed, Angel took his leave and returned to the station. On his desk, at the top of a small pile of papers was a message taken by Cadet Ahaz. It read:

'Sir. Your wife telephoned to say that she must stay in Derby a few more days as her mother is having an operation tomorrow. She said that she hoped you were all right and that you were remembering to feed the cats.'

Angel pulled a disagreeable face and grunted. He screwed up the paper and threw it in the wastepaper basket. He leaned over and pressed a button on the phone.

'Is DS Crisp there?'

'Yes, sir.'

'Send him through.'

He took off his suit coat and hung it on the back of the chair. He leaned over and felt the radiator; it was stone cold. His nose wrinkled as if there was a nasty smell in the place, he went over to the window, opened it wide and took a deep breath of the incoming air. 'That's better.'

There was a knock at the door.

'Come in.'

It was DS Crisp. He was carrying a clip of papers.

'Grab a seat, lad. Is that the witness's statement?'

'Yes, sir.'

Angel took the sheets and began reading. 'Does he give a good description of the man? Could he recognise him if he saw him again?' he muttered.

His eyes raced down the first page.

'No, sir. He said there were no lights. It was too dark. It was unexpected and it all happened so quickly.'

Angel lowered the statement and threw it down on the desk. His face was scarlet. 'Then it's no use, is it? It reads like the small print on my mortgage — and makes about as much sense!'

Crisp looked up at him as Angel, still standing, leaned over to him putting the flat of his hands on the desktop. 'It won't do, lad. It won't do. *I want to know what sort of a person we are looking for!* What he looked like. How big he was. How tall he was. Didn't he get *any* impression about the villain's height? Was he seven foot nine or three foot two? He must have had some idea. Did he smell of anything? Alcohol? Tobacco? Curry? Fishermen's Friends? We're clutching at straws here! But we are hunting a murderer! Did he have any facial hair? A moustache or a beard? Was he bald or had he a big thatch? You can get an impression even in a bad light. Was he young or was he old? Was he a young lad of sixteen sprinting up the path at the speed of light to Sycamore Grove or an old codger of seventy panting and wheezing and coughing his way up there? Yes. Did he cough? When surprised, did he gasp? Did he make any noise at all? Can't you get *any* information from this man?' Angel handed Crisp the statement. 'Here lad. Take this back to him. See if he and you can come up with something useful.'

Crisp stood up and glared at the DI.

'And hurry up. I may want you to go to Wales tomorrow.' Angel sat down and started rifling through the pile of papers. 'And have you had a result from Mac about that car?' he continued.

The DS turned towards the door. He stared at Angel with steely blue eyes. 'Not yet sir.'

'Have you phoned him?'

'No.'

'Well, see to it, lad. See to it.'

'I did find a pair of navy blue gloves in the car. I passed them onto him. There was no sign of a video. And I didn't find a gun.'

'Right. No gun. No video. The videos in the house were all of Batman and Robin. I'll have a word with Mac. Off you go. And on your way out, tell that Cadet I want him, pronto.'

The door closed with a bang.

Angel looked up, shook his head, pushed the papers away and picked up the phone and dialled a number. 'Dr Mac, please.'

'Speaking.'

'It's Michael Angel. How's it going?'

'Och, I know who it is. And I know what you're wanting.'

'Three months in Lanzarote would do very nicely. Can you give me a sick note, Doctor?'

Mac ignored the wise cracks. 'Just let me get ma notes.'

Angel pulled his notebook from his pocket and clicked his pen.

'Are you there?'

'Yes.'

'That unidentified female corpse in the park. She was about forty-five. Weight, 120 pounds. Height, five foot two. Good physique. Brown hair. Brown eyes. Wearing good quality clothes, more for hard wearing than for appearance. There are no identification labels on any of her clothes. No pockets. No handbag. Nothing to help with an ID.'

'You've already told me all that. I think I know who she is.'

'Oh? Good. Anybody I've heard of?'

'No.'

'Well, I don't think she's married. Anyway, she's a *nullipara.*'

'She's a what?'

'She hasna borne children,' Mac said patiently.

'Oh.'

'*Nullipara* is Latin. Did they not teach you anything at that school apart from cooking and needlework and hockey?'

'They didn't waste time teaching us a dead language. Anything else?'

'Aye. Like I said, for some reason her right stocking was inside out and not fastened to her suspender belt, but she has not been interfered with.'

'What's the significance of that then, Mac?'

'It beats me. But I'll give it some thought.' Angel knew he would.

'Anything else?'

'I think she worked at a job where she was on her feet a lot.'

'A nurse?'

'Aye. That would fit. She'd be from a place near or by the sea and she was a non-smoker. Her lungs are as pink as a new born babby's.'

'North Wales?'

'Aye. That'd do. There's nay many chimneys there. She had had a meal six or seven hours before she died. She had taken a compound of some sort, either with the meal or soon after. But that didn't kill her. It would slow down her metabolism, but it didn't kill her. Her blood showed a high content of diamorphine hydrochloride. That's pure heroin to you, Mike. And that's what killed her. And there's a small bruise on her ankle, of no particular significance.'

Angel nodded. 'She died from an overdose of heroin?'

'Aye, by injection. If she was a regular "druggie" there'd be injection marks on her arms or other parts of her body, but I can't find any. I've been over every inch of her skin with a magnifying glass. I'll have another go tomorrow. It's bound to be there somewhere.'

'So someone else, the murderer, administered the jab then?'

'Oh yes.'

'Someone with expertise? Someone in the medical profession? But *she* was a nurse.'

'That's interesting. Mmmm. It's probably a coincidence. These days, if you were illiterate and a druggie, you would know how to wield a hypodermic, wouldn't you?'

'Aye. And that's half the world!'

'She had been dead, more than three days, less than a week.'

'How about last Friday?'

'Could be. Could be.'

'Mmm. Where would a murderer stash a body? He'd want rid of the evidence, wouldn't he?'

'Who knows? I canna help you there, Michael. Her coat was quite dusty. If you find a location where the body is from, I would almost certainly be able to determine it.'

'Thanks, Mac. Thanks very much.'

'Are you wanting anything else?'

'No. That's pretty comprehensive.' Then without a pause, Angel said, 'Have you any dope on that car yet?'

'Give me a chance, man. I thought you'd want the corpse doing first.'

'That's right. That's right. But I've got a joker in jail and I want to get him sent down.'

'I'm surprised you're stuck at that — a man as enterprising as you. Well, Crisp found a pair of thick navy blue woollen gloves in the car, Mike. Now that's pretty significant in the middle of a heatwave, isn't it?'

'Yes. But are they the gloves worn at the Pettigrew and Shaw break-in?'

The Scotsman said, 'Yes. The fibres caught on the screw on the door knob at Pettigrew and Shaw and the woollen gloves taken from the Volkswagen car match.'

Angel's chest swelled as he breathed in deeply and he nodded with great satisfaction. 'Thanks, Mac.'

As he replaced the phone, he pursed his lips thoughtfully. The forensic evidence suggested that the dead body was that of Fiona Thomas. He was now faced with finding her sister, Miriam, and organising formal identification.

There was a knock at the door. 'Come in,' Angel barked.

It was Cadet Ahmed Ahaz. 'You wanted me, sir?'

'Where have you been? You're harder to find than a threepenny bit in a Christmas pudding.'

Ahmed smiled and then looked puzzled. 'What's that mean, sir?'

Angel ignored the question. 'Look lad, I want you to get me a Nurse Miriam Thomas at the Moorside Hospital, Pontylliath, North Wales on the phone. If she's not on duty, find her phone number and follow it through. I want to speak to her. It might be a matter of life and death.'

'Yes sir.'

'And I want you to get me some more milk to take home for those two cats.'

'Right sir. Anything else, sir?'

'Yes lad. I want a reel of cotton suitable for sewing a button on a shirt. White. You know what I mean?'

Ahmed nodded.

Angel pulled a long face. 'I'm getting a bit fed up with playing at housekeeping, lad. But that's what you have to do in an emergency. I'll be glad when Mrs Angel's mother is better and she comes back. Now off you go. Chop-chop.'

Ahmed nodded, turned to leave and then turned back. 'My mother would sew you a button on, sir,' the young man said tentatively, his gentle eyes shining bright. 'I told her that Mrs Angel was away attending her sick mother in hospital. She said that I was to say that anything she can do to help, she would be happy to do.'

Angel leaned back in the chair. A big smile began to spread across his face, then suddenly he looked severe and frowned. 'That's very kind, Ahmed. Please thank your mother for me. I can sew a button on, for goodness sake.'

'It is nothing, sir. My mother would help anybody,' he replied with a smile. 'Oh sir, you will remember I have reserved a table for dinner for you at The Feathers tonight.'

'Ah yes, lad.'

Ahmed rushed off.

Angel smiled and pushed himself away from the desk. He was looking forward to dining at The Feathers. It would be a change from cooking for himself.

He made his way down the olive green corridor to the custody suite and spoke to the duty jailer who had a tray holding four cups of tea.

'Where is the prisoner brought in yesterday by DS Crisp?'

'Cell number one, sir,' he replied.

'How is he? What's happening? Anything?'

'Very quiet sir. He says nothing. He asks for nothing.'

'Is he eating?'

'Oh yes, sir. And drinking. It's the tea round now. I was just taking him a cup.'

'Oh aye? Give it me here. I'll take it. Is there a spare one for me?'

'Help yourself, sir.'

'Ta.'

The policeman put the tin tray on his counter top, went up to the suite door, locked it and then, after peeping through the grill, opened cell number one.

'There you are, sir. I'll leave the door open, shall I?'

Angel nodded. 'Aye, lad. Ta.'

The policeman returned to delivering the mugs of tea.

Angel went through the cell doorway holding a beaker in each hand. 'Here you are, lad. I've brought you some tea.'

The thin young man was still wearing the navy suit and blue shirt. His long, black hair framed his white face and his eyes had dark circles under them.

Angel handed the mug to him.

He didn't say anything. He looked closely at the Inspector, then at the beaker and took it from him. He pulled a face as the hot mug burned his fingers and swiftly turned it round with the other hand and took hold of the handle.

Angel paused and took a sip of the tea. It was a bit too sweet for his liking, but he thought it was good — for prisoner's tea.

'Now then, lad. I'm Angel. I am the one bringing the charges against you.'

The man said nothing but continued to look at the Inspector.

'And you'll need a solicitor to represent you in court. Then you could let *him* do the talking. I mean that's what you'd be paying him for, isn't it?'

He paused again and sipped the tea slowly. The young man looked bored.

'Unless, of course, you are going to apply for legal aid. Mmm. You might think about that. It's very expensive mounting a defence in the light of the evidence we've got stacked against you and your mate. But, well, you'll have to see what your solicitor advises, won't you, lad?'

The man looked down at the red tiled floor.

Angel paused and then continued. 'Of course for us to get you your solicitor we'd need to know your name.'

Angel paused and sipped his tea. The young man looked back at him briefly then looked away. The Inspector leaned over to a chair by the wall and with one hand, picked it up, turned it round and slipped it between his legs from the front and sat down. 'That's better. It's like being at home, here, isn't it?' He pursed his lips, leaned forward over the back of the chair and forced a smile. He looked into the big, brown, sad eyes of the young man.

'Yes, I'd need to know your name to be able to instruct a solicitor. I mean I couldn't instruct a solicitor to defend you if I couldn't tell him who you are, could I? It stands to reason.'

He sipped the tea. The man gazed at the green painted wall.

'I suppose you could invent a name. A sort of alias. Let's think of an outlandish name. Mmm. Yes, well, how about Elvis Presley? I mean nobody in their right mind would be called Elvis Presley, would they? Yes, Elvis Presley would be a good choice, wouldn't it? Yes. It's a good one. Shall I put your name down as Elvis Presley then? What do you think, lad?'

The young man looked down at the tiles.

Angel continued. 'Take your time. Oh. You don't fancy Elvis Presley? All right. We must think of another. Evel Knievel's a good sounding name. Do you fancy that? Then there's Robinson Crusoe. There's another unlikely name. How about that? Sounds good, doesn't it? Robinson Crusoe. What do you think?'

Angel put the mug on the cell floor and leaned back in the chair. He folded his arms and looked across at the man who looked back at him, expressionless.

There was a few seconds silence.

Angel drummed his fingers. Eventually, he said, 'I give up. I don't think I'm getting anywhere with you, lad, am I? It seems to me that you will be happy to stay rotting in jail while your mate roams free. I don't understand it. Fancy you chumming up with him? Mighty mouse!'

Angel still failed to provoke any response. He would try another stab in the dark. 'Whatever would your mother say about this?'

The man looked up at Angel. The corners of his mouth turned up in a short-lived insolent grin.

Angel knew he had been rumbled. He pursed his lips. His voice hardened. 'Right lad. I can see how hard boiled you are.'

'No comment,' the young man suddenly said crisply.

Angel's eyebrows shot up. 'Oh. You have got a tongue, lad? I was beginning to think you had caught it in the till at that petrol station you and "Shortarse" robbed on Saturday.' Angel swept up the mug from the floor and stood up. He looked down at the man and then said quietly, 'You know assaulting that girl was not a good idea.'

'No comment.'

CHAPTER 7

'Was everything all right, sir?' the waiter said as he cleared the empty wine bottle and pudding plate away with the flourish of a serviette.

'Very nice,' Angel said to the waiter as he emptied the wine glass of the last drop of the half-bottle of Liebfraumilch and dabbed his mouth with a well-starched napkin.

'Coffee, sir?'

'Oh no, lad. No thanks.' The waiter turned to go. 'Just the bill.'

'Yes sir.'

The waiter arrived two minutes later with a silver salver bearing a long folded paper, which he deposited on the table. Angel reached out for it, unfolded the bill and looked at the bottom figure. His eyebrows shot up. 'I didn't want to buy the place,' he grunted to himself.

The couple on the next table looked across at him. He smiled at them weakly and fumbled around his wallet and pockets for money, which he left on the plate. Then he stood up and made his way towards the restaurant door. A waiter appeared from nowhere and said, 'Good night, sir.'

Angel nodded. 'Good night.'

He strolled into the big hallway of The Feathers and passed an illuminated sign that read 'Bar'.

A young man in a smart, light blue coat called out from behind the shiny white counter. 'Good evening Mr Angel. Can I get you anything?'

Angel turned and peered at him. 'Do I know you, lad?'

The young man smiled. 'My auntie lives next door to you. She introduced us last Christmas when I was visiting her.'

'Oh yes. I remember,' he lied. 'Your name is, er…Peter, Paul, Patrick—'

'Lance,' the young man prompted.

'Lance, that's it, Lance. On the tip of my tongue. Yes. Nice to see you. I'll have a pint of bitter, Lance,' he said pointing to a particular pump.

'Right, sir.' The young man selected a glass from a tray and began to fill it from a pump. 'Have you had dinner here, sir?'

'Yes.'

'Very nice.'

Angel pulled a note out of his wallet and slapped it on the sterile white counter top. 'What you doing here, lad. I thought you were at university.'

'I am, sir. This is a holiday job.'

'Oh.'

'I go back in October.'

The bar was not busy and as Lance was filling the glass, Angel glanced round the room.

'You're a policeman aren't you, Mr Angel? A detective?'

'Yes.'

There were three couples seated in cosy alcoves designed for four at the far end of the room. At the other end of the bar a tall man with a long cigarette was leaning against the bar drinking something green in a small glass. Angel thought he recognised him. A strikingly beautiful young woman in a big pink dress appeared at the door. She looked into the room, recognised the man, smiled and ran up to him. He didn't see her coming. She grabbed him by the sleeve and kissed him gently on the cheek. He pulled away from her and looked anxiously round the bar. He was not pleased.

Angel turned quickly back to Lance. In the mirror behind the bar, Angel saw them move quickly to an alcove at the far end of the room. He recognised the man. It was the solicitor, Peter Wexell. But who was his glamorous friend?

'There you are, sir,' Lance said, putting down the glass of brown liquid with an ample white head. He picked up the money. 'Are you on duty now, Mr Angel?'

'Never off duty, lad.'

The DI heard an electric bell ring from somewhere behind the bar. Promptly, from the same direction, a waiter in a blue blazer appeared, he lifted up a portion of the counter and went across to the far alcove. Seconds later he returned. He poured out two small glasses of the green liquid and took it on a tray to the alcove where Peter Wexell and the young lady were seated.

Lance put Angel's change on the bar top. 'Thank you, sir.'

Angel picked up the money. He leaned over to Lance. 'Who's the flashy young lady with the man in the expensive suit? They've just disappeared into the end alcove.'

Lance smiled knowingly. 'I noticed her. She's an eye knocker, isn't she? I don't know, sir. But I'll ask.' He went into the stillroom at the back of the bar.

Angel sipped the beer and nodded approvingly. It was very nice. He put the glass down on the counter top and then counted the sparse change he was still holding in his hand. He pursed his lips, shook his head and dropped the coins into his trouser pocket. He promised himself it would be a long time before The Feathers had any more of his hard earned money.

Lance returned, his eyes twinkling. 'That couple Mr Angel — he's a solicitor in town called Wexell, from Pettigrew and Shaw's, on Eden Street. He doesn't know who she is, except that he's heard Mr Wexell call her "Lola". They've been here several times in the past fortnight. They have a couple of drinks and then leave. They don't stay long.'

'Thanks, lad.'

The young man hesitated a second and then, leaning over the bar, in a hushed voice said, 'Are they wanted for something, Mr Angel?'

Angel pulled back and forced a smile. 'Oh no, lad.' he replied. 'No. I'm just curious, that's all. Nothing more,' he lied.

He emptied the glass and placed it back on the bar top. 'I must get off. I'll tell your Aunt and Uncle I've seen you, er, Lance.'

'Thank you, Mr Angel. Goodnight.'

* * *

'Come in,'

Cadet Ahmed Ahaz entered the office.

Angel looked up from his desk. 'What is it, lad?'

'Did you enjoy your evening at The Feathers, sir? Was the meal good?' he asked breezily.

'The meal was very good, lad, thank you. Why?' he said putting down his pen.

'You'll be going there again then, sir. Do you want me to reserve you a table?'

Angel shook his head firmly. 'No, lad. I'm not paying *their* prices. You need to be a footballer to afford to eat there. Besides, nobody can beat my wife's cooking.'

'Is she still away, sir?'

'Yes lad. And I'll be glad when she's back. Which reminds me, Ahmed. Will you find out if there is a laundry in the town? There used to be the old Co-op laundry on Leeds Road. I used to see their vans running up and down. See how it works. Do they have a special collecting day, or what? I shall be wanting some shirts washing and ironing if Mrs Angel is away much longer.'

'Yes, sir.'

'Now what did you want, lad?'

'You asked me to get Nurse Miriam Thomas on the phone, sir.'

'I did. It's very urgent.'

'Well,I got her number from the exchange and rang her several times. She has apparently not arrived home because there is no reply. There is an answerphone that I left a message on to contact you. Then I telephoned the hospital in Pontylliath where she works, and nobody knows where she is. The last time anybody saw her was last Friday at six o'clock in the evening when she went off duty. She should have been at work on Monday morning. She has not arrived and they have had no messages from her. The ward sister says it is unusual because she is so reliable. She also said that her sister, Fiona Thomas, had not reported for work either and they had not had a message or sick note from her. I didn't explain that — er.' Ahmed stopped speaking. He didn't need to complete the sentence.

Angel jumped in quickly. 'Quite right, lad. Quite right.' His jaw stiffened, things were not looking good. He would despatch Crisp to Pontylliath immediately. He must find Miriam Thomas before anything happened to her. Crisp would be able to get on the spot information.

Ahmed continued. 'And I've just heard from Swansea about the Volkswagen Passat, sir. They are false number plates.'

'Predictable. What about the chassis number.'

'Filed down, sir. Undecipherable.'

Angel wiped his hand across his mouth, 'Predictable.'

'And there are twenty-two of this model at this age on the stolen car register. From all parts of the country.'

'Hmm.' He grunted, looking down at the desk. 'It's not going well, lad.'

'No, sir.' The young man said.

Angel leaned back in the chair and gazed briefly at the ceiling, then suddenly he reached over to the phone and picked it up. 'Send DS Crisp in here.'

'Yes, sir,' the distorted voice on the phone replied.

He turned to the Cadet. 'There's something else I want you to do.'

'Yes sir,' Ahmed said eagerly.

'Yes. Get me the phone number for the rates office at Bromersley Town Hall, pronto.'

'Yes, sir, pronto. I will sir.' Ahmed dashed off, as Detective Sergeant Crisp came in.

'I was just coming to see you, sir.'

'Sit down, lad.' Angel noticed some cat hairs on the sleeve of his new suit. They would have belonged to Butch and Sundance. He started picking them off as he asked, 'What did you manage to get out of that witness then.'

'Well, he eventually said that the man was average height.'

'How tall is that?'

Crisp shrugged. 'That's the best I could do, sir. He was average height and probably between forty and fifty years of age. He didn't notice anything unusual about his hair. He didn't know whether he had a beard or moustache, or whether he was bald or not. He didn't think he was wearing a hat or a cap, and he wasn't near enough to detect any specific smell.'

'Is that it?' Angel said, dropping the cat hairs into the wastepaper basket.

'Yes sir.'

'It fits half the population of the world!'

Crisp glared at him.

Angel pushed the pile of papers in front of him to one side to rest his arms on the desk. 'I want you to go to Pontylliath. I'll send a letter of introduction to the local force by email. Find Miriam Thomas and when you find her, stay with her, don't let her out of your sight. Her life might be in danger from whoever murdered her sister, Fiona. Got it? And phone me. Cadet Ahaz will give you the address. And see what you can find out about the dead woman. And see what you can find out about a hospital Sister called Violet

Rae, who was there in 1981. She is wanted for fraud and drugs offences. Try and get a description of her from older members of staff who may remember her or if she has any family still living there. Get a photo if you can. And keep in touch. Right. Off you go. It should be nice there at this time of the year, but I'll want you back in a couple of days.'

DS Crisp nodded. 'Yes, sir.'

He went out as Cadet Ahaz came in.

'I've got that phone number for the rates office you wanted, sir,' he passed Angel a sliver of paper.

'Right, lad. Now see if you can sort that laundry out for me.'

'Right sir,' Ahmed dashed off and closed the door.

Angel dialled the number and was soon speaking to the Rates Office Manager, who promptly gave him the name and address of the owner of 71 Sheffield Road. Angel found the man's telephone number from Directory Enquiries. The private landlord explained that he owned a few houses in the town to provide him with an interest and an income in his retirement. The leasing of the house and the collection of the rent was in the hands of a local estate agent's, and that he didn't personally deal with the tenants. The rent of the house was paid monthly to the estate agent's office. Angel asked for the name and telephone number of the estate agent's and was soon speaking to the proprietor.

'The rent is always paid in cash. The tenants of number 71, most unusually, put cash in an envelope and drop it in our letterbox on the first of each month. They never miss. I wish all our clients were as good payers as these people are.'

Angel's eyebrows shot up. 'Do you take up references on your tenants before they move in?'

'Well, it's not always necessary. You can see what they're like when they apply to look over the property. Besides that, they pay a month's rent and insurance in advance. They have to leave a bond of two hundred pounds and sign a repairs lease before we entrust them with the keys.'

'And did these people sign a lease?'

'Most assuredly, Inspector.'

'And who dealt with them.'

'I did, I think.'

'So you will know what they look like?'

'Well, I can't remember them off-hand.'

'But you will know their names.'

'The name will be on the lease, but I need to find it. Hold on a minute. It's here somewhere.'

Angel noticed a gentle throbbing sound in his ears. This always happened when he was excited. This could be the breakthrough he was waiting for. He would like to remove that insolent look off that young man's face in the cells. He moved the handset to his other ear to enable him to mop his forehead with his handkerchief.

'Are you there, Inspector?'

'Yes sir. I'm here.' He could hear the rustle of paper.

'Mmm. Yes. I was the one who dealt with this couple.'

'And you have their names?'

'Oh yes. I remember them. Mr and Mrs Mouse. Unusual name. They are newlyweds.'

Angel's head dropped. 'A married couple? Are you sure you have the right house?'

'Yes, Inspector. 71 Sheffield Road.'

Angel knew this was another dead end. 'And I suppose his first name was Michael and his wife was called Minnie?' he said flippantly.

'Oh? Yes, you're right. How did you know that, Inspector?'

* * *

Angel drove the car out of the police station yard, down a side road into Eden Street, the main shopping thoroughfare, and joined the flow of traffic through the town. It was market day and the town was busy. The street was crammed with cars parked on meters on both sides and progress was tedious. Shoppers swelled over the pavement into the road and some darted without warning between the convoy of slow moving vehicles. As Angel meandered past McDonalds, Marks and Spencer's, the North Eastern Bank, the Exco chemists, the Bromersley Building Society and the 'Hollywood' hairdressers, the traffic lights at a pedestrian crossing changed to red. Angel pressed on the brake, scarcely noticing that he had come to rest outside the offices of Pettigrew and Shaw. Shoppers bustled across the front of the car from both sides of the road in a frantic race to beat the clock.

The sun beat down on Angel's face. He wound down the window and switched on the fan, staring thoughtfully ahead, he dreamily thought about what he might see on television that night. He was glad to leave the office and be going home, even though it was to an empty house. It had been a long, tough, useless day — a frustrating day. No evidence uncovered; no arrest made. He knew he wouldn't relax. His mind would be on the murder of Fiona Thomas and the robbery at the service station and he would be bemoaning the lack of progress on both fronts. He was thinking the only useful work he had done was to send Crisp to Pontylliath. He was still not happy with DS Crisp, and would be glad when Ron Gawber returned from the course at Hendon. But he had to rely on Crisp, he had no choice in the matter.

Crime fighting wasn't easy anymore. Criminals were getting too smart. There were too many 'true-life' forensic crime-solving programmes on the telly. Everybody knows about fingerprints, consequently hardly anyone left them around anymore. Crooks were even getting too clever for CCTV cameras, they simply stole the videotape, or sprayed the lens with ink, or covered it with a towel or smeared it with jam.

He was beginning to think he had lost his touch. He was doing all he could to find out who murdered Fiona Thomas and at every twist and turn he was confounded: either the line of enquiry led to a dead end or he was bound by Judges' Rules, or Chief Constable's orders. Whoever heard of stopping search warrants of potential crime scenes because the press might shout!

Where had she been between ten o'clock on Saturday morning, when she left the Lowbridges, and 11 p.m. on Sunday? And where was her sister, Miriam Thomas now?

From out of the crowd, an old lady emerged with a shopping trolley, which she pulled across the road in front of his car. She was quickly overtaken by a smartly dressed man, who had just come out of the North Eastern Bank. He bounced across the road in his inimitable way. Angel recognised him: it was Peter Wexell. He was dressed in a suit that must have been made by a tinsmith, it was that sharp. Angel watched his every step across the road, onto the pavement, and into the offices of Pettigrew and Shaw. He was walking fast and carrying a small parcel. He reached the double doors of his offices, raised an elegantly manicured hand and pushed his way into the building.

A car horn pipped from behind. The lights had turned to green. Angel gently let in the clutch and moved along the street. At the next lights, he turned off into Manchester Road and changed into top gear. Two minutes later he was in the country and motoring along an open narrow road empty of traffic. It was such a beautiful evening, not a cloud in the sky. A warm breeze flowed through the car window and ruffled his hair. He wound it up a tad.

The foothills of the Pennines, leading to the moors, are a beautiful part of Yorkshire. Dry stonewalls holding back expanses of green hills with a sprinkling of low farmhouses, typify the landscape. The road narrowed and twisted as he approached the T-junction to the residential estate where he lived. He changed gear, glanced up and saw the windscreen of a car behind filling his mirror. 'Stupid idiot,' Angel grunted, commenting on the closeness of the big black car behind. He glanced in the mirror again. His eyebrows lifted as he recognised the driver, the moustache and hairline easily recognisable behind black sunglasses. It was Peter Wexell.

'Trying to kill himself!' Angel muttered.

A bend in the road permitted the high-powered black car to overtake the policeman and surge ahead. The fast car effortlessly ate up the road as it climbed the Pennines towards Manchester.

As Angel reached the T-junction leading to his bungalow, he made a spontaneous decision. He didn't turn. Instead, he cancelled the indicator and carried straight on behind Peter Wexell. He didn't know what made him do it, probably plain old-fashioned curiosity. The reason didn't matter, he didn't have to be home at a fixed time; it wasn't as if his wife was expecting him and there wasn't a meal spoiling. On the contrary, he was going to have to cook himself something. That was nothing to look forward to. It was such a beautiful evening, a run in the country would be very enjoyable. If he happened to be able to find out what Peter Wexell was up to, so much the better, and if not, well, he'd have had some fresh air and a pleasant run over the moors on a July evening. He lived so near the Pennines but rarely enjoyed them. He recalled that on summer Sundays in years past, he and his wife had enjoyed parking the car in a lay-by and walking a mile or two on the moors taking a rug and a picnic. They hadn't done that for years.

As the road twisted and turned, he caught a glimpse of Wexell's car belting along the quiet road ahead, leap-frogging heavy vehicles travelling to Tintwhistle, Dukinfield or places in Cheshire or Lancashire. Eventually, it was gone. Angel was content to travel at a slower pace. Maybe he'd catch up with him, maybe he wouldn't. He pressed the car to climb a short hill at thirty miles an hour and was happy to keep his foot steady and let gravity determine the speed down the other side. At the brow of a hill, he looked across at green fields, wide stretches of pine trees and the reservoir with its silver twinkling reflections. He smiled, summer was the best time of the year. He was due some holiday soon: when his wife was back and he could leave the Fiona Thomas case, they would go up to Scotland.

Suddenly, round a bend and coming from the opposite direction towards him was the black car. It was being driven fast. He could see the driver, it was Peter Wexell. Angel turned away from the window to avoid being identified as they crossed.

Angel pursed his lips, he drives like a madman. What on earth was he doing on the moors? It wouldn't be to enjoy the scenery. He wouldn't be able to appreciate it driving at that speed. He appeared to be returning to Bromersley, but what was he doing up there? If he had had a rendezvous, it had been a quick one. He was an extraordinary person. And so was Lola.

CHAPTER 8

'What is it?' Angel said, looking up from his desk.

'It came by post, sir,' Cadet Ahmed Ahaz said as he closed the door.

'Oh?'

'It is addressed to you, sir,' Ahmed put a small parcel on the desk.

The Inspector looked at the packet bearing his name and address, care of Bromersley Police, neatly printed in ink on a white label stuck to the brown paper.

He peered at it as he ran his tongue round his mouth and across his teeth. 'Has it been scanned?'

'Yes sir. There's no metal. It looks like a book.'

Angel picked it up with the tips of his fingers. He turned it upside down and then back again. It was wrapped in several layers of brown kraft paper and sealed with opaque sticky tape. There was no indication as to who had sent it. It weighed about six ounces. He shook it, there was the slightest rattle, hard but not metallic. He brought it up to his face and sniffed at it. There was no smell and there was no leak of any substance: he was thinking of acid or caustic soda.

He glanced at Ahmed. 'It's not a book, lad.'

He pulled out the desk drawer, found a sharp penknife and began to cut round the edge of the packet, as if he was filleting plaice, handling it as little as possible.

Ahmed looked on. His eyes slightly closed.

'I warn you, lad,' he said with a grin. 'If it *is* a bomb, you'll have such a headache, it'll take tablets bigger than Moses brought down the mountain to cure it!'

'Yes sir,' he said, shaking his head.

At length, the Inspector was able gently to shake out the contents. A black plastic video cassette dropped onto the desk. It was not labelled. He shook the brown paper to see if there was an enclosure. There wasn't. He carefully picked up the wrapping and put it into a clear view plastic envelope and sealed it. He passed it to Ahmed. 'Label it, and take it to Dr Mac immediately.'

'Yes sir,' Ahmed said and made for the door.

Angel picked up the phone and pressed a button. 'Is there anybody from Scenes of Crime in there?'

'Yes sir.'

'Send him in to me, will you? And tell him to bring his dusting kit.'

A young man appeared at the door almost immediately. He was carrying a black fitted attaché case.

'You wanted me, sir?'

'Dust this for me, lad.' Angel said indicating the videotape.

The man opened his case on the floor. He took out a brush and a plastic flask of aluminium powder and painted the video case on both sides, handling it by his gloved fingertips. It took only a minute. 'It's been wiped clean, sir. There's nothing there.'

'Thanks lad. It's what I expected.'

The young man cleaned the powder off the videotape with a duster and began to put his brush and flask of powder away.

'Is that video player in CID working?'

'Yes sir.'

Angel picked up the tape and dashed out of the room.

Seconds later, he was in the CID office running the video. The pictures were out of focus and the tape scratched slightly, but it was clear that it was the missing security tape from Bardsley Service Station. The shots were taken from two cameras: one sited on the roof of the pay office and the other from inside it, and they were programmed to alternate recording every few seconds. The tape showed the forecourt and pumps, and then the picture changed to show the inside of the pay office and the cash till.

When Angel had absorbed the pattern of the tape, he ran it fast forward until he found the arrival of the two robbers in the Volkswagen estate car on the forecourt at pump number one. He already knew the number plate was false, so he learned nothing there. He saw the two men, one tall and one short, with their backs to the camera, leave the car pulling on balaclavas and gloves and then running to the pay office. He was pleased to note that the picture certainly looked very much like the taller of the two men who was tucked away in a cell. He noticed him putting his hand to his mouth and then quickly removing it before pulling down the woollen balaclava and putting on gloves. Then the picture cut to the two masked robbers entering the pay office. There was a close-up of the head and shoulders of the tall one reaching up to the video recorder to take out the tape, and then the screen went black. He replayed the tape in slow motion from the point where the two men had left their car and ran across the forecourt. He played the tape at normal speed four times. Then he put it on slow play and watched it a frame at a time.

At length, he leaned back in the chair, and smiled from ear to ear. There were no pictures that he could use in court, but he thought the tape provided him with a tiny piece of information that he could work on to get the robber they were holding charged with robbery with violence.

He leaned forward and took the videotape out of the player.

Ahmed came into the room, seeing the Inspector he came straight across to him. Angel saw him coming. 'Ah lad, did you see Dr Mac?'

'Yes sir. He says he'll ring you if there's anything on that parcel wrapper.'

'Right. I'm going up to Bardsley Service Station, if anybody wants me. I've got something urgent to attend to there. I don't expect to be long.'

Angel was at Bardsley in five minutes. He parked his car away from the pumps and went into the pay office. Behind the counter was Mrs Mulholland. She beamed as he came through the door. 'Now then, Inspector, what can I do for you?'

'How are you getting on? How's that lass of yours — Jane?'

'Oh she's not so bad. They let her out of hospital yesterday. Her face is still sore. She had to have that tooth out, and she's still weak but I reckon she'll be all right in a couple of weeks. Mind you, she's too scared to come back in here. She'll never come back in here on her own.'

'No,' he said sympathetically. 'I'm not surprised, Mrs Mulholland. She's a brave lass to stand up to those two.'

'Are you any nearer catching them, Inspector?'

'We've got one.'

Mrs Mulholland's mouth opened and then closed. 'Ooh. I hope you'll send him down for a long time.'

'It's not up to me, love. I just try to catch them.'

'And I've heard you're right good at it too, Inspector,' she replied earnestly.

He smiled and licked his bottom lip. She had more confidence in his ability than he had himself. He rubbed the lobe of his ear between finger and thumb. 'Tell me, Mrs Mulholland, how often do you sweep this frontage?' He glanced out at the forecourt briefly and then turned back.

She paused a second and thought what an unusual question for a policeman to ask. 'Well, I go round with a rubbish bag every day, and pick up any paper and suchlike that may have been dropped. People are so untidy. But I don't sweep it often. It gets dusty, of course, but the wind blows it away. It's worse in the winter, when snow with mud falls from under the cars while they're standing being filled up. But in the summer, it's not really necessary. Why?'

'You haven't swept it recently?'

'No. Does it look dirty?'

'No. No. Not at all.' Angel smiled. 'Mmm. Oh, just wondered.' He turned to the door, paused, turned back and said, 'I'll just have a look round before I go, Mrs Mulholland. Remember me to Jane, will you? I hope to see you again soon. With some more good news.'

'Goodbye, Inspector.'

With a wave of the hand, he closed the pay office door and walked slowly across to pump number one, his head bowed searching the ground. At one point he squatted down and pressed his thumb, screwing it round on something on the concrete floor. He nodded and then stood up and turned towards his car. He put the key in the lock and looked back to where he had squatted. He rubbed his hand across his chin and got into the car.

Mrs Mulholland, who had been watching him through the paydesk window, shook her head as he drove away.

He was soon back in his office. The phone was ringing as he came through the door. He snatched it up. 'Angel.'

'It's Crisp, sir.'

'Yes lad. What have you got?'

'There's no sign of Miriam Thomas sir. The hospital staff are quite worried about her.'

'They're not the only ones.'

'She should have reported for work on Monday and she didn't show and they've still heard nothing. I have been to the flat she shared with her sister. Her belongings appear to be there, except there are no suitcases. There's no sign of her packing up and leaving or anything like that.'

'Right lad, keep digging. Find out if the sisters have any relatives. What have you found out about Violet Rae?'

'Nothing yet, sir. Nobody remembers her. The staff are all pretty much under forty and they didn't know her. Some had heard about the death of the male nurse by a patient in 1981, but they don't remember Violet Rae.'

'There must be somebody. Try the local newspaper. Ask to look back at old records of the day. And get a photograph. There must be a photograph of her when she passed her exams and got her cap and gown and bedpan, or whatever.'

'Right, sir.'

Angel replaced the phone. He pursed his lips and blew out a long sigh. It looked as if Miriam Thomas was missing. And she was last heard of in Bromersley — on his patch.

He didn't like that.

There was a knock on the door.

'Come in.'

It was Cadet Ahmed Ahaz.

'Come in lad. I was just going to send for you. Sit down there. What did you want?'

'Dr Mac phoned, sir. He wants you to ring him back.'

'Oh? Right.'

'And I have got a reel of white cotton for you. For that button.'

'Right lad. Ta.'

'And the laundry you asked about has closed down, sir. It went bust two years ago.'

'What?' he bellowed, waving his hands in the air. 'Well,that's marvellous! How on earth am I going to get some clean shirts while Mrs Angel is away?'

He stood up and walked across the tiny office to the window and back. 'I don't mind telling you lad, I'm fed up with this. It's like camping out. I'll be glad when her mother gets better and she can come home where she belongs!'

Ahmed didn't know quite where to look. He began counting the number of terracotta tiles on the floor.

After a few moments, Angel slumped in the swivel chair and sighed noisily. 'I'll have to buy some new shirts. That's all. There's no other way. And that'll set me back a few quid.'

Ahmed muttered, 'I am sorry, sir.'

Angel turned to the Cadet and asked, grumpily, 'Have you any more bad news, lad?'

'No sir,' he said innocently.

'Well, I've another job for you. I want you to report Miriam Thomas to Missing Persons. Write this down. She is aged about forty-two. Worked as a Nurse at Pontylliath Hospital, Wales. Brown hair. Brown eyes. Height five foot two. Weight a hundred pounds. Missing since Saturday last. Got it?'

'Yes sir.'

'Get that off straight away.'

'Yes sir,' Ahmed said and eagerly made for the door.

'Hang on, lad. Hang on. I haven't finished.' Ahmed turned back.

'Aye. Will you also get me some chewing gum?'

Ahmed's eyes widened. 'Chewing gum?'

'It's not for me, lad.'

'Yes sir. What flavour?'

Angel made a face. 'I don't know, do I? The most popular flavour, I suppose. What's that? Peppermint?'

'Peppermint then sir. Anything else?'

'Aye. I want to send some flowers to that lass that got knocked about by those two hoodlums. She's out of hospital now. Jane Mulholland. Put a card in. "Get well soon. Kind regards. DI Angel." And get them to send the bill to me, here. All right?'

'Where shall I order them from, sir?'

'I don't know. Oh yes. The best place is that little flower shop on Market Street. The one with all that lace and ribbon display in the window.'

Ahmed looked blank.

'Don't you know it, lad? It's run by those two poofs.'

* * *

Angel picked up the phone and dialled a number. It was soon answered. 'Mortuary.'

106

'Hello Mac. It's Michael Angel. You wanted me to ring you.'

'Oh yes, Mike. It's about that brown paper wrapper.'

'Oh yes?'

'Didn't you look at it?'

'I didn't want to contaminate it, Mac.'

'There are no prints, but you didn't expect any did you?'

'No. The address is written in old-fashioned ink. You ken? From out of a bottle.'

'I ken. I can just about remember what ink is.'

'Presumably by someone who uses a posh fountain pen. And it was posted in Bromersley yesterday.'

'Thanks, Mac. Thanks very much.'

'All part of the service. Do you want to know anything else?'

'Yes. The name of the person who sent it?'

'I'll leave that to you. I wouldn't want to put you out of honest employment.'

'There is something, Mac.'

'What's that, laddie?'

'I'm not having any luck with this Fiona Thomas murder. Have you found out why an intelligent, sensible, strait-laced woman was going around wearing a stocking inside out?'

'It's got me, Mike. But I hadn't forgotten. I haven't given up on it yet.'

'All right, Mac. Thanks for your help.'

'Cheers.'

Angel slowly put the phone back in its cradle. He leaned back in the swivel chair, stretched out his arms and arched his back. He looked up at the ceiling for inspiration and made a decision. It wasn't a difficult one. It was time, he decided, to call on Peter Wexell.

Angel parked his car on a meter in Eden Street and put a printed cardboard 'Police' sign on the inside of the windscreen. He made for the mahogany painted entrance to the offices of Pettigrew and Shaw. In the entrance hall, he faced double glass doors with the word 'Reception' painted on them. He pushed open the left hand door into a big reception room with high walls and a vaulted ceiling. The lower parts of the walls were wood panelled, above the panelling were a dozen larger-than-life-size oil paintings in ornate gilt frames depicting different Pettigrews, some in red robes and wearing mayoral chains, some in morning dress, and others in breeches with ugly wives and miserable children dressed in duck egg blue or mustard coloured coats and pants, and some had a dog, a grey whippet in a big black collar, laid in front of the fireplace. Angel made his way past comfortable leather easy chairs and settees, which were placed around the floor in twos and threes. The reception area was empty of visitors. The only people there were a trio of pretty girls at the far end of the room working intensively at computers that were positioned on valuable antique desks behind a tall barrier with a counter top. He ploughed through the thick Chinese carpet towards them. The girls appeared not to notice his presence, but by the time he arrived at the enquiry counter, one of the budding Miss Worlds had risen from her computer and was smiling into his face. She came up very close, maintained a long look straight into his eyes and, in a dreamy voice, said, 'Hello. Can I help you?'

Angel smiled. He was momentarily disarmed, but he was under no illusion that he had made any personal impression on the young lady.

'I would like to see Mr Peter Wexell, please,' he said in his best Richard Burton voice. He presented his card from an ivory and tortoiseshell case, which he kept for such occasions.

Her slim, white, manicured hand took the card as if it was a cheque for a million pounds and read it. She bestowed another smile on him, tilted her head slightly so that her hair swirled round and bounced on her suntanned neck. 'Have you an appointment, Inspector Angel?'

'No.'

'That's all right. I'm sure he'll see you. Excuse me.' She turned back to her desk and picked up a phone. It was answered immediately. 'There's Inspector Angel to see you, Mr Wexell.'

She replaced the phone and returned to Angel. 'He's coming immediately, Inspector.'

'Thank you.'

'It's a pleasure.'

Angel turned away from the reception desk. He couldn't help smiling. All this old world courtesy and charm from beautiful women was beguiling. It must be difficult to get angry in the place. He thought what a shame it was that such charm and beauty should be wasted on the young, and underutilised in a solicitor's office in an industrial town in South Yorkshire. She could be a model throwing it about in Paris, Milan, New York or wherever.

He looked across at the leather chairs and was contemplating where he might sit, when the double entrance doors swung wide open and Peter Wexell in smart suit, white shirt, moustache and big smile came into the room. He walked quickly across the carpet to within a yard of the Inspector before he spoke.

'How nice to see you, Inspector,' he held out his hand to shake it. 'Please come into my private office,' he said turning and taking Angel by the elbow. He spoke as if they were blood brothers and hadn't seen each other since the last family wedding.

He glanced back to the receptionist. 'Thank you, Gloria.'

'It's a pleasure,' she replied sweetly with a further tilt of the head. She turned away to her computer.

Wexell and Angel went out through the doors and along a corridor to the first door, which was partly open. It led to a small office with desk and chair, two filing cabinets, two stationery cupboards, a notice board covered with papers and a year's chart stuck on the wall. Wexell ushered him through it to a door at the end, which led into his office, a large room with an arch shaped window reaching to the floor. It was furnished like a sitting room cum study complete with TV and bar. In front of the huge window was a partners' desk with telephone and papers neatly arranged on it in columns. A young lady was waiting by the desk holding a letter. When the men came in, she smiled.

Wexell said, 'Is it ready, Ingrid?'

The woman nodded and put the letter down on the desk in front of him.

He began to read it. He glanced briefly at Angel and said, 'Do, please excuse me, Inspector. I have to get this letter off. Won't be a moment.'

Angel nodded and looked round the room. 'Sit down, Inspector,' the solicitor said, with his eyes on the letter.

Angel slowly unfastened his coat and sat down in a comfortable round-bottomed armchair upholstered in green leather. He looked out of the big arched window at the colourful show of flowers in front of the town hall on the opposite side of the road. Then he saw Wexell, who was still standing, open the middle drawer of his desk, take out a fountain pen, unscrew the top, sign the letter and return the pen to the drawer. He observed that the pen was indeed a fountain pen and that the ink was black. He pursed his lips. As usual, Dr Mac's observations proved invaluable.

Ingrid picked up the letter and left the room, quietly closing the door.

'Now then, Inspector. Sorry about that. What can I do for you? You have my complete attention,' he said, moving into the big swivel chair behind the desk.

Angel pursed his lips, took in a deep breath and then slowly blew it out. He deliberately took his time.

Wexell gazed at him expectantly across the polished desk, and without looking down, adjusted his shirt cuffs to show an inch of starched white below the jacket sleeves.

'I got a parcel this morning,' Angel said smoothly when he could not drag out the pause any longer. He looked closely at the solicitor, who returned the look, his face revealing nothing.

'Oh?'

Angel didn't reply.

The silence embarrassed Wexell. He had to break it. 'What was it? A gift?'

'No. No,' Angel replied slowly. 'As a matter of fact it was a videotape.'

'A videotape. Oh?' Wexell said, trying to look surprised.

'Yes. And I've come to thank you for it. You were right to send it to me. I am most grateful.'

There was a pause, then a smile slowly developed and spread across Peter Wexell's suntanned face. 'What makes you think I sent it?'

'Forensics,' Angel said confidently.

Wexell grinned, but his eyes weren't smiling. After a moment he nodded and said, 'You are very clever, Inspector. My duty to help the police and all that,' he said with a wave of the hand. 'I came by it. Played it. It was obviously a security tape.'

'And how did you come by it? It is very strange for you to be in possession of a security tape of a service station that had recently been robbed, isn't it?'

'Well, yes. I suppose it is. The fact is, it came to me in error.'

'Obviously. It seems the thieves who stole your tape also took the security tape from the service station and mixed the two up. After arranging to return your tape to you, they actually sent you the wrong tape.'

'Inspector, you know that I am anxious to have the tape that was stolen from this office returned to me. Well, I was using my own efforts to have it returned. After all, you didn't seem to be making any progress. My explanation as to how I came by that tape could be wrongly construed by a zealous prosecuting counsel as aiding and abetting a criminal in the execution of a crime. I thought that sending the tape to you was the best thing to do.'

Angel pursed his lips. 'As I have said, I am thankful. But what criminal are you referring to?'

The solicitor smiled. 'I don't have to incriminate myself, Inspector. I am saying nothing more.'

'Mmm. You know that if I choose to get difficult, I could have you subpoenaed.'

'You could, but you won't. Because you know that if you put me in the witness box, I wouldn't say anything I didn't want to say. And let me point out, you have no witnesses.'

'We have the parcel itself. We can prove it came from you,' he lied.

Wexell shook his head and continued firmly. 'But you can't prove that I am withholding any information. In any case, it's only a trivial offence. It's not worth making a fuss about.'

'That's for me to decide.'

'Well. Inspector, I expect over the years, you have chosen not to prosecute someone who had helped you, or there were some other extenuating circumstances why you didn't prosecute a criminal, even though you would have been pretty certain of a conviction?'

Angel wasn't going to admit that to Wexell. 'You know that a police officer has to proceed with a prosecution if he believes he can get a conviction. If he doesn't, he is guilty of an offence himself.'

'I know the law, Inspector. And that's why I'm not prepared to incriminate myself by going into the matter any further. You have to understand, to put it as modestly as I can, that being a figure of some importance in this town, and having built up a practice based upon integrity, I could not risk being charged with a criminal offence. Apart from myself, it would have a catastrophic effect upon my wife, my partners and subsequently this practice. I am not stupid.'

'You forget that I have forensic evidence to show that the tape came from you.'

'So you say, but I don't have to dig myself in any deeper. In any case, I don't know anything that would bring a criminal to book. I have no name, no address, not even a description of the man who sent me the tape.'

'Even so, I'd very much like to get him behind bars. We have conclusive evidence that the two men who broke into your offices and stole that tape are also the same pair that robbed a service station in broad daylight. The tape you sent to me shows pictures of that robbery. The pictures are indistinct and probably won't in themselves make evidence, but it helps to link that crime of armed robbery to the burglary of your offices. And, can I point out, that one of the two men was armed and that they assaulted a young woman who had to have an operation and five days in hospital to recover from injuries at his hand.'

Wexell licked his lips.

Angel gripped the arms of the chair and leaned forward sticking his jaw out. 'We are not dealing with a couple of tuppeny-ha'penny housebreakers here, Mr Wexell. These are hoodlums that could end up doing a life stretch for murder if they are not brought to heel. I am holding one of them at the station right now, but between you and me, I am having difficulty making a case against him stick.'

'I wish I could help you, Inspector. But what I know is hardly going to make any difference.'

'The other one is armed and a vicious man. He could murder someone before the week is out, or may already have done so. If you are negotiating with him, you are playing with fire. Will you tell me what you *do* know to help me get this pair put away?'

Wexell pulled the face of a man in pain. 'I have committed no crime other than negotiating with a criminal to try to have my property returned to me.'

'I believe you,' Angel lied.

'Will you undertake not to bring any charges against me?'

'That would be a deal,' he winced. 'I can't do deals.'

'Then I can't help you, Inspector.'

Angel's jaw tightened. He drummed his fingers on the chair arms. After a few seconds, he leaned across Wexell's desk, smiled and said, 'Tell you what. There's more than one way of skinning a cat. Could you not tell me about a hypothetical client, whose confidentiality prevents you from giving me his name?'

The solicitor peered closely at him.

Angel leaned forward and, by way of explanation, added, 'Let's say you have a client who came by a videotape. *He* could have given it to you to return to the police, couldn't he?'

Wexell looked above Angel's head for a moment in thought, then he lowered his eyes to look into the policeman's eyes. He smiled and nodded knowingly.

CHAPTER 9

There was a knock at the door.

Wexell was glad of the interruption. 'Come in.'

It was the secretary carrying a tray of tea. She put it on the desk.

'Thank you very much, Ingrid. Leave us, I'll pour.'

She smiled and left them quietly.

Wexell waited for the door to close and then he began. 'Well, Inspector, as you suggest, I have a client who had a videotape of his work and life and business interests stolen in a robbery at his place of work.'

Angel nodded and smiled encouragingly.

'A few days after a robbery, he got a letter from the robber.'

'Where is it?'

'Burned, I'm afraid.'

Angel pulled a face and shook his head.

Wexell continued. 'It said that the writer had a videotape that I — my client — might be interested in and that he wanted a thousand pounds for it. If he wanted its return, he was told to get the money in small used notes, wrap it in a brown paper parcel, put a notice in the *Bromersley Chronicle* under the Personal Column to read, "To Hubert, Peter will play," and then to await instructions. My client did all that, and on Wednesday afternoon at about five o'clock, my client got instructions by phone to take the parcel out to the Manchester road and put it under the Bromersley boundary signpost. And that was done.'

'Yes,' Angel said, smiling. 'I saw you up there driving like a bat out of hell at 5.30 on Tuesday. Did you see anybody or anything?'

'No. My client said he saw nothing,' Wexell said carefully.

'What was the voice like?'

'Ordinary, but he had a cockney accent.'

Angel nodded. It fitted the information he already had. 'And how did your client get his tape back?'

'It was in his letterbox the following morning. He was delighted. However it was the wrong tape. Externally, one tape looks just like another.'

'So your client was a thousand quid out and in possession of the wrong tape?'

'Precisely.' Wexell picked up the silver teapot and pointed it at a cup.

'I see. Then what happened?'

'He put a notice in the paper again. Saying, "To Hubert. Wrong parcel but Peter is still willing to play." Wexell pointed to the teacup. 'Help yourself to sugar and milk, Inspector.'

'Ta.' Angel dug the apostle spoon into the sugar bowl.

'It worked. The robber phoned and said that he had the tape but it was going to cost my client another thousand pounds. He agreed to pay. So the man said he was to make up the money in a brown paper parcel as before and await instructions.'

'And when are you expecting him to phone?'

Wexell shrugged. 'Anytime.'

Angel's jaw dropped open. 'Anytime? Anytime now?'

He nodded.

Angel hurriedly lowered the teacup and dived into his pocket for his mobile. He banged a number onto the panel of the phone. Then he turned to the solicitor and said, 'Excuse me, sir. I had better do this now.'

Wexell's jaw tightened. 'I don't want surrounding with blue uniforms and buttons, Inspector. It would frighten him off.'

'Get me Superintendent Harker.'

'He's out, sir.'

'Is DS Crisp back yet.'

'I haven't seen him. He's in Wales.'

'I know he's in Wales,' he roared. 'I sent him there. Who is in CID?'

'I'll put you through.'

There was a pause.

Angel's eyes flashed back to Wexell. 'Don't worry, sir. We *have* done this sort of thing before.'

A small voice answered the phone. 'CID. Cadet Ahaz speaking.'

'Who's there besides you?'

'Oh, it's you, sir?'

'Yes, it's me, lad. Who is there besides you?'

'Nobody, sir. It's dinnertime. I was just going to have my lunch.'

'I hope you're not planning on having kippers, lad. I want you to do something for me right away.'

'Oh no, sir. I mean, yes sir?'

Angel spoke very precisely. He knew time was probably short. 'Listen carefully. Switch on your mobile immediately, and bring it, and a pair of handcuffs to Pettigrew and Shaw's solicitors, on Eden Street. And take a taxi. And be quick about it. Got it?'

'Yes, sir.'

'Meet me there. I am in Mr Wexell's office. Hurry, lad.'

Angel switched off the mobile and dropped it in his pocket. There was a knock on the door.

'Come in.'

It was Ingrid. And she wasn't smiling. She looked at Wexell. 'Sorry to interrupt. There's an urgent message for you.' She passed a small folded piece of paper to the solicitor.

Wexell took the paper and read it. His eyebrows shot up. He turned to Angel and said, 'It's him. On the phone.' He nodded towards the instrument on his desk.

Angel's eyes lit up. 'Ah,' he grunted and pushed himself out of the chair.

'Thank you, Ingrid,' Wexell said as he rose to his feet.

She made for the door.

'Right. Now take your time,' the policeman said coolly. 'And I want to hear, if I can.'

They watched the door close behind Ingrid. Then Angel nodded to Wexell and he snatched up the phone. Angel put his head near the solicitor's.

'Peter Wexell speaking.'

'You took your time,' the hard cockney voice said.

'I was with a client.'

'I don't want no tricks, Wexell. Got the money?'

'Yes. Have you got the tape?'

'Course I 'ave. You won't need your car this time. You can leg it down smartly to the centre of tarn to the phone box at the corner of the market building and Cod's Head Alley. Put the money on the shelf in there and disappear. And hurry up. If you're not there in three minutes, I'm off. And you can wave goodbye to your tape.'

There was a loud click.

Wexell replaced the phone and immediately bent down to a desk drawer. He took out a small paper parcel. 'I'm off, Inspector.'

'Give me a minute's start. That's all. Have you got a back exit?'

'Oh yes. I'll get the girl to show you.'

'Good. You go out by your front door, put the money in the telephone box and then come straight back here, in case you're being watched. And don't rush. He'll wait a minute.'

118

'Right.' Wexell opened the door.

The secretary was standing at her desk in the anteroom shuffling some papers.

'Ingrid, will you quickly show the Inspector the rear door to the car park?'

She nodded and made for the door. Angel was straight behind her.

Wexell watched them chase along the corridor and down some steps. He saw the policeman reach into his pocket for his mobile. He looked at his watch.

Angel reached the precinct three minutes later. The area was crowded with hundreds of shoppers bearing plastic bags of all colours and sizes. Groups of giggling girls walked linking arms in lines of up to five; long-faced men carried bags for their weary looking wives; young women with babies pushed prams with tired youngsters hanging onto the handle; middle-aged women thrust shopping trolleys dangerously around the feet of old people; a boy ambled along nibbling a hamburger out of a paper and skilfully kicking an empty lager can along at the same time. Everything was normal for a market day in Bromersley. 'Hubert' had deliberately chosen the busiest time of the week.

Angel positioned himself so that he could see the telephone box door in a reflection in the busy delicatessen shop window at the opposite side of the precinct. The confused smell of freshly ground coffee and not so fresh fish drifted around the door. He looked at his watch. Four minutes had passed. He hoped to see a short man hovering around the telephone box. There was no one.

Just then, Peter Wexell arrived from out of the crowd. He opened the telephone box door smartly, put the brown paper packet of money on the shelf, closed the door, turned round and walked off. He was lost in the throng in seconds.

There was a slight stir in the precinct as an enormously fat woman wearing a long blue coat with a fur collar, a black hat skewered with an evil looking hatpin with a big pearl on the end of it, and mittens came into view. The state of the coat suggested that she wore the same clothes in the summer as she did in the winter. She perspired in the heat and emitted a punishing smell of cabbage water, which hung around in the nostrils for some time even after she had passed by. She was pushing a child's pram overloaded with a dirty pedal bin, a damaged guitar with a string of turquoise coloured beads hanging from it, an umbrella, a packet of streaky bacon, a 1989 copy of *Yellow Pages*, a brown paper bag of Brussels sprout peelings, two loaves of bread, a bottle of Sheffield Sunny Smooth Sherry, and many other interesting items peeking out from underneath. The shoppers didn't seem to see her coming, but they steered out of the way as she advanced towards them and then closed in again when she passed. Nobody was seen to observe her coming but, when they had passed her, some looked back at her and subconsciously pulled a face.

Angel knew her, it was Elspeth Bottle. She had been involved in minor skirmishes with the police for years. It was usually for shoplifting or drunk and disorderly. She had spent several nights in the cells at Bromersley Police Station annoying the duty Sergeant by repeatedly singing 'Three Little Maids from school' until six o'clock in the morning. Angel was always inclined to let her go without charge. She was usually more trouble in the station and in the Court than the offence warranted.

When he saw her, he gritted his teeth. 'Go away, Elspeth,' he said under his breath. 'Go away. Don't muck up my pitch!'

Elspeth Bottle was only five yards away from the telephone kiosk. She had observed Wexell depositing the packet, and she could see it through the glass window. She aimed straight for it. She jammed her pram by a drainpipe against the wall, yanked open the door, snatched the loot, stuffed it in the pram between the guitar and the bottle of Sheffield Sunny Smooth Sherry and waddled like a duck being chased by a fox up Cod's Head Alley. At the top, the pram went round the corner so fast, it careered on two wheels and the pedal bin bounced up and down precariously.

Angel's eyes swept around the precinct. There was no sign of a short man near the telephone box. There was no sign of anyone near the telephone box. There was no sign of Cadet Ahaz either. He ran his hand across his mouth. He must not lose that money. That was the lure he hoped was going to lead him to his next arrest. He sprung into action. He raced across the precinct, weaving his way between shoppers, prams, pushchairs and trolleys. He passed the kiosk and thrust his way up Cod's Head Alley. When he reached the top, he stopped and looked each way. Shoppers pushed into him from both directions. It was the busiest pedestrian intersection in Bromersley on market Day. Elspeth Bottle was nowhere to be seen. One way led to the rear entrance to the Market Hall, and the other way led to a multiple chain store, smaller shops and the Bus station beyond. He opted for the Market Hall. He shuffled sideways to speed his progress and slowly made his way through the crowd, treading on more than one set of toes, until he eventually arrived at the back entrance of the building.

The semi-open section of the modern concrete market contained sixty colourful stalls with unshaded electric light bulbs over men and women on duck boards throwing produce into brown paper bags and yelling out unintelligible announcements such as, 'Oy de pell de pow,' and, 'Lass to med you bee.' People were milling around, drifting in every direction, occasionally stopping to look up at the colourful display of fruit, vegetables and flowers and trying to decipher the hand scrawled signs hanging over the produce.

Angel's eyes scoured round the hall looking for the huge, blue coated Mrs Bottle. He went through an arch into another big hall with more stalls selling dry goods and clothes. He struggled past 'Norah's for Knickers' and the 'Northern Continental Gaslight Company'.

Angel looked across the hall at the assortment of shopper's heads; he stood on his toes and panned to the left and then to the right and then back again like a searchlight. Then he suddenly spotted a black hat with a pearl ended hatpin sticking out of it anchored to a mop of black hair, below it a blue coat with a fur collar. Yes. It was Elspeth Bottle. He sighed with relief. She was in front of the Market Café. It was two stalls against a wall, with water plumbed to a geyser over a sink behind a big silver urn. You could get sausage rolls, pork pies and sandwiches there. The old man running it was filling a cup from the urn. The tea was weak, short of milk and in dirty cups, but people leaning at the counter were drinking it. She kept bobbing up and down, in and out of view. Angel couldn't see what was happening. He made speed for the café and pushed through what he thought was a gap in the shoppers. A young boy daubed an ice cream down the front of his new Reid and Taylor worsted. He growled at him, pulled a face and carried on. He wasn't about to lose her again. She had a thousand pounds in that pram and, more importantly, she could be leading him to the little thug who had struck terror into young Jane Mulholland and committed other crimes. Angel could still see the frail girl in the ambulance holding her bloody face and bravely telling how she tried to hold onto the cash till in the petrol station. There would be no escape for him.

Angel was now only a few feet from the café. He could see Elspeth Bottle's enormous frame and hear her voice. She spoke surprisingly pleasantly. Her speech was clear and she had an adequate vocabulary. 'I've got it safe. I've got it safe. Don't you worry about that, Mister. Twenty pounds and it's yours. Now pay up, else I'm off.'

A loud cockney voice was yelling hysterically. 'Hurry up, you silly old cow, what have you done wiv it? Where have you put it? I saw you myself put it in the bloody pram. And I said a fiver! Now where the 'ell is it?'

Shoppers passed the front of the café hardly bothering to glance at the two characters leaning over the pram and shouting. Mrs Bottle had the bottle of Sheffield Sunny Smooth Sherry in her hand and the copy of *Yellow Pages* for 1989 under her arm. The guitar was sticking up at a dangerous angle in the pram. The remainder of the pram contents were on the floor.

The little man's scarlet face came up out of the pram. 'I got to go! I got to go!' he yelled urgently. 'Where the 'ell is it?' he screamed at Mrs Bottle.

Then Angel saw him. His deep, loud voice didn't match his stature. He was five foot four inches tall. He had big teeth and heavy, bottle-bottom glasses. He was dressed in a sharp navy blue suit with a grey pinstripe, bow tie, black oily hair and black leather shoes.

A man in a blue-and-white striped apron came from behind the big silver tea urn. It was the man who ran the little cafe. He stood with his hands akimbo at the entrance. 'Hey, you two,' he said authoritatively, pointing at the pram. 'Take that thing and 'op it. You're ruining my business. Nobody is going to stop here while you two are shouting the odds. Now buzz off before I send for a copper. And do your courting somewhere else!' Then he returned to his position behind the urn on the counter, lifting his eyes skywards at a brave solitary customer waiting to be served.

The little man's jaw dropped, then tightened. He turned back to Elspeth Bottle.

'All right. All right. You win, Missus. Twenty quid it is.' He dug a hand into his inside pocket, pulled out a wallet and began fumbling inside it. 'Give me the packet quick. Here's twenty quid,' he said sullenly.

Angel saw the big American Class ring on his finger. It was exactly what he had wanted to see.

Elspeth Bottle smiled and thrust her ample hand down into the pocket of the blue coat.

Angel took a last look round for any sign of Cadet Ahaz. There was none. He had to go it alone. He squeezed forward, was briefly jostled and then ejected between two large ladies, like a cork out of a bottle. He found himself next to the pram. He promptly reached over to the little man, put his hand on his shoulder, and securely gripping him, looked at the woman and said evenly, 'Is this man bothering you, Elspeth?'

She looked round at the policeman. 'Mr Angel!' she said, her big, white face brightening with pleasure.

The little man's eyes were popping out of his head. He closed the wallet and started to struggle. "'Ere, get your hands off me!' he said indignantly.

Mrs Bottle leaned over to the policeman. 'How nice to see you. Nah. It'd take more than a shrimp like him to bother me, Mr Angel.' The cabbage water reached his nostrils. He pulled a face, closed his mouth and leaned away from her.

The little man took hold of the policeman's forearm and tried to release his grip. Angel maintained his hold.

'Will you let go? Get orf. Get orf!'

Angel tightened the grip. 'Be still, lad. Be still. You're not going anywhere.'

Mrs Bottle returned to retrieving her valuables from the floor and packing them in the pram.

'What's it all about then?' Angel said.

'He owes me twenty pounds and he won't pay up,' she said stuffing a bowler hat at the side of the guitar.

'Does he?' Angel said, looking down at the red-faced man and affecting a smile.

'It's a fiver,' he chirped.

'It's twenty,' Mrs Bottle alleged, busily heaving the old pedal bin on top of the pram and wedging it to make it safe.

The policeman gripped the collar tighter. His fingers sunk into the shoulder pad. 'Now don't be a mean little bastard,' he said, still holding the smile. 'Pay the lady.'

'What's it got to do with you, Lofty?'

Angel dropped the smile. 'I am a police officer.'

The little man's eyes opened wide briefly. He promptly stopped struggling, opened the wallet, found a twenty pound note and held it out to Mrs Bottle. She grabbed it, unfolded it, looked at it, smiled and shoved it in her pocket. She then pushed up her mittens with the palm of her hands and grabbed the pram handle.

'Look I've paid her. What more do you want? Now let me go, Constable.'

Angel tightened his grip. He spoke through his teeth. *'Inspector*, lad. *Inspector*. My name's Inspector Angel.'

He swallowed. 'Look 'ere, Inspector, you don't want to believe anything that old bat tells you.' He made another attempt at breaking Angel's grip. 'I've done nothing wrong, let me go.'

'I can't do that, lad. I can't do that. You've got a very important appointment to keep with a lady.'

The man blinked through the bottle bottoms. 'Appointment? A lady? What lady?'

Angel beamed down at him. 'Her Majesty.'

'Her Majesty? Uh? What do you mean? Where?'

'It depends.'

'What on?'

'Where there are vacancies. Her Majesty would want you to be comfortable.'

'Oh. What are you on about?'

'Oh yes. Well, there's Maidstone, Durham, Strangeways, Pentonville, Armley. Or perhaps you'd like somewhere more modern, in the country, like Doncaster.'

The little man grunted and made a further vigorous attempt to wrench himself free.

A familiar voice rang out behind Angel. It was Cadet Ahaz. 'There you are, sir. Couldn't see you. Heard the row. You said by a telephone box.'

'That was an hour ago,' he growled. 'I thought you must have been choosing your eight gramophone records.'

'What's that, sir?'

Angel ignored the question. 'Have you brought any help?'

'There's a van and two uniformed PCs outside, sir.'

'Well, fetch them in here, lad. There's no need for them to loll about in the precinct topping up their suntan!'

Angel noticed that Elspeth Bottle had found a chink in the crowd and was endeavouring to push her pram towards the main exit. 'And stop that woman. She's coming with us. Did you bring the handcuffs?'

Ahmed handed them to him and rushed after Mrs Bottle.

125

The little man looked at the handcuffs. "'Ere, what are you going to do wiv them?'

Angel looked down at him. He pointed to the big ring dominating the man's hand. 'They're for you. They're bracelets. *I know* how much you like jewellery.'

CHAPTER 10

There was a knock at the door.

'Come in.'

It was DS Crisp. 'Have you five minutes, sir?'

Angel looked up from his desk. 'Oh? It's you. It's about time. Back from your world tour promoting your new album, are you? Come in, lad. I've as long as it takes. Sit down. What have you found out? Were Pontylliath police helpful?'

Crisp took the seat nearest to Angel's desk. He had a cream file, which he held on his lap.

'They were helpful, but they didn't know much. All the lads and lasses at the station were too young to remember the incident in 1981, but they let me look in the files. No one in Pontylliath nick could remember Sister Violet Rae. And I wasn't able to find a relative. I went to Pontylliath hospital and spoke to the Manager. He was instrumental in getting me a photograph of her taken in a group.'

Angel's eyebrows shot up. 'A photograph? Where is it, lad?'

Crisp opened the file and pulled out a large print with eighty-five people, mostly women and girls in uniforms, nurses, sisters, matrons, auxiliary nurses, cleaners and doctors all crowded onto it. The photograph was taken outdoors at the front of the hospital with the personnel placed in tiers four deep. The back row was presumably standing on chairs, the next row standing, the next sitting and the next kneeling. At the bottom of the photograph was printed, 'Staff of the Pontylliath Hospital for the Criminally Insane — 10 May 1981.' A sheet of tracing paper, with a penned outline of the people on the photograph and their names, was fastened with sticky tape. Angel found the outline of Sister V. Rae and then whipped it over to see the photograph of her. The average height of the others in the same row suggested that Sister Violet Rae was about five foot four inches tall. She was slim and dark-haired. The image was too small to make out anything special about the face.

Angel grunted. 'Mmm.' He turned the photograph over. 'It isn't very good. Who took this? Is there a name anywhere?'

'The local newspaper. I enquired. The photographer is dead and the plate was presumably destroyed years ago.'

Angel growled and dropped the photograph on the desk. 'Couldn't you find a live photographer? Well, we now know she existed, that she was average height, dark-haired and slim. I suppose you'd say she was not unattractive.'

'And very young to be a Sister.'

Angel wiped a hand across his mouth. He reached over to the phone and pressed a button.

A voice answered. 'CID Cadet Ahaz speaking.'

'Come in here, lad.' He replaced the phone and turned to DS Crisp. 'Notice anything about the date?'

'1981, sir.'

Angel picked the photograph up again. 'Aye. The same year that that male nurse was killed. This would be a fair reproduction of how Violet Rae must have looked just before she disappeared.' He peered closely at it. 'Does it remind you of anyone, lad?'

'No.'

'Mmm. Don't you think it has a vague look of…?'

There was a knock at the door.

'Come in.'

Cadet Ahmed Ahaz came into the office. 'Ah yes. Come here, lad. Look at this.' Ahmed looked down at the photograph and blinked.

'See that woman there?' Angel said.

Ahmed stuck a long brown finger on the print. 'That one, sir?'

'Aye. Can you put this in that machine of yours and blow it up?'

'Yes sir. That can be scanned all right. How big do you want it?

'As big as you can, up to where it loses definition. That's a photograph of Violet Rae taken in 1981.'

'Oh? The woman we're looking for?'

Angel smiled at him and winked. 'You're quick, lad. You're quick.'

Ahmed grinned. He picked up the photograph and went out.

Angel turned to Crisp. 'Well, did you get anything else, lad?'

'Yes sir.' He reached out for the yellow file. 'I got a Photostat of the local newspaper report of the death of the male nurse dated 20 May 1981. That's a week after it happened.'

Angel took it eagerly. It read:

Patient kills Nurse

Male Nurse Derri Evans, 25, of Abergele Road, was brutally killed by schizophrenic Gavin Meredith, a patient at Pontylliath Hospital for the Criminally Insane on Wednesday last.

A spokesman at the hospital said that Nurse Evans went to the secure single cell to administer a routine injection, when Meredith savagely attacked him with a metal bedstead.

He suffered serious injuries to the head and died shortly afterwards.

Nurse Evans had been working at the hospital for two years and was a popular member of staff. He had been due to marry fellow Nurse Miriam Thomas in June.

A hospital spokesman said that it was a tragic accident and that Gavin was a much-liked, conscientious nurse and would be sadly missed by his friends.

No criminal action is to be brought against Gavin Meredith who is being held at Her Majesty's pleasure for the murder of his wife in 1977.

Security at Pontylliath Hospital is under review.

Angel read the report again. 'Mmm. There's nothing new there. That's pretty much what Miriam Thomas told me.'

Crisp pulled out another sheet of paper. 'And I've got a copy of a newspaper article printed a week later on 27 May 1981.' He passed it to Angel.

'Ta.'

It read:

Missing Nurse in £20,000 drugs swindle

Sister Violet Rae of the Pontylliath Hospital for the Criminally Insane has disappeared. She was reported missing following the opening of an enquiry into a mammoth drugs and equipment swindle at the hospital.

Rae, aged 24, of New Flats, Broadway, Pontylliath, was due to face questions before a tribunal at the hospital on Monday morning.

Up to £20,000's worth of drugs, bandages, plasters, hypodermic syringes and other specialised equipment used to treat patients has been syphoned away from the hospital.

Also it has been revealed that patients have not always received full doses of drugs prescribed by doctors.

On Sunday afternoon, Violet Rae's flat was found to be cleared of her clothes and personal items, after her landlord had received her keys through his letterbox and visited the flat to find out what had happened.

The investigation was opened following the tragic death of Nurse Derri Evans on 13 May (Reported in last Friday's edition of the *Pontylliath Times*). According to the Coroner's

Office, Sister Rae is wanted for manslaughter, theft, fraud and drugs offences.

A hospital spokesman said that the death of Nurse Evans had raised serious implications in relation to the wellbeing of patients and subsequently the security of members of staff. He said that a closer supervision of the administering of drugs by nursing staff, as well as new stock recording systems had recently been installed.

The police have stepped up their search for Sister Violet Rae.

Angel put the paper down. 'And after all this time, haven't those singing leek eaters any idea at all where she is?'

'None, sir. They have not had a single lead. She disappeared into thin air in 1981. She had no living relatives. I think they believe that she is now either abroad or dead. I tend to agree with them.'

Angel shook his head slowly. The corners of his mouth turned down. 'Oh no, lad. She's not abroad or dead. Sister Violet Rae's here in Bromersley, laughing at us. I'll bet she's got a cosy nest organised for herself somewhere. She's probably bunked up with a man, where she thinks she is perfectly safe. Maybe the man — whoever he is — has no idea of her history.'

'Do you think she's married, sir?'

Angel shrugged. 'Who knows? So much time — twenty-one years — has passed. She's had time to build a whole new identity for herself. I believe she was recognised by Fiona Thomas and that she murdered her because of that. She is desperate to keep her identity secret. She is a very dangerous woman. We have to be very careful.'

Crisp said, 'I don't suppose Miriam has turned up, sir?'

'Not in Bromersley, she hasn't. I must confess, I am getting quite worried about her. After all, Miriam told me she thought her sister had gone missing here, and, of course, she has proved to be horribly correct. If she went looking for her sister she could have ended up the same way. If only we knew who it was that Fiona contacted. That would give us a clue to Violet Rae.'

'There's been no sign of Miriam in Pontylliath since last Friday, when she cancelled her milk. She told the milk woman that her sister was away and that she was going to join her, and that they'd both be away a couple of days.'

'That all fits. What is their home like?'

'They share a flat near the hospital.'

'Did you manage to get into?'

'Yes sir. Miriam left a key with a neighbour and she let me in. I had a long chat with her. She said she was probably their best friend. She knew nothing unusual about them. They had a big circle of friends, all women. All similar age group. She could only speak well of them and their parents. Good respectable people. Two sisters. Always together. They lived for their parents, and when their father died some years ago, they had their mother move in with them. She lived with them until she died recently. The sisters were devastated, particularly the elder girl, Miriam. They enjoyed their work and were dedicated to nursing. It's a small town community. If there had been anything to know, she said, she would have known it.'

Angel shook his head. 'I don't know about that. When the front door is shut, nobody knows what goes on behind it. Nobody knows, for instance, that my wife and I are keen Morris dancers. And that we put on leather shorts and floral hats and get out our sweeping brush handles every Friday evening for a practice dance around the bidet. You didn't know *that,* Sergeant, did you?' he said with a straight face.

Crisp smiled at the very thought of it.

'So don't be taken in by convention. Things are not always what they seem. You said you gained access to their flat.'

'Yes sir. There was nothing unusual about it. It was comfortable and well set up. Entirely a woman's home. Smart, clean, spotless. Just what you'd expect of two spinster sisters living together. No signs of the presence of any man.

Or male influence. No photographs. A very womanly place. Lots of frills and furbelows, cut flowers in every room. Flower vases that hang on the wall with flowers in them. And unusual displays of flowers all over the flat. Hanging baskets on the balcony outside. As a matter of fact, there were flowers all over the place.'

'Mmm. Flowers, eh? So what? Did you find any letters, correspondence at all among the petunias?'

'I had a look in the drawers and cupboards. There didn't seem to be any correspondence around the place. There was no bureau or desk. No address book. There was some post on the mat so I had a look through it. Nothing of interest to the case — circulars, a catalogue and the gas bill.'

'Anything else?'

'No sir.'

There was a knock at the door.

Angel looked up. 'Come in.'

Cadet Ahaz burst in with a big smile carrying some papers.

'Have you got that blow up?'

Ahmed smiled showing off his even white teeth. 'Yes sir.' He put the papers on the desk in front of Angel.

The Inspector looked down eagerly. 'Mmm.'

'I did several, sir, showing different magnifications. The early ones come out pretty well. You can see increases in stages from ten per cent to 800 per cent. The bigger ones lose definition of course.'

Angel fingered through the scanner prints carefully. Crisp stood up and looked over his shoulder.

The Inspector said, 'Anybody you know, lad?'

Crisp rubbed his chin. 'I don't know, sir. I don't know,' he replied slowly.

The Inspector finally selected one in the middle range. He put his finger on a print. 'That one.'

Ahmed nodded.

'Print a dozen. I'll give you a circulation list later.'

Ahmed looked confused. 'How many's a dozen, sir?'

'Ten, lad.'

'I'll print twelve to make sure.'

Angel gaped at him and shook his head. Ahmed rushed off.

The phone rang. 'Angel.'

It was Dr Mac. 'Oh Michael, I think I've found out why Fiona Thomas had her stocking on inside oot. I thought you'd want to know.'

The question had been at the back of Angel's mind for some time. 'Yes Mac, tell me.'

'You will recall that I couldn't find where the injection into the woman's body had been made?'

'Aye.'

'I've found it now. Most unusual place. It was between the toes!'

Angel's eyes shone. 'Ah! Between the toes.'

'The stocking may have been removed. I think the murderer was after concealing the needle mark. And as the stocking was not put back on correctly, it suggests, only suggests mark you, it was possibly the work of a man. After all, a woman would know about these things, wouldn't she?'

Angel beamed. 'It makes sense, Mac. It makes sense. Thank you very much.'

'All part of the service.'

'Aye. Well, while you're on, Mac, can you tell me how you get hold of the stuff she was injected with? Diamorphine hydrochloride, wasn't it?'

'Och. With difficulty, I hope. It is a seriously dangerous drug. It's pure heroin. In monitored doses it is a highly effective painkiller, but too much is certain death. GP's occasionally prescribe it and administer it themselves or through a nurse. But, it is mostly administered in a hospital environment. All pharmacies would stock it. But it would be locked safely away in the cupboard. Illicitly, it's obtained by fraud or by stealing. When a pharmacy has been broken into, you can bet that all the diamorphine hydrochloride is taken.'

'So you need to be a thief or know a thief to get hold of it?'

'Or a druggie. Or a bent doctor or nurse.'

'Thanks Mac.'

Angel slowly returned the phone to its cradle. He rubbed the lobe of his ear between finger and thumb. It seemed all roads led to Sister Violet Rae.

* * *

The duty Police Constable unlocked the door in the custody suite.

'Thanks lad,' Angel said and strode into the cell.

He heard the door close and the jangle of keys behind him.

The little man resting on the bunk bed looked up through his bottle-bottom glasses, turned the corners of his mouth down and said, 'Oh, it's you.' He slowly stretched his arms and got to his feet.

Angel stood in the doorway looking across at him. 'Yes lad.'

'About time,' he said breezily in a broad cockney accent. 'Come to let me out, have you?'

Angel didn't react. He slowly took a wallet out of his pocket and opened it. He read the name showing. 'Edward Arthur Skinn.'

The little man's eyes shone. 'Here! That's mine.'

Angel closed it and threw it on the bunk. 'You can have it, lad.'

Eddie Skinn leaped on the wallet and opened it up. 'There was money in here.'

'It's all there, lad,' Angel growled. 'A hundred and twenty quid.'

He turned his back on the policeman, counted the money, stuffed it back in the wallet, put it in his pocket and then looked back.

Angel said, 'You ought to be grateful.'

Eddie Skinn looked up at the policeman and stuck out his chin. 'I don't have to be grateful for having my own money returned to me, do I?' There was a pause and then he added, 'But I still ain't saying nothin'.'

'Of course not. You're not even going to admit you've been caught red-handed with the video *and* the money, even though we've got witnesses. Are you?'

'Witnesses? Huh. I don't know what you mean.' He patted his coat pocket. 'This is my money. It's got nothing to do with anybody else.'

'I'm talking about the thousand pounds.'

'I don't know anything about any thousand pounds.'

'The thousand pounds that Mrs Bottle collected from the telephone box for you,' Angel said patiently.

'I don't know what she's been saying to you, but I don't know nothin' about any money she was trying to sneak off wiv. You want to watch her,' he said, pointing a finger. 'She's a sly old biddy, she is.'

'So that's not your money then?'

Eddie Skinn didn't reply at once. His eyes slid to one side and back. 'No.'

'Well,what were you making all that fuss about in the market?'

'Aaah,' he snarled and ran his hand through his hair. 'Look, I'm not answering any more questions. I want a solicitor. I'm entitled to a solicitor. You shouldn't be asking me anything without it being recorded. I don't know nothin', and I haven't done nothin'.'

'What do you want a solicitor for? You haven't been charged with anything yet. At the moment, you are simply helping police with their enquiries.'

'Am I? Huh. I know you lot. Look here, if you've anything to charge me wiv, get on with it. And if you haven't, you've no right to hold me. You should let me go. I could sue you.'

'Don't worry Eddie, I wouldn't do anything against the law. You ought to know that. A charge sheet is being prepared.'

'It's about time I knew what you was cooking up.'

Angel reached for a chair from the corner of the cell, pushed it backwards between his legs and sat down. He looked the little man up and down and pursed his lips as he thought out what he wanted to say. He wanted it to be just right. He didn't want to fluff it. He spoke slowly and carefully, selecting each word. 'You must be an important man to need a solicitor,' he began. 'You must be a big wheel. The leader of the gang. The brains behind the outfit.' He looked at Skinn closely. 'Your mate in the next cell said that *you* were the big boss.'

'What does *he* know?' he said quickly with a sneer, and then he looked back at the policeman. 'I've more brains than he has, that's for sure, whoever he is. Anyway, I don't know what you're talking about. And I don't know who you're talking about either. Who've you got next door? Ernie Wise?'

'Of course, he'll probably get off with Community Service. After all, you were the one with the gun. You were the one who assaulted the girl.'

'What girl? What gun? And why should he get off with Community Service? What are you on about?'

Angel put his hand in his pocket and slowly took something out. Eddie Skinn looked down at his hand.

Angel kept his fist closed.

The little man continued to stare at it.

Angel watched his face. After a few seconds, he saw the policeman was watching him so he looked away.

Then the Inspector said, 'Do you chew gum, Eddie?'

'Chew gum? No,' he snapped.

'Your mate does,' he said and then added quickly, 'Oh, that's right. He said you didn't,' he lied.

The little man stared at him with a fixed jaw.

The lie had paid off.

From the expression on his face, Angel observed that Eddie Skinn's brain must be making and breaking connections faster than an electric bell circuit. The policeman took his time. He slowly opened his fingers and smiled. 'I got this for him.'

In his hand was a blue-and-white packet of chewing gum.

Skinn looked down at the small package and then sniffed. 'How is it he's got you running for him? And how is it he'll get off with only Community Service? And what else has he been saying? And who is he? He's not my mate. I don't even know the man.'

'I can't tell you what he's said, Eddie. But he has told me a lot about you. About your days in London.' It was a risk, but Angel now thought it was worth taking. He knew the man's accent was unquestionably cockney.

Skinn raised his eyebrows almost imperceptibly and then lowered them. His jaw tightened. Then he began to speak icily, 'If anybody is telling any lies about me…' He stopped.

Angel continued smoothly, 'He was telling me about that woman.' He thought he was on safe ground, there was always a woman. He pursed his lips.

The little man jumped to his feet. 'What woman?' he shrieked. 'If he's been telling you about…' His voice trailed away again and his jaw dropped as he considered the situation.

Angel noted his hands were trembling slightly.

Skinn turned away. He walked across to the cell window and looked at the steel bars and the white opaque glass, shining with the hot sun beating onto it. He removed his spectacles, breathed on the lenses and wiped them vigorously with a handkerchief. It took a minute or so.

Angel didn't speak. He just waited, looking at the back of the little man in the well-cut suit.

Eddie Skinn returned the handkerchief to his pocket and said quietly, 'I'm saying nothing. What do you think I am? Huh?' Then he spun round, his face scarlet and his eyes shining. He pointed a finger at Angel and said, 'But you can tell Larry Dott that if he finks he can gob on me and get away with it, he's got another fink coming!'

That was a worthwhile breakthrough and was the payback for observing that the man on the security video had discarded a wad of gum at the service station before going into the pay office.

Angel remained impassive. Years of experience had taught him not to show any reaction when an important piece of information was elicited from a suspect. He stood up and replaced the chair against the wall.

'Well, Eddie, that's all the time I can spare you today. I'll tell Larry what you say. I don't think he'll like it.'

CHAPTER 11

Angel walked into the cell. He heard the door close behind him and the solid click of the key turn in the lock. He looked down at the lanky young man stretched out on the bunk.

The young man raised himself up on his elbows.

'Hello *Larry,*' Angel said with a big smile and emphasis on the 'Larry'.

The man's mouth dropped open. He looked absolutely stunned. He licked his lips lightly and said nothing. Still staring at the policeman, he sat up, swivelled round on the bunk and put his feet on the floor.

Angel, smiling confidently, reached over for a chair, pushed it between his legs from the front and sat down resting his arms on the back.

'It was easy really,' he continued. 'We've got your chum, ever-ready Eddie, next door. He told me. Oh yes, we caught him trying to do a deal with a stolen videotape yesterday. Silly man. And, among other things, he told me you liked chewing gum, so I brought you some.'

Angel plunged into his pocket, pulled out the blue-and-white packet and held it out to him.

Larry Dott looked at it but didn't take it. He remained motionless on the bunk bed, his hands resting on the edge of it. He looked at the wall, his mouth still open.

Angel pursed his lips and said, lightly, 'It's just like me, generous to a fault.' He tossed the packet onto the bed and looked back at the pasty face of the young crook in the crumpled suit, a strand of greasy hair partly covering his left eye.

Larry Dott seemed to be listening but he was looking at the wall and shaking his head ever so slightly.

Eventually Angel said, 'Hey. I hope you are all right, lad. I hope you are not sickening for anything. Getting a GP to visit here is not easy, you know. And the police surgeon isn't much good. He's more used to treating police horses than humans.'

Dott stared at him blankly.

'I can't recommend him,' Angel added. 'That smell of formaldehyde can put you off.' He paused a few seconds. 'Do you know, Larry, we once had an old lag in here suffering from a strange thing called "Stripes" disease. He was in this actual cell. About two years ago now. Yes. His face and his hands were alternately coloured white and brown in stripes? Up and down in stripes. Nowhere else on his body, just his face and hands. They took him to the hospital for tests. They tried scrubbing him with a scouring stone but it didn't do any good. They tried painting the white stripes with creosote but that didn't work either. They tried all sorts. Eventually they did find out what had caused it. And do you know what it was? Well, he'd served that much time in prison, that the sun had burned him through the bars, leaving him tanned in stripes. Anyway, the doctor said he thought he would be all right, but that if he ever got out of prison, he should never stand next to a zebra because he might find himself put in a zoo, in which case, he could spend the rest of his life behind bars! Funny really.'

Larry Dott still didn't react.

'Never mind, lad.'

Angel reflected that getting this man talking was more difficult than he had anticipated. He ran his tongue around his mouth thoughtfully, and then he pointed to the untouched chewing gum on the bed and said, 'When you've been here for a month or two, you'll enjoy that. It will help pass the time. And it's something to do with your mouth when you are not talking.'

Angel smiled, paused and then said, 'Anyway Larry, you needn't worry about not talking. I know it's standard practise to say nothing. It's supposed to hinder us and it leaves the field clear for your solicitor to concoct some fairy-tale. But in this case you needn't worry about not talking. Because we have your good friend Eddie Skinn. Now he's a cockney, and cockneys love to talk. And Eddie makes up for your silence. Oh yes, *He* talks. Now there is a talker. He talks all day and all night. He talks about everything and everybody. He talks about you. And I must say, Larry, that some of what he says isn't very nice. It seems you've been leading him astray, Larry. Yes. He says he was innocent before he met up with you. You've been a bad influence on him, Larry. He used to be as good as gold. Pure as the driven snow. That's what he says.'

There was the slightest movement of Dott's mouth. Nothing significant but it was a start. Angel thought he was going to need a barrel of WD40 to loosen this locked tongue.

'For instance, he said it was you that hit that girl at the service station across the face with that gun.'

Suddenly Larry Dott spoke. Quietly and evenly he said, 'I didn't hit anybody with any gun. I don't have a gun. You didn't find a gun on me, did you? I haven't done anything wrong. I want a solicitor. And you have no right to hold me without charging me.'

Angel's eyebrows moved upwards. 'Oh. It's alive. Thank goodness. I was beginning to think I should ring the abattoir.'

Dott's face went red. He spoke quietly through fixed teeth. 'You can't fool me, Mr Policeman. And Eddie Skinn *wouldn't* talk. You're only saying these things to get me talking!'

Angel's eyes flashed, the smile vanished. 'I have already told you that he gave me your name,' he bellowed. 'I couldn't invent it! I couldn't invent a name like Larry Dott, could I? John Smith maybe. Or Mickey Mouse, but not Larry Dott. He told me you liked chewing gum. Could I invent that? He told me about his days in London. He told me about the gun. He told me about that woman. And lots of other things besides,' he lied.

Larry Dott's mouth opened again. Then he smiled. It was not a genuine smile, 'Huh. You're bluffing.' Dott shook his head, shaped his mouth like a gobstopper and exhaled noisily. Now I *know* you're bluffing. He would never talk to you about his mother!'

Angel's ears pricked up. That was a welcome titbit he could use. A lovely juicy morsel of information he could take back to the cell next door. So Eddie Skinn's mother is 'the woman' he was so touchy about.

Angel barged in. He spoke at his persuasive best. 'Oh yes, lad. He's got a thing about women. He's not very tall. Don't you realise? He probably feels inadequate — he's got a complex. It's often inherited.'

Dott looked at the floor, shook his head and muttered, 'You must have got him in a right state. I would have thought he would have kept his mother out of it.'

'No. It's just that when you are up against a wall, you try and protect yourself. And he is up against a wall. Assault while in the course of robbery could be a four-year stretch. That girl was badly knocked about, you know. Young lasses like that are fragile. They are not up to being whipped with a gun. Did *you* assault the girl at the service station?'

'No. What service station?'

'Why? Have you blagged more than one?'

Larry Dott's mouth tightened.

'Bah!'

The mood had changed.

'No comment' he added.

Angel said, 'Where's the gun?'

'No comment.'

'Are you going to answer all my questions like this?'

'No comment.'

* * *

'Listen, lad. I want you to go to London. Start at that address in Hackney — the one on Eddie Skinn's driving licence, and see if you can dig up his mother.'

DS Crisp's eyebrows shot up. 'His mother?'

'Yes, lad. Don't sound so surprised. I know he's a little monster but even *he* must have had one.'

'Yes sir.'

'Now, if you draw a blank try the phone book. Then there's the electoral roll at the town hall. There can't be that many Skinn's even in yon place. And when you find her, tell her the situation we have here. I have a feeling she might be very useful in extricating the truth out of the little maggot. And going down there, you'll have to smarten yourself up a bit. We don't want them thinking we still shave with broken bottles. I should chuck that suit out for a start. There's enough grease in those trousers to make a pan of chips.'

The phone rang. He reached out for it. 'Well, get off, lad. And keep in touch.'

Crisp sighed and made for the door.

'Hello. Yes?' Angel said into the mouthpiece.

'There's that solicitor, Mr Wexell, on the line for you, sir.'

Angel pulled a face and then raised his eyebrows. 'Right. Put him through.'

'Is that Inspector Angel? I am sorry to bother you, but I wanted to know if you recovered my videotape from the man you have in custody.'

'Yes, Mr Wexell, we did.'

'Ah, good. I wonder, if I called in, could I pick it up?'

'I'm afraid not, sir.'

'It *is* in your possession though, isn't it?' Peter Wexell said anxiously.

'Yes sir. It is perfectly safe with us. You will understand that it is evidence and will have to be held by the court until the case is heard. Incidentally, we also have your packet of money, the thousand pounds unopened. We would like to hold onto that for the time being also. That also is evidence. Of course, being money, if you need it, arrangements could be made to…'

'Oh no. That's all right, Inspector. As a matter of fact, I was thinking under certain circumstances that money could go to a police charity.'

'Oh? That's extremely generous of you, sir. But, what do you mean, "under certain circumstances"?'

'Oh. Well, that tape is only of interest to me, and my family. Any tape would do to hold as a nominal piece of evidence, wouldn't it? I mean one videotape in a box looks very much like another. If you could see your way clear to letting me have the tape back, you could keep the one thousand pounds until it is no longer evidence and then you could give it to your favourite charity. I know the police are generous people and have their favourite charity.'

Angel pursed his lips. 'Well,sir. It might be necessary to play the tape, for instance to prove that it is the stolen one and that, indeed, it does belong to you.'

Wexell's voice grew louder and was pitched an octave higher. 'Surely not. I mean it's private property. Nobody has more right to it than I have. It is a very private and personal record of history of the practice and my career and so on.'

Angel wondered what the fuss was all about. 'I am very sorry, sir. What can I do? My hands are tied.'

'If I spoke to the Chief Constable, do you think he would make an exception?'

'You could always try,' he said, knowing it would be a waste of time.

'Right Inspector, thank you.' Wexell rang off quickly.

Angel replaced the phone. It rang immediately.

'Angel.'

'I have got the Pontylliath police on the phone, sir. The caller is asking for DS Crisp, but he's not in CID and nobody knows where he is. Is he with you?'

'No. What does he want?'

'He says it's to do with the Thomas murder case.'

Angel's pulse quickened. Was this the call he was dreading? Had they found Miriam Thomas? Was she still alive?

'I'll take it,' he said quickly. 'Put him through, please.'

There was a click, and a Welsh voice said, 'Hello?'

'This is Inspector Michael Angel of Bromersley CID. DS Crisp is on my team and he's out on a job for me. I can take any message.'

'Oh, right now, Inspector. There's an interesting development in this murder case. In the process of going through the women's flat, a letter has turned up in the post this morning addressed to Fiona Thomas, and it's from Bromersley.'

'Oh? Aye lad. Go on.'

'Yes well, it's from a woman in Bromersley and postmarked yesterday, and we were wondering if you could see your way clear to interviewing her on our behalf. It might save us coming over. It would also assist your inquiries. It might be more quickly explained Inspector, if I read the letter out to you.'

'Right lad. Go ahead.'

'It's dated yesterday's date. It's handwritten. It says,

Dear Miss Thomas,

We were very disappointed that you did not come to our meeting to judge and to talk to us last Saturday afternoon. I have been awaiting a communication from you. You said you would be here for two o'clock and all our displays were ready for you. Our members had made special efforts to present a high standard of floral work on the subject you set, for you to judge and you never arrived. We waited until 4.30 but some of the blooms began to drop. By five o'clock the display was a disaster. We have not heard from you and we are very grieved that you have not even had the courtesy of telling us that you were not coming. We have had judges and speakers over the years from all over the country but we have never been let down like this. It is too late to arrange another date as our programme for the season is now fully booked.

It would be nice to have some explanation and apology from you.

Yours sincerely,

Emily Mulholland (Mrs).

Chairman Bromersley Ladies Flower Arranging Club.

'The address is given as Pitduck Farm, Sheffield Road, Bardsley, Bromersley.'

'That's very interesting. Thank you, lad. It might be the missing piece. Yes I'll see to it myself, and I'll send you a copy of my report,' Angel replied.

'I hope it leads us somewhere, sir.'

'I hope so. Have you managed to turn up anything at all about the whereabouts of her sister, Miriam?'

'No, sir. A complete blank. Not a whisper.'

'You will let us know if you hear or see anything of her?'

'Certainly, sir.'

'Thanks very much. Goodbye.'

'Goodbye now.'

Angel replaced the phone and wiped his hand across his mouth. Was this the break he had been waiting for? He remembered Emily Mulholland. Maybe she could fill in the blanks about Fiona and Miriam Thomas.

Twenty minutes later, Angel turned his car off the main Sheffield road opposite the service station at Bardsley, and up a narrow track to Mulholland's farm. The lane was a hundred yards long and bordered on both sides by sandstone walls, eaten into by two hundred years of wind-driven acid rain. At the end, he turned right through an open gate in the wall into the farmyard and stopped behind a battered Land Rover parked outside the house. Before he could knock on the door, a face appeared from behind the Land Rover. It was Mrs Mulholland. She was wearing a blue overall and holding a spade.

'Oh. It's you, Inspector Angel. What brings you out here?' She asked with a straight face. She wiped her sweaty forehead on her sleeve and then leaned on the spade handle like a practised workman. 'Have you got both of them robbers that assaulted our Jane?'

Angel smiled as he looked down at her chubby red face. 'As a matter of fact, Mrs Mulholland, we have.'

She blinked, then she sniffed and said, 'Are we going to get back the money they took?'

'Don't know about that, love. If they've still got it, there's a chance.' He pursed his lips. 'How is Jane?'

Mrs Mulholland tightened her grip on the spade. 'She's in bed. She is not very strong, you know, Inspector. And she won't work in the petrol station any more. She's too scared. I can't blame her. I didn't bring her into this world to be pushed about by thugs. My husband is running it for the time being. He fits it in, as best he can with looking after the farm. I don't know how he does it. And I help him all I can.'

Angel nodded sympathetically. 'Tell Jane I asked after her. She was very brave trying to stand up to those men.'

'Or daft.' She nodded towards the door. 'Did you want to come in?'

'No. I'm all right. It's nice out here. Don't mean to disturb you.' He glanced round the farmyard and across the stonewall at the rich green hills in the distance and put a hand up to shield his eyes from the sun's searching rays. 'You know, you're lucky to live up here, Mrs Mulholland.'

'It's a lovely day today sure enough, but it's not much fun in the winter, Inspector, I can tell you. Trudging down this lane in a foot of snow.'

'No, I don't suppose it is.' Angel smiled and looked at the spade. 'Doing a bit of gardening?'

She made a disagreeable face. 'As a matter of fact, I've just buried a cat.'

Angel looked into her eyes, licked his lips and then blew out a short sigh. 'Oh?'

'Come here.' She turned and went over to a narrow border of flowers under the house window.

Angel followed her round the front of the Land Rover. She pointed to an area of freshly moved earth drying off in the sun. Angel looked down and along some stocks and a bed of sweet peas climbing up a wooden trellis. About four feet away, he saw a small, hand painted sign, white on black, by a clump of wallflowers. It read, 'Tilly. Much loved. 1990 to 2001.'

Angel said, 'Tilly.'

'That's our old cat, Tilly. This one was called, Henrietta. She was our Jane's.'

Angel said, 'What was the matter with her?'

'I don't know. I took her to Mr Niven, the vet.'

'I know him. He looks after our two cats.'

'He's the best vet round here. He said something was wrong with her blood. He did tests, but...' she shrugged. 'Jane's really cut up about it.'

'I'm sorry.' He looked down at the flowers and the small pet's cemetery. 'Two dead cats,' he reflected. It reminded him of the reason he was there. 'Mmm. Two dead cats.'

'What's that?'

'Nothing.'

Mrs Mulholland looked down at the plot and said, 'She's been dead for two days. She was in a box in the barn. I had to bury her today. In this heat, she ponged something terrible,' she added, wrinkling her nose.

'Billy Niven would have disposed of it and saved you the trouble.'

'Oh no. I had to do it. I wanted to do it, for Jane. My husband will make a little sign for it when he can find the time.' She swallowed then looked up at Angel, forced a smile and added, 'We're daft.'

Angel said, 'No.'

She saw a stray dandelion in the flower border and leaned down to pull the root out.

Angel took a deep breath. He thought he might now try to approach her about Fiona Thomas. 'It's not often we get summer's like this and weeding is a full time job,' he began. 'And I expect you like flowers a lot. I believe one of your interests is flower arranging?' he asked tentatively.

'I don't have much time for it, but yes, it is. Why? How did you know about that?'

'Oh, it came up. You see we are investigating the murder of a lady I believe you know.'

'Oh? Who?'

'A Miss Fiona Thomas.'

Mrs Mulholland's mouth opened then closed. She looked up into the policeman's eyes. 'Fiona Thomas, did you say?'

He nodded.

'Oh.' She shook her head quickly a few times and bit her lip. 'No wonder she didn't come to our meeting last Saturday.'

'How long have you known her?'

'I don't *know* her. I didn't know her. Never met her. She is on the national register as a judge of floral arrangements so she must know her stuff. She was recommended, otherwise we would not have asked her to come all the way to Bromersley and agreed to pay her.' She closed her teeth around her bottom lip and then muttered, 'And I wrote her such a stiff letter.'

'You weren't to know. You didn't see her last weekend at all then?' he asked fingering his earlobe.

'I have never seen her, Inspector. I wrote to her and booked her. It was all done by post. She just failed to turn up at our meeting last Saturday. That's all I know.'

'Oh,' Angel said, looking down. 'Do you know anybody who saw her last weekend? It's very important.'

'No. Oh how awful. Tell me, where was she murdered? She comes from Wales, doesn't she? Whatever happened to her?'

Angel sighed, this was leading him nowhere. 'I don't know. I thought you were going to be able to tell me. Do you know anyone who knows her or who has seen her recently?'

'No. They must know her at the central office of the flower club in London, I suppose. She's judged some big events all over the country by what they say. How did she die?'

'Poison,' he said slowly, stroking his chin. 'Did you know her sister?'

'I didn't know she had a sister. Why?'

'She's disappeared.'

'Oh? How long has she been missing?'

'Since last Saturday.' Angel lowered his eyes, shook his head and muttered. 'It is very worrying.'

CHAPTER 12

Angel slumped in the chair and reached over for the phone. 'Cadet Ahaz.'

'Yes, sir?'

'Come in here, lad, quick. And bring me a cup of tea.'

'Right sir.'

He replaced the phone and pushed the pile of papers in front of him to one side. He pulled open a drawer, took out a white paper bag and opened it up. Inside was a teacake sandwich. He took it out of the bag, removed the top slice and peered at the filling. He pulled a face, replaced the top and took a bite out of it. Still holding it with one hand, and chewing away he drummed the desk rhythmically with his other hand. After two choruses of 'The Entry of the Gladiators,' he stood up and went to the door. As he opened it, a smiling Cadet Ahmed Ahaz arrived with a tray with a mug on it.

'Where've you been, lad? It's taken you long enough. Have you been dressing your verruca?'

'No sir. I haven't got a verruca,' Ahmed said, his smile gone.

'Well, waken up. And look lively,' he said, waving the sandwich in the air. 'There's more life in this potted meat pasty!'

Ahmed looked crestfallen, 'I had to wait at the machine, sir.'

'Well, bring yourself in here and sit down,' he growled. He took the tea off the tray and carried it back to his desk.

The young cadet sat opposite him and then pointed to the papers, 'There's a message from your wife, sir.'

'I've read it, lad. It's worse than *Les Miserables*. Which reminds me, you'd better get some more milk for the cats. And I'll have to think of something for my tea.'

'Right sir.'

'Is Superintendent Harker in?' he said spraying Ahmed with crumbs.

'Yes sir.'

'When I've finished this, I'm going in to see him,' he said taking a hurried sip of the tea. 'Have you heard from Sergeant Crisp?'

'No sir. He hasn't been in all day.'

'I'm expecting him to phone,' he said, taking another bite of the sandwich. 'And get Dr Mac for me, will you lad?' he said nodding towards the phone and chewing vigorously.

Ahmed came up to the phone and tapped in a number.

Angel took a look at the remaining crust of the teacake and pulled a face. He pushed it into the paper bag and dropped it in the wastepaper basket.

'It's harder to swallow than Crisps' expense vouchers.'

'He's on the line now, sir.' Ahmed passed the phone to Angel.

'Ta.' He took the handset. 'Is that Mac?'

'Aye. Speaking.'

'Michael Angel.'

'Ah yes, Mike.'

'Mac, I still haven't been able to find that missing woman, Miriam Thomas, sister of that body you have there.'

'I can't help you there, laddie.'

'No. But I was thinking. This heat wave. If she has been murdered and her body was being kept unrefrigerated in this weather, say for a week, it would be in a hell of a state, wouldn't it?'

'Well, it would depend on the cause of death. The face and limbs would begin to turn blue or dark brown. It may leak urine. There'd not be much else to see.'

'Yes, Mac, but it would begin to smell something dreadful, wouldn't it?'

'Unrefrigerated, in this heatwave, enclosed for seven days? I would say so! Most foul.'

Angel rubbed his chin. 'Mmm.'

'Of course, it's only about one year in twenty we get summers as hot as this for as long as this.'

'Aye. But I mean you wouldn't want to live in the same house with it, would you?'

'I've known cases where you wouldn't want to live in the same street! But it depends just where and how it is kept.'

'I thought so. Just checking. Thanks, Mac. Goodbye.'

'Goodbye.'

Angel slowly returned the phone to the cradle and wrinkled his nose as he remembered corpses he had seen in the past. He looked up at Cadet Ahaz. He was standing by the door, motionless and holding the tray with the empty cup on it. He was staring back at Angel, his mouth open.

'What's up lad?'

Ahmed hesitated. 'Well sir, I do not like to think that that woman who came to see you here in this office a week ago is dead somewhere.'

Angel shook his head. 'I don't, lad, but she may be. Now hop off and get that milk for me. And try not to break that computer again.'

'It isn't broken. It crashed,' Ahmed muttered. 'And I didn't break it in the first place,' he added as he noisily closed the door.

Angel smiled as he stood up and knocked a few breadcrumbs off his shirtfront. He wiped his mouth and fingers on his handkerchief and glanced in the mirror. He straightened his tie and ran his hand over his hair and went out of his room and down the green corridor to the last door on the right to Superintendent Harker's office. He knocked on the door.

'Come in.'

'Have you a minute, John?'

'Come in. Sit down.' The white-haired man rubbed his hands like a moneylender. 'Have you found that woman yet?'

'No. And as long as the embargo on house searches is on, I don't expect I ever will,' he said as he lowered himself into the chair.

Harker smiled. 'Come on Mike, it's not as bad as all that. And the *embargo*, as you insist on calling it, is not on every house search, only in circumstances where he thinks it's not absolutely necessary.'

'It's because Wexell is a big noise solicitor, isn't it? I don't know what the Chief sees in him.'

'It's not that at all.'

'Do you know, Wexell phoned me yesterday to ask if he could have that videotape back that was stolen from his office. I said he couldn't. Immediately he had the neck to ask if he spoke to the Chief did I think *he* would let him have it back. Of course, I said he might!'

'Well, he won't,' Harker replied quickly with a grin.

'I know. But what a cheek!'

'You're getting very touchy these days, Mike.'

Angel dismissed the comment with a wave of the hand. 'Does the Chief really know how difficult he has made my job? And doesn't he realise that I understand the fine points of this case better than he does?'

'Don't be difficult, Mike. The Chief has said no, so it's no. There's no point in going on about it.'

Angel sighed, ran his hand over his mouth and said, 'Right, sir.'

'Now then, is there anything new?'

'No John. No. No new evidence. Miriam Thomas has not been seen or heard of for six days now. You'd expect her to be around, concerned for her sister's welfare, but she has disappeared into thin air. The Pontylliath police are looking out for her. She has not been back to her flat.'

'Should we mount a campaign to find her?'

'No sir. I don't think that's necessary. Not yet, anyway.' Then he added in a low, sombre voice, 'If she has uncovered the identity of Violet Rae, I think I know where we'll find her.'

Harker's eyebrows shot up and he stared at him.

Angel massaged the lobe of an ear between finger and thumb, and then he made a decision. 'John, I want the stake-out van, the CCTV stuff with four cameras and four monitors and two men from the dayshift to man it?'

'For Sycamore Grove?'

'Yes.'

Harker frowned. 'That's more expense, Mike, and we are way over budget now.'

Angel pulled a face.

Harker said, 'To observe both houses at the same time?'

'Yes.'

'How long for?'

'Forty-eight hours?'

'Is that long enough?'

'It is.'

'It's not long enough. It may not work.'

Angel nodded. 'It will.'

'You'll need much longer.'

'I won't need any longer.'

Harker looked into his eyes.

Angel stared back.

After a pause he said, 'Very well, Mike. You can have that set up for forty-eight hours, provided no greater priority crops up.'

Angel looked shocked. 'What's got a greater priority than a multiple murder?'

The big man impatiently shuffled some papers about on his desk. 'What are you up to? What exactly are you wanting to achieve? Who are your suspects?'

'Well, obviously sir, I want to find out the identity of Violet Rae. That will lead me to the murderer of Fiona Thomas, and will explain the whereabouts of Miriam Thomas. That's what I'm up to. As for suspects? I've more suspects than a postman has rubber bands. The common features of this Violet Rae woman are, that she is not very tall, was attractive (may still be), in her forties and is a qualified nurse. Well, obviously there's Peter Wexell's wife, Olga. There's Mrs Lowbridge — there's so little known about her. And in a desperate moment, I even thought about Mrs Mulholland, the woman from Bardsley Service Station. Anyway, they all fit the profile except that I don't know that any of them is a qualified nurse.'

Harker blew out a loud sigh. 'Right. Get on with it then.'

'Yes sir.' Angel reached for the chair arms. The Super put up a hand to hold him back. 'How long do you intend keeping those two jokers in the cells for that service station job?'

'Why? Is there a problem?'

Harker shook his head and breathed in, making a slight hissing sound. 'You worry me sometimes. Have they seen a solicitor? Have you made a case? Have you consulted the CPS? Are you going by the book?'

Angel looked him straight in the face. 'Don't I always go by the book?'

'No.'

Angel smiled. 'Well, I am this time, sir. Bloomfield has been to see them both. He came in this morning.'

'Good. Have they applied for bail?'

'Not yet, but they will. And I'll object to it.'

Harker shook his head again and his lips tightened. He threw the pen he was holding onto the desk, 'Look here. I don't want a PC tied up playing jailer, providing three-star room service and running up a meals bill.'

'Would you like me to fill it full of drunks to make it worth your while?'

'There's no need for that, Mike. You know how it is.'

'I do know how it is, sir. I feel sometimes I'm not here to catch crooks. I have to jump more hurdles than Red Rum, and I'm still expected to get convictions.'

'You're being touchy again.'

'I should think I am.' Angel pursed his lips and breathed out noisily. 'Look John, one of those two has a gun. And I haven't found it. And I don't want him running loose round the streets of Bromersley with it. He's already hit a teenage girl in the face in the course of that service station robbery. God knows what might happen next time he feels the need of a few quid. Now it's taken me a bit of time and a whole lot of trouble to get those two villains caged, and I'm in no hurry to release them before they've been disarmed and the system has been given the opportunity to civilise them. I want that man and that gun safely disposed of. And I *have* to keep those two in isolation. I don't want them comparing notes. I've uncovered a slight fracture in their relationship, if I get the opportunity to exploit it, I could get a confession. That's the only way I can see that I am going to get a conviction.'

Harker looked straight into Angel's eyes. 'I can give you three days, Mike. Then you must either charge them or let them go.'

Angel shook his head. 'Is that it then?'

'That's it.'

Angel stood up and slowly crossed to the door. He opened it and, still holding the knob, he turned back.

The Super looked up. 'Is there something else?'

'Yes sir.' Angel ran his tongue around his mouth and looked down at the big man. 'You know, I have often thought that I should have married you, sir.'

Harker stared at him.

Angel added, 'Then I could have come to work and left you at home.' He closed the door.

A smile appeared on Superintendent Harker's face.

Angel stepped sprightly down the green corridor. There was a lot to do. He had the green light to proceed with the obo. But only he knew the ruse he had devised to discover the identity of Violet Rae and the whereabouts of Miriam Thomas. The Super only knew half the plan. Angel had no intention of divulging the other half!

He reached his office door.

Cadet Ahmed Ahaz was running along the corridor from the direction of the CID office. His eyes lit up when he saw the Inspector.

'What is it, lad?'

'A phone call, sir.'

'Sergeant Crisp?'

'No sir. A Mr Niven. He says he's a veterinary surgeon and that you phoned him yesterday.'

'Ah,' Angel said eagerly. 'Yes, that's right, lad.' He went into his office and reached over the desk for the phone. 'Is that Billy Niven?…Aye…Have you got them then?…Yes. Good…Will you wrap them up separately, nice and tight?… Right…I'll pick them up today. Thanks very much, Billy… Goodbye.'

Angel replaced the phone and rubbed his hands like an undertaker at a centenarian's birthday party. He looked at the puzzled face of Cadet Ahaz.

'What's happening, sir?'

'I'm a bit pushed right now, lad. But I'll tell you all in good time. Suffice to say, I've got a rat. I've got a trap. All I need is the cheese!'

* * *

Inspector Angel pressed the bell on the door of 1 Sycamore Grove. He stood under the portico out of the hot sun and swatted away a persistent wasp. He looked round at the high stone wall at the far end of the small front garden, generously covered in dark green ivy. He glanced up at the large trees in Jubilee Park and appreciated how well the lower branches overhung the wall of Sycamore Grove gardens. They made the top of the wall the ideal covert place for two

CCTV cameras to observe the front doors and garden paths of both 1 and 2 Sycamore Grove. A noise drew his attention back to the house.

The door was opened slightly. Tal Lowbridge peered through the chink. When he saw who it was, he pulled it wide open.

Angel switched on his Sunday smile. 'Good morning, Mr Lowbridge.'

'It's you, Inspector. What brings you here?'

'Just passing, Mr Lowbridge. Nothing special,' he lied. 'Can I have a word?'

'Of course. Come into the sitting-room.'

'Thank you.'

'I wondered who it could be,' Lowbridge said, as he closed the door and led the policeman across the hall, past the staircase, the doors to the other two dayrooms and the stairs down to the basement. 'I thought it must be somebody selling something. We get a lot of that round here. My wife's out at the shops. I thought she must have forgotten her key again. She's always doing that. Did you want to see her? I don't think she'll be long.'

'No. No. Just a couple of questions, Mr Lowbridge. That's all. I'm sure you'll be able to supply the answers.'

Angel remembered the highly polished oak table, the glint on the brass fittings on the doors and the smell of polish. They went into the small sitting-room. The double doors on the veranda were open. A slight breeze on the sunny warm morning blew the fresh tang of cut grass and pollen through the window. 'Another beautiful day, Inspector.'

'Very nice.'

'I love these hot summers.'

'Indeed.'

'Please sit down.'

'Thank you.'

Lowbridge unfastened the blue-and-white apron he was wearing, pulled it from his front and tossed it on to a chair.

'I was busy in the kitchen, preparing veg for a party of twenty French schoolteachers coming in next Friday. There's no rush. Now, what is it, Inspector?'

Angel pursed his lips and then said, 'Mr Lowbridge, there's one aspect of the inquiry I didn't touch on before. I wondered how Fiona Thomas had come to stay with you. I mean, did she telephone or write?'

'Neither. She just arrived. I opened the door to her and booked her in myself. Violet was out.'

'Well, how would she come to choose to stay here? She could presumably have stayed at any one of a dozen places in Bromersley, couldn't she?'

The question was immaterial, and Tal Lowbridge's answer inconsequential. Angel wanted the opportunity to look out of the veranda window at the back garden. He could see below that there was plenty of foliage and trees in which to conceal a CCTV camera, and that there would be no difficulty in positioning it to monitor the back door, which was immediately below the veranda. Hiding the linking cable to the van might prove a problem, but the engineers had had trickier places than this to cover. He was satisfied that there was no insurmountable problem.

'Inspector,' Tal Lowbridge began, 'we subscribe to all sorts of magazines and tourist advertising. We are on the Internet and we are on the accommodation list at the town hall. That's how we get our custom. She could have obtained our address from any number of places.'

Angel turned back from the veranda and nodded. 'I see.'

Lowbridge said, 'She simply asked if we had a room and how much it was. I asked her if she wanted us to provide dinner. She said she did. I took her case, showed her to her room and that was that.'

'Did she say where she was from? Or what she was doing here?'

'No. And I didn't ask.'

'While she was here, did she stay all the time in her room?'

'No. I saw her wandering around the garden shortly after she arrived. She seemed interested in the flowers. And she spent some time in the visitors' lounge, watching television. I had to switch it on for her.'

'Did she make any phone calls?'

'No. Not from our phone. She may have had her own mobile.'

'And she had dinner with you?'

'Not *with* us. I cooked it. Violet served it in the dining-room, and she ate on her own. At seven o'clock.'

'What did she have?'

'Hmm. It was Friday, wasn't it? That would be fresh salmon, poached, potatoes, peas, followed by home-made apple pie and custard, and coffee. We had the same ourselves. There was nothing wrong with it. It was very nice.'

'I'm sure,' Angel said. 'Sounds very appetising. Well, thank you very much, Mr Lowbridge. There's just one more thing. Did you see her take any pills or tablets while she was here? Perhaps at the table with her meal, or with a drink.'

'No.'

'That's all I wanted to ask.' He pushed down on the chair arms and rose smartly to his feet. 'Thank you.'

Lowbridge moved quickly to the door. 'How is the case going, Inspector? Are you anywhere near finding the murderer?'

'Oh yes,' he said, nodding hard and following him into the hall. 'I expect to be making an arrest very soon.'

Angel lingered at the top of the basement steps. Then suddenly he stopped abruptly. Lowbridge turned back. When Angel observed that he had his full attention, he stuck his head up high, turned up his nose and sniffed several times. Lowbridge stared at him. Angel's timing was perfect, he then pulled a disagreeable face, put his head through the doorway to the basement steps and sniffed again. Again he pulled a sour face and shook his head. Four pairs of tramlines appeared on Lowbridge's forehead, and the skin on the back of his hands tightened. He followed Angel around, sniffing

162

anywhere and everywhere for half a minute or so. Then he stopped sniffing and turned back to look at the man. At that moment, Tal Lowbridge's patience ran out.

'Whatever's the matter, Inspector?' he exploded, his face as red as a taxman's pencil.

Eventually, waving a hand, Angel said deliberately, without conviction, 'It's nothing. Nothing. Please excuse me. I must be mistaken. I'm very sorry.' He looked at his watch. 'My! Look at the time. I must be off.'

When the door closed behind him, he stood under the portico, wiping his face with his handkerchief, wearing a smile that would have delighted Burt Lancaster's dentist.

That was only the beginning of the cat and mouse game he was to play.

He sauntered round the front of the house, along the gravel path through a shared wicket gate into the garden next door, and up the path to 2 Sycamore Gardens, the home of the Wexells, and pressed the doorbell. He waited more than a minute and then wondered if there was anybody at home. He was about to press the bell again when the door opened and the glamorous Olga Wexell appeared.

'Oh, hello, Inspector,' she drawled, pulling off the mirror sunglasses. She was in blue shorts, white top and sandals, her face, arms and long legs much browner than before. 'Sorry to keep you. I was down at the pool. I can only spare five minutes, I am expecting someone.'

'That's all right. I won't keep you a minute, Mrs Wexell.'

'Well, come in then. Have you come to tell me that you have found the murderer of that poor woman?'

'Not yet, I'm still working on it,' he replied breezily, stepping into the hall. 'It's just a matter of time.' He looked round at the large, framed oil paintings on the walls looking down at him.

She closed the door and stood at the bottom of the mahogany staircase with one hand on the banister. 'You sound confident.'

'Oh I am, Mrs Wexell. I am.'

She nodded and smiled. 'Now what exactly did you want?'

'It was your husband I wanted to see really.'

'He's at the office, at this time. I thought you would know that.'

'Of course, but I was next door and I thought if he was in, I could kill two birds with one stone.' He turned away, 'I'll catch him at the office.'

She licked her bottom lip. 'Of course, if there's anything I can do to help…'

'No. No. I'll see your husband. Thank you.'

'You should make an appointment, Inspector. He's very busy.'

'Of course.' He forced a smile and turned to go. That was the moment. He swiftly turned back.

She looked up at him. He lifted up his head, gently sniffed and then pulled a long face.

'What's the matter, Inspector?'

He didn't reply.

She began to sniff while looking around. 'What is it?'

He still didn't reply. Continuing the game, he made a beeline to the top of the basement stairs and looked down them. She came up behind him.

He sniffed and took the opportunity to look at the swimming pool and garden through the window at the top of the steps. The position of the back door was the same as the house next door. He could see that it would be easy to conceal a CCTV in the trelliswork of the gazebo, providing a clear view across the swimming pool to the back door. He sniffed again, pulled a sour face and looked at her.

'What is it, Inspector?' She asked, her mouth turning down at the corners. She continued the sniffing. 'Is it something downstairs? I can't smell anything.'

Eventually he brought the routine to an end. 'It's nothing. Nothing at all,' he said deliberately without conviction. 'I must be mistaken. I do apologise. I have a very sensitive nose.'

Mrs Wexell's face relaxed, apparently relieved he had reached that conclusion.

There was the distant sound of a door opening and then closing.

Olga Wexell looked back at the basement stairs. 'That'll be my guest. You'll have to excuse me, Inspector.'

'Yes, of course.'

A woman's voice called from down the stairs. 'Hello! Hello! Are you there?'

'Yes. I'm coming, Lola.'

When Angel heard the name 'Lola' his eyes lifted almost imperceptibly and immediately returned to normal. He experienced the sensation of a marble dropping in his head, rolling along a track and rattling into a slot. Lola. Yes, that was her name. What was *she* doing here?

'Goodbye, Inspector.'

Angel hesitated. He would have liked to see Lola again. He would have liked to ask her a few pointed questions, but he could hardly have asked them in front of Olga Wexell!

The door was wide open. 'Goodbye, Inspector.'

'Er, goodbye, Mrs Wexell.'

He crossed the step. The door closed quickly behind him.

CHAPTER 13

Angel came back to work shattered, after a weekend attempting to repair the damage of an unrelenting sun by 'greening up' his lawn with a hosepipe, shopping for bargains at Tesco, washing out vests, pants and socks in the sink with the last two squirts of Fairy Liquid, changing the sheets on the bed, vacuuming the hall and sitting-room, and preparing and cooking two main meals.

That Monday morning, he was seated at the desk, attacking the pile of letters, reports, witness statements and other bumf that had accumulated over the previous week, trying to make sense of it all, and was about as happy as a piglet with no teat.

The phone rang.

The Inspector reached for the handset, 'Angel.'

'It's me, sir. DS Crisp.'

'I've been waiting to hear from you. Where the hell are you, Mars?'

'I'm on the train. Just left Kings Cross. I went to the address you gave me. Eddie Skinn doesn't live there anymore. It's his mother's house. He doesn't have a permanent address.'

'*I know* he doesn't have a permanent address!'

'Anyway, I made contact with the mother, told her the score, and she insisted on coming up to see him.'

'Oh that's *very* cosy! Well, what are you ringing up about? Did you want me to come and serve you both with toasted pikelets and tea?'

'We arrive in Doncaster in two hours, sir. Will you send a car to meet us at the station?'

'I suppose so. But I'm up to my eyes in it. And, by the way, you're working tonight, *all* night. So you'd better get some kip on the train while you've a chance.'

'Oh? Yes, sir.'

He banged down the phone and blew out a noisy sigh. 'I could have done without that!'

'What's that, sir?' Ahmed asked.

'Never mind, lad. Get me the duty Sergeant in charge of STS, chop-chop.' He pointed to the phone.

'What's STS, sir?' the cadet asked, picking up the handset.

'Special Technical Services, lad,' he growled. He swivelled the chair round to look at the young man square on. 'Didn't those nuns teach you anything besides kicking, scratching, drinking, swearing, bribery, drug taking, and the love of God at that convent school? And while I'm speaking to the STS, ring the garage on the CID phone and find out if anyone can collect Crisp from Doncaster station. Then get me a street map of Bromersley. There's one in the CID office somewhere. And then get me a cup of tea. And I want some milk again for the cats. And you'd better get a quarter of boiled ham for my supper.'

Ahmed looked bewildered, 'I don't know if I can remember all that,' he muttered making for the door.

'Then when I've had a cuppa, I'm going down to the cells. Come on, lad. Hurry up! Step lively. Imagine Joan Collins is just behind you looking for a new husband!'

Ahmed's eyelids clicked upwards and stayed there. He scarpered out of the office and hurriedly closed the door.

* * *

Angel walked into the cell. The door clanged shut behind him.

He looked down at the little man on the bunk bed. 'Now then, lad.'

Eddie Skinn leaped up and peered at him through his thick glasses. 'Oh, it's you. Time's up, eh? You've come to let me out?' He grinned as he reached for his coat and stuck his arm in a sleeve. 'I'm not surprised. I knew you couldn't hold me. Wiv no evidence and no witnesses. You've just been marking time, haven't you? Hoping for som'ing to turn up, and nuffin 'as. Trying to kid me on wiv what Gobbo is supposed to have said next door.'

Angel stood looking down at him with his eyes slightly closed. He yawned.

Skinn collected a packet of cigarettes and a disposable lighter from the bed and stuffed them in his pocket. He folded up a newspaper and pulled up his tie while continuing the rhetoric.

'Bloomfield said he'd have me out of here in no time. He said you wouldn't be able to hold me and he was right. He's not a bad bloke, for a Yorkie. I'll be glad to get out of here and back to London. And you needn't bother with all that father and son chat: the warning of a bleak future for the likes of me, and all that crap; the golden doors of opportunity will fly open if only I give 'em a chance; if I work hard and stay out of trouble and keep my finger on the pulse, my shoulder to the wheel and my nose to the grind-stone, by the time I'm sixty-five (if I'm not dead) I'll be able to afford my own kennel on the Isle of Dogs. And I'll get a watch for years of loyal service as a closet walloper, a coffin carrier or a refuse disposal operative or whatever the rich bastards of this world would let me do, because they don't want the job themselves.' Angel shook his head slowly.

Eddie Skinn slurped the last drop of tea from a mug and continued. 'A man is innocent until proved guilty. Eh? Yeah! That's right. It's only fair. I agree with all that stuff. I believe in good old British justice. You can't beat it.'

He put the mug down on the table, looked round the cell and then up at Angel.

'Right, Colonel. Ready when you are!'

Angel reached out for a chair. He planted it in front of the door and sat astride it leaning over the back. He looked at the little man and shook his head again. 'Have you finished?'

Eddie Skinn's breezy smile left him. 'What's all this then? Let's go. Come on. Let's go,' he said, pointing at the cell door with a rolled up newspaper.

'You'd better sit down, lad. I think you're in for a shock.'

Skinn stared across the cell. He put a hand in his jacket pocket like James Cagney pointing a gun and said, 'You can't hold me any longer. You haven't a shred of evidence against me.'

Angel shook his head slowly. 'Don't act daft, lad. We've got bucketsful of evidence. We've got proof that you broke into Shaw and Pettigrew's office. We've got a thread of navy blue wool which was caught on the brass screw of a doorknob in the office, which is an identical match with a pair of gloves we found in your car.'

'Huh! I expect the glove company make about fifty million pairs of identical gloves every year. Anyway, who says they're *my* gloves? You'll have a job to make that stick!'

'DNA from the gloves will prove they're yours. We've got a videotape — the one you sent in error to Shaw and Pettigrew — showing you and Larry Dott crossing the service station forecourt and entering the pay office.'

'It's fuzzy. It don't look nothing like me. And we was — the robbers was wearing balaclavas. I've seen it, don't forget.'

'Even if you can't be identified from it, how come it was in your possession?'

There was a pause. It was just a moment. Then Eddie Skinn said, 'I found it.'

Angel grinned. 'You *found* it? You'll have to do better than that, Eddie.'

'The robbers must have frown it away.'

'Yeah. Like they did the one they stole from the safe at Shaw and Pettigrew's?'

'Yes.'

'That you tried to sell back to Peter Wexell for a thousand pounds?'

'Yes. *No*. You're trying to confuse me.'

'Now come on, Eddie. You'll really have to do better than that. I know it was you who sent that security videotape, taken from the service station, to Peter Wexell by mistake. You know I do. Who else could it be? And you know I can prove it was you that tried to sell him his own tape you had stolen from his safe. I know. I was there. And it was the same MO, the same wrapping paper and the same voice on the phone.' Angel paused to add emphasis to his next point. 'And *there* you have the connection! There's the connection between the solicitor's office burglary and the service station robbery. And you and Larry Dott did both jobs. That'll be good enough for any court.'

'Huh! We didn't. And you'll never make that stick.'

Angel sniffed. 'Then there's that ring,' he pointed to his hand. 'You were seen wearing it during the robbery — by a very reliable witness.'

'There's millions of rings like this around. You'll not make that stick either. It's just a coincidence. There's a chap in Hackney who's got forty of these. He collects 'em!'

'Of course we'll make it stick. Don't you worry about that, lad.'

Eddie Skinn glared at him. 'Bah!'

'Now Eddie, the time has come for you to make two decisions.'

'What?'

'You have to decide how to plead.'

Skinn's face went scarlet. 'Are you thick? I shall plead not guilty,' he yelled.

Angel sighed and shook his head. 'Now you know how judges get ratty about timewasters who cause the court to go unnecessarily through the fending and proving of every little detail of a case? Take it from me, Eddie, you'd be far better off pleading guilty. You'd get a shorter sentence.'

Skinn's mouth opened wide, 'What you talking about? I ain't guilty of anythin',' he bawled.

Angel, unperturbed continued, 'And the second thing you've to decide, is what you're going to do about Larry.'

'What do you mean? What about Larry?'

'Well, are you going to let him off the hook?'

'No!'

'Or are you going to give evidence against him?'

'Yes. *No*!'

'Like he's going to give against you?'

'What?' he yelled.

'Well, he says you had the gun. And it was you who was waving it about. And it was you who hit the girl with it.'

'He's a bleedin' liar. I never touched the girl. And I haven't got a gun.'

'That's not what he said.'

Angel was herding him towards the corral.

'I haven't got no gun. I've never had a gun. How many times do I have to tell you?' He stopped and thought for a second. He forced a smile. 'And as long as you can't prove there was a gun, you haven't much of a case, have you?'

That was true, but Angel wasn't going to admit it. At the moment he wanted to get Eddie moseying along the trail to the enclosure. He just sat there looking at the little man.

'We've got a very strong case, for a very serious offence.' Angel lingered a moment before he dropped the whopper. 'Now that Larry Dott's coughed,' he lied.

Skinn responded quickly. 'Why? What's Larry Dott been saying then?'

Angel was almost ready to close the gate. 'All sorts of things,' he said, deliberately taking his time. Then he said it. 'He was also telling me about your mother?'

There it was. He watched Skinn closely.

The little man's jaw stiffened. His face went red. His clenched hands began to shake. 'Whatever I told him, I told him in confidence, not to be spieled to any struggling copper who's down on his luck. It's got nothing to do wiv him. It's got nothing to do with anybody. It's *my* business. I do the best I can, it's not been easy since my dad died. But it's got nothing to do with him. Nothing!'

Angel just looked at him.

After a moment he recovered. 'What about my mother, then? What did he tell you? What did he say? What about her? Eh? Eh?'

Angel waited.

'What about her then? What did he say? Come on. If you know so much, tell me!'

He pursed his lips. 'She's coming to see you.'

Eddie Skinn stared across the cell. 'What?' he screamed looking at Angel.

'She's coming up from London to see you.'

'What? She's coming to see me? Here? In this cell?'

The little man tipped his head back to look up at the ceiling. He put his hands to his forehead. Then he looked down at the floor while his stubby fingers massaged his scalp. He removed his spectacles, rubbed his eyes and then dropped his hands limply to his side. After a few seconds, he shook his head slowly, put his spectacles back on and said, 'What have I done to deserve this? What have I done to deserve this?'

Then he started walking up and down. It was four paces this way and four paces that. There isn't much room in a Police Station lockup.

'What's up, lad?' Angel said. 'You're not having a nervous breakdown, are you?'

Eddie Skinn ignored him. He was thinking aloud. 'Coming to see me *here*? In this place? In this cell? She'll go bananas. She'll go off her trolley. She'll go stark, staring mad!' He turned to Angel. 'You'll have to stop her. You'll have to stop her. She can't come here.'

'I can't stop her lad. She wants to visit her little boy. And it's right that she should be allowed to see you, isn't it? Her son and heir. The fruit of her womb. And you are entitled to one visitor anyway, lad. It's the law.'

'I don't want to see her. My visitor was Bloomfield. If my ration is one, I've had it. It was Bloomfield. Tell her that.'

'She's coming a long way.'

'I don't care. It's the same distance back. What did you have to tell her I was here for? She doesn't know anything. She can't help you.'

Angel looked at the sweaty little man and said nothing.

Suddenly he came up close to Angel, looked directly into his face and pointed a finger at him. 'You fink my mother can help you convict me, don't you? But she doesn't know nothin'. Do you know what, Mr Inspector? You're goin' to need a bleedin' miracle to convict me.'

Angel thought a miracle highly desirable but not very likely. 'Oh, I don't know about that, lad,' he replied nonchalantly.

Eddie Skinn came up close to him again. 'If you're waiting for a confession, you'll have to wait a long time. The only way you'll get a confession out of me is if you was to hold a bright object in front of my eyes and twirl it.'

Angel shook his head very slowly. 'I don't think so, lad.'

'Huh!'

'In fact, I think you're very close to it now.'

'Ha!' he said, forcing a laugh.

'You know lad, I think that if I was to say to you that I would keep your mother away from you, which is not my natural inclination after all, a man should not be separated from his mother — you would happily go into that Interview Room, tell my sergeant all about your activities at Bardsley Service Station, and at Pettigrew and Shaw's, leaving nothing out, and that you would tell him all about the gun, and that you would let him write it all down, I believe that you would sign it, like the good mother's boy I am sure you are.'

Eddie Skinn's mouth opened and closed as he considered what to do next. Then he grinned. But it was not a genuine smile. 'You must be joking? You must be out of your tiny mind. You Yorkshire coppers are the limit. You've eaten that much tripe and onions, the vinegar's pickled your brain.'

Angel pursed his lips and then nodded. 'Possibly. But I don't think so.'

'Either that, or…' he broke off. He'd thought of another insult. 'You know Inspector, you're much nearer the Arctic Circle than we are in London. And I reckon them reg'lar freezing temperatures you have coming down them Pennines has numbed your brains.' The cockney grinned with satisfaction at his own impertinence.

The banter was suddenly interrupted by a very loud raucous call that could be heard throughout the Station. 'Edward!'

The smile left the little man's face. His eyes widened as he listened.

'Edward! Where are you?'

It was the gruff imperious tone of a female sergeant major with a sore throat.

'No!' the little man said, aghast.

Angel's eyebrows went up.

'She's here! You didn't tell me she was here,' the little man squeaked.

Angel looked at his watch. Crisp must have arrived with Mrs Skinn. 'I didn't know she'd arrived.'

'Well, don't let her in here. I can't do with her in here.' He began pacing up and down the cell again.

'I told you, lad. I can hardly stop your own mother visiting you, now, can I?'

'Tell her you had to let me go and you don't know where I am,' he said, waving an arm frantically.

'I can't do that.'

Eddie massaged his chin. He made four more laps, then stopped and came up to Angel's chair. His left eye was twitching. 'Didn't you say you'd do a deal?'

Angel pursed his lips then he said quietly, 'I don't do deals.' Then he added quickly. 'But admit to those two jobs. Admit to the gun and say where it is. Leave nothing out. On paper. Sign it. Now. And I'll keep your mother away from you.'

'How will you do that? Are you sure you can do it? She's very difficult.'

'So am I,' he boomed.

'You wouldn't trick me, Colonel, would you?'

'What have I to gain? I just want to clear up those two offences. I'm not even going to ask you about offences you might want taking into consideration. That would be up to you. And I'm not interested in any arrangements you want to make concerning your mother. I'll simply tell her she can't see you. But you must tell the truth lad, the whole truth, and leave nothing out.'

'Edward!' The bellow came down the corridor.

Angel could hear protestations from DS Crisp and then some heated response from the rasping woman's voice followed by some other voices. 'No you can't go down there, Madam. No. You mustn't. This way. Thank you.'

The loudest voice of them all yelled, 'I want to see my son! I have a right to see my son!'

Eddie Skinn pulled a pained face, ran both hands through his hair and looked at Angel. 'Right, Colonel. You're on.'

* * *

'Ah, Crisp. Come in, lad.'

'Sorry about the racket, sir. I've had a right job,' he said, brushing his jacket sleeves with his hands. 'She's kicked my shins.'

'Aye. Where is she now?'

'In reception. I've told the PC on the desk on no account is he to let her through the security door without permission. And I've got a WPC to sit with her. I've told her she can't see her son at the moment. So, of course, she insists on seeing you.'

'Mmm. No point in putting her in the holding cell by the main door?'

'She'd raise merry hell and do no end of damage, sir.'

'Aye. Right. Well, I'll see her shortly. But I want you to take a statement from Skinn, now, while he's bursting. I've said

175

that I'll keep his mother away from him provided he coughs to both jobs, the gun and everything. Now make sure he tells you about that gun. It's absolutely essential to support Jane Mulholland's evidence. It would jeopardise her credibility if we can't produce the gun. And I want to know where it is now. I want it for evidence and I want it out of commission. Go to him directly, before he starts feeling brave.'

'I'm on my way, sir.'

The door closed.

* * *

'Now then lad. Are we talking today? You've seen Mr Bloomfield. I presume he's advised you?' Angel pulled the chair from against the cell wall and sat astride it.

Larry Dott glared at him from the bunk bed. 'He said be cooperative but don't say anything stupid. He also said that all interviews should be in an Interview Room and be recorded, to stop you from twisting my words round and making out I said things I didn't.'

Angel smiled. 'Tut, tut, lad. As if I would.'

'He also said that I didn't have to say anything, and that I could wait until he came and that you could interview me when he was here.'

'Oh no, lad. No. No. That's not right. We're not running a hotel. This isn't your five star Hilton, you know. We don't do room service here. I'm not on a hook at the back of the door, lad, to be picked up and put down whenever it suits you. Oh no. And don't get the impression you're here for the season. You're not here for long. Oh no. You're out of here and off to Strangeways for a spell, just as soon as I can arrange it.'

Larry Dott muttered something unintelligible and ran his hand through his long, dark hair.

'Now, lad, let's get on,' Angel said quickly. 'Time's money. Where did you hide that gun?'

176

Larry Dott hesitated slightly, 'You're always on about a gun. I've told you, I don't know anything about a gun.'

Angel's eyebrows went up. 'Don't mess about, lad. I've got a very nasty case of murder to deal with. I haven't time for this.'

'I don't have a gun. I've never had a gun.'

'That's not what Eddie said. He said you had a gun.'

'No. I've never had a gun. It was his gun.'

'Ahh.' Angel smiled. 'At last. We're agreed there *was* a gun. Well, where is it now?'

The young man ran his hand through his hair again. 'I don't know,' he said edgily. 'I don't know.'

'Look Larry, if you have nothing to do with the gun, it will go easier on you if you tell me where Eddie Skinn has hidden it.'

'I don't know where he's hidden it!'

'Did he have it in the house you and he lived at?'

'Yes. He had it on him. Sometimes he would carry it about. If it wasn't on him when you picked him up, I've no idea where it is now.'

'Is that the best you can do, lad?'

Larry Dott nodded.

Angel blew out a sigh, 'Right.' He shook his head, stood up, put the chair back against the wall and turned to the door.

The white-faced young man looked up at him. 'You mustn't believe everything he tells you, you know.'

'I don't, lad,' Angel said, his jaw set. 'I don't.'

* * *

Angel reached over for the phone and pressed a button. 'Reception.'

'You've got a visitor for me there, haven't you? A Mrs Skinn?'

'Not 'arf, sir.'

'She's with a WPC, isn't she? Will you send her down to my office?'

'With very great pleasure, sir.'

Angel replaced the phone and wondered at the PC's unusual reply. He looked at the pile of papers on his desk, but he couldn't apply himself to anything until he had dealt with the woman. He rubbed his hand across his mouth, then stood up and crossed to the door. He opened it as the procession of a WPC, Mrs Skinn and a PC arrived.

He knew instantly it was Eddie's mother. She looked like him. The same height, the same figure, the same spectacles; even the voice was similar. She had similar hair but more of it, and was wearing a smart, navy blue suit and carrying a large, matching leather handbag.

Their eyes met. She pointed at Angel, looked at the WPC and rasped, 'Is this 'im?'

He stepped forward and smiled. 'I'm Inspector Angel. You are Mrs Skinn, I believe? Please come in.'

He nodded confidently at the WPC and the PC, 'Thank you.'

They hesitated, looked at each other and then went hurriedly up the corridor.

Mrs Skinn sailed into the room, glanced around it and then looked back at the Inspector.

He closed the door and with an open hand indicated the chair by his desk. 'Do please sit down.'

She put the handbag on the floor and settled herself in the chair.

Angel went round the desk and sat down. 'Now then, Mrs Skinn. What can I do for you?'

'I want to see my son, Edward.'

'So I understand. I have to tell you that your son has been charged with armed robbery and burglary. And we'll probably find a couple of lesser offences to charge him with later.'

Her mouth twitched. She looked down at her hands, clasped them and said nothing. Angel waited a few seconds.

'I'm sorry to have to tell you this, Mrs Skinn.'

She looked into his face. 'That's all right, man. You have to speak the truth.' She nodded and then said, 'He always has been a trouble to me.'

Angel didn't react. There was another pause.

'Will he go to jail?'

'Yes.'

'For how long?'

'It depends on the judge. Probably between two years and five.'

'Oh!' she wailed and shook her head several times.

Angel saw her eyes fill with tears.

She leaned down, pulled up the big handbag and rummaged deep inside. She eventually found a packet of paper tissues, unravelled one and applied it to her eyes. 'I don't know what his father would have said if he'd still been alive.'

The scene affected Angel but he did not show it. He waited.

Eventually she said, 'Is there anything I can say or do to help him?'

Angel hesitated and then said, 'You could give evidence.'

She peered at him. 'What sort of evidence?'

'You could say something good about him. To mitigate his sentence.'

The tears had gone. She thought a moment and then said, 'He's my son. I gave him life, I brought him up. But I don't know anything good to say about him.' She dabbed her nose and put the tissue in the coat pocket. 'I will have to see him,' she said, and then she sniffed.

'Well, that's not possible at the moment.'

'Why?'

'He's making a statement.'

She looked up surprised. 'He's admitting to what he's done?'

'Yes.'

She considered the situation and then asked, 'Tell me, Inspector. Will he definitely go to prison?'

'Yes.'

There was a pause.

'Definitely?'

He nodded.

She sucked her top lip and then made a decision. 'I don't think I could stand to see him in a prison cell. That is, of course, unless he wants to see me.'

Angel permitted himself a wry smile.

'You will let me know what happens, Inspector?'

He nodded.

She looked at the wall, expressionless for a moment, then she turned back to the policeman.

'I shall go home. I shall catch the next train back.'

Angel nodded and said, 'I think it's for the best.'

'And there's something else, Inspector.'

She leaned forward again and dragged up the handbag. She opened the top flap, put her hand inside and came out with a heavy object wrapped in a bright yellow duster. It rumbled noisily as she placed it on the desk in front of the policeman.

'You'd better have this for safe keeping. I don't like things like this around the house. I found it in a biscuit tin buried in the garden. I saw him fiddling around with a spade. He buried it last week when he visited me, I knew it must be something fishy — he's never done any gardening in his life. I dug it up when he'd gone. He thinks I'm stupid.'

Angel unravelled the yellow duster. Inside was the missing piece of evidence that was going to put Eddie Skinn and Larry Dott away for a few years. It was a Smith and Wesson Revolver 128.

CHAPTER 14

Cadet Ahmed Ahaz opened the office door. He stood there with his hand on the knob. 'It's Inspector Moxon from the STS, sir.'

Angel looked up from his desk and smiled. 'Oh good. Not Foxy Moxey from the brains department? Come on in, lad.'

A big man with a big smile came in carrying a clipboard. 'Hello Mike.'

Angel stood up and shook his hand.

'Come in, lad. Sit yourself down,' Angel said. He turned to Ahmed. 'I want that copy of the plan of Jubilee Park and Sycamore Grove.'

'It's here, sir,' Ahmed said, putting the A4 sheet he had been holding on the desk.

'Ta, lad. Stay and listen in. This'll be an education.'

Ahmed smiled and remained standing by the desk.

Inspector Moxon took up the chair by the desk. 'And how's the missis, Mike? Haven't seen her for ages.'

'I haven't seen her for ages myself — well, it seems like ages. Her mother's in hospital in Derby. She's away keeping an eye on her. She's been away over a week now.'

'Sorry to hear that. If you get fed up of being on your own, you can always come to our house for a bit of bread and drip. Our kids have left home so there's only the two of us. You'd be right welcome.'

'That's very kind. I might take you up on it. I am getting a bit browned off with all this shopping and cooking. And how is Sandra?'

'She's fine.'

'Good.'

Foxy put his elbows on Angel's desk, took a pen out of his pocket and pulled up the clipboard. 'Now what's this job about?'

'Aye, well, have a look at this plan.'

'Mmm. Jubilee Park, eh?'

'I want to keep obo on these two houses next door to each other, back and front. I want to see and record all the comings and goings through four doors day and night for forty-eight hours.'

'Mmm. Are these the two houses hatched in red?'

'Aye. I thought you could park the van under the trees there. It would be completely hidden from the house by this wall. You could run the cable round the side of the park then over the wall about there. Then run it up to the gazebo.'

'Is that the gazebo?'

'Yes. There. There's some trelliswork where you can conceal a camera and fasten it onto a stanchion. And then run another cable parallel and on into the orchard next door, and you can screw a camera bracket onto a tree somewhere round here.'

'Yes. That looks all right. How far is it from the van to the orchard?'

'About a hundred and fifty yards.'

'Mmm. That's the back doors, what about the front doors?'

'Aye. Well, this wall is about ten feet high. I thought that both cameras could be mounted about ten yards apart on top of it.'

'How thick is this wall?' Foxy asked as he wrote something on the clipboard.

'It's stone. About two feet, I guess.'

'That's wide enough. Mmm. Mmm. And you want four monitors in the van. And the facility to view and record all four cameras independently as required.'

'Aye. That's it exactly.'

'Are there any existing lights or street lamps? Are these doors you want to monitor illuminated by any artificial light at all?'

'No.'

'Mmm. They'll have to be infra-red lenses then.'

'Will they?'

'Mmm. Do you want any sound?'

'Eh?'

'Do you want to overhear or record anything? You might as well. We can drop mikes over the wall to cover the two front areas at night. It's only about forty feet, and they wouldn't be seen. You can pull them back over by their own cable for daylight obs.'

'Aye, right.'

'Mmm. Sound from the back would be more difficult. The distance from the doors.'

'Don't bother. I really expect any critical movements to be through the front doors. Sound is helpful. It will give us forewarning.'

'Exactly.' Foxy scribbled something onto the clipboard. 'And when did you want this operation to start?'

'The Super's only given me forty-eight hours, so it's got to be set overnight tonight, and then tomorrow night.'

'Hmm. Doesn't give us much time. But we can do it, I suppose. Who's on the team?'

'There's a DS, this Cadet and me, overnight. And the Super's giving me two DCs for the day shift.'

Ahmed looked up from the plan when he heard his name mentioned. Angel noticed. 'You're working tonight, lad. You've not been on an obo before, have you?'

'No sir,' he said with a big smile.

'Good experience for you.'

Moxon didn't seem impressed. 'See what you feel like in the morning, son.' He returned to his clipboard. 'Mmm. The van will be in the park and can be seen all day tomorrow? We'll have to paint something on the doors, or stick posters on it, or something. Keep nosey parkers at bay. What can we put?'

'Er, how about, "Joint Universities Natural History Study." It sounds suitably academic and innocuous, doesn't it?'

'Can't you think of something shorter?'

'Yes. JUNHS. But it doesn't have a sense of conviction, somehow.'

Foxy grinned and wrote something on his clipboard. 'And for my records, what are you calling this operation?' He asked with his pen poised.

'I dunno. Haven't given it a name.'

'Well, think of something, Mike. I've got to put something down.'

'Well, what?'

'Anything. Anything short.'

'All right, how about TDC? Is *that* short enough?'

'It'll do. What's it stand for? The Difficult Case?'

'No. Two Dead Cats.'

* * *

'Come in, lad. Come in. Sit down. How did you get on?' Angel said, closing a paper file and tossing it onto a pile at the corner of the desk.

Crisp smiled triumphantly. 'I've got it here, sir,' he said, waving a sheet of paper. 'Eddie Skinn's coughed to both jobs and he's fully implicated Larry Dott.'

'Ah,' Angel beamed. 'That can go to the CPS now.'

Crisp hesitated. 'Er…there is one thing, sir.'

Angel's eyes steadied on him. 'Aye? What?'

'He didn't say anything about a gun.'

Angel groaned. 'Well, he wouldn't volunteer it, lad, would he?'

184

'I pressed him hard and he denied all knowledge of it.'

Angel grunted and threw his pen on the desk. 'When I left him he was willing to admit to owning a gun. In fact, when I left him he was willing to admit he was Osama bin Laden rather than face his mother!'

Crisp shook his head.

Angel looked straight into his eyes. 'You know, lad, you're going to have to brush up your interviewing techniques.'

Crisp's mouth tightened. 'Do you want me to have another go at him?'

'No. We haven't time to do everything twice. As it happens, your luck's in. His mother made me a present of his revolver. So now we have enough to have them both sent down for four years at least.'

Crisp breathed out a long sigh.

Angel went on. 'What about CRO. Have you heard from them?'

'I was coming to that, sir. There's nothing known re either of the Wexells, nor the Lowbridge woman. But Tal Lowbridge has done time.'

Angel's eyebrows shot up.

Crisp referred to a page of the papers he had tightly clasped in his hand. 'And he had an alias.'

'I'm not surprised with a name like that.'

Crisp smiled. 'His actual name is Tiberius Angelus Lowbridge. No wonder he shortened it to Tal.'

Angel's jaw dropped. He leaned back in the swivel chair and smiled. *I know* him. Of course. He was a barber. My! He's changed. Put on a lot of weight. Had a shop at the top of Canal Road. Well, and I never recognised him.'

'That's right, sir.'

'He didn't shorten his name. Tiberius was hardly an appropriate name for a barber in Bromersley, now was it? His customers did it for him, from the way it was painted up on the shop door. In brown paint on frosted glass, I remember, "T. A. Lowbridge. Gentlemen's Barber". T A L, Tal. His shop was straight off the pavement. It was that near the road, it used to get slarted with snow when the Tracky buses passed. Aye. Fancy me forgetting. Mind you, it is over thirty years. Went there as a lad, when we lived on Canal Road. He's cut my hair a few times.' Angel looked up at the ceiling and then at Crisp. 'He was done for receiving. Or was it handling, gold bullion or something. What was it, lad. Have you got it there?'

Crisp said, 'Both, sir.'

'Aye,' Angel nodded. 'He was a warm lad, but no real evil in him. He'd been a sort of coin dealer cum bullion dealer in a small way for years. While he was cutting hair, he'd buy grandma's old wedding ring and sell the odd sovereign to the old codgers that came in to have their hair cut or their beards trimmed. There was nothing known until two lads from the Met came up following a lead from some big job at Gatwick Airport or somewhere. I remember they arrested him and took him down in handcuffs. Made quite a show. But he was only a minnow. He didn't get long, did he?'

'He got twelve months.'

'Mmm?'

Crisp nodded. 'When he came out, his business had gone. Next thing, he's married to a lass a lot younger than himself. No children.' Crisp handed the papers to Angel.

'That's all, sir.'

The Inspector chucked them onto the pile at the corner of the desk. He pursed his lips. 'Nothing else known, eh?'

'No sir.'

Angel sniffed. 'Mmm. Well, we'll see what tonight brings, eh?'

The phone rang.

'You'd better get off and get rested up.'

'Right, sir.'

Angel reached over for the handset. 'Angel.'

The door closed behind Crisp.

'Who did you say?' the Inspector said into the phone.

'The Chief Superintendent of where?' His eyebrows shot up. 'Pontylliath ah! Yes, I know it's in Wales...Yes, I'll hold on. What a lovely musical voice you have, Miss. It must be all those leeks you've eaten while keeping a welcome in the valleys, eh?…The Chief Superintendent? Of course I'd be pleased to speak to him. Put him through…Good afternoon, Chief Superintendent…No, sir. I regret to say I have no news on Miriam Thomas. In fact, I'm extremely worried about her.'

* * *

There was a knock at the door.

'Come in,' Angel called, his head stuck into a letter. He was still working feverishly trying to clear the deck for the obo coming up that night.

The door opened, it was Ahmed. 'Miss Lola Spedding to see you, sir?'

Without looking up from his desk, Angel mumbled, 'Yer what, lad? Who?'

'Erm,' Ahmed muttered while moving his body weight from one leg to the other and back. 'Miss Spedding, sir.'

Angel continued reading.

Ahmed coughed delicately into his closed fist.

Eventually, Angel looked up at him.

The young man's eyes moved to the door and back. 'You told me to fetch the lady from reception, sir,' he said uneasily. 'The young lady. Friend of Mr Wexell. Er — You know, sir?'

Angel's brow furrowed as he peered at him.

Ahmed put his open hand to the side of his mouth and whispered. 'The pretty lady. She's outside.' He said with a jerk of his head to the door.

'All right, lad. All right. Don't get excited. Keep pulling faces like that I'll have to book you into the Betty Ford Clinic.'

Ahmed looked down at the floor.

Angel stood up. 'Come in, Miss er…'

'Lola Spedding, Inspector.' She bounced cheerfully through the door wearing a light coloured summer dress, big straw hat and sandals. She smiled, first at Angel, then at Ahmed and said, 'Hello.'

Ahmed looked away.

Angel smiled and nodded.

'Please sit down,' he said to her indicating the chair by the desk.

'Shut the door, lad, you'd better stay.' He pointed to the chair by the wall.

Angel detected a pleasant perfume, strange to Bromersley Police Station and very welcome on a hot sticky day.

He found himself unexpectedly smiling as the tall, beautiful woman sat next to him. 'Now then, Miss Spedding. What can I do for you?'

She flashed the even, white teeth again. 'I'm sorry to bother you, Inspector. I am sure that you are busy with all sorts of serious crimes and criminals and things, but I understand that you have a tape belonging to Peter, Peter Wexell.'

Angel pursed his lips. 'I may have,' he said guardedly.

'Oh? Peter said you definitely did have the tape.'

Angel said nothing.

She paused.

He looked into her big blue eyes.

She smiled again. 'It's a family tape. All about members of the family, partners in the practice, relations, pictures taken on holiday, friends, that sort of thing.' She stopped, frowned and added, 'Have you looked at it?'

'No.'

'It is here?'

'There *may* be a tape here, to which you are referring. If there is, I suppose it rightly belongs to Mr Wexell.'

'Oh yes, Inspector. That's right. He has sent me to collect it. It's perfectly all right. I know all about it, Peter told me. I am here on his behalf. It was stolen from the safe in his office ten days ago. He was offered it by the thief, at a price. You cleverly intercepted it, caught the thief and recovered the tape. I have come to collect it. Can I have it, please?'

Angel shook his head.

Lola dropped the smile.

'No, Miss Spedding. I'm afraid you can't. Such a tape would be needed as court evidence. The case has not been…'

Her eyes flashed. 'He's paid you a thousand pounds for that tape.'

'No, he hasn't. Nor could I accept money for it, anyway.'

'He's paid you a thousand pounds for that tape and now you won't let us have it. You want the money *and* the tape.'

No one should ever accuse Michael Angel of dishonesty. A hot sensation in his stomach, expanded across his chest and spread upwards. Heat radiated from his face.

'I do not want either his money or his tape,' he said through tight lips. 'It is needed to prove a case of robbery and fraud. Both the money and the tape will be returned at the end of the court hearing, and not before.'

She breathed in noisily and filled her ample chest. She glared at Angel who glared back.

Then Angel pushed back his chair and rose to his feet.

Lola squared her shoulders and said, 'You're not the senior police officer here, are you?'

'No.'

Lola Spedding stood up. 'Well, I want to see him, whoever he is.'

'My immediate superior is Superintendent Harker. His superior is the Chief Constable. I don't know if either of them will see you, but you can ask at reception.'

'I will do that.'

Angel turned to Ahmed. 'Take Miss Spedding back to Reception.'

Ahmed's big eyes were wider than usual as he looked at Angel. He nodded and went to the door.

Angel saw the woman's smile was replaced by the dark face of despair.

He softened, 'I simply cannot do what you ask. It is the law.'

The anger left her. She spoke evenly and quietly. 'I really don't know what Olga Wexell will say to me. She is on the tape a lot. It is a private tape, you know. It was not shot for other people to see. Don't you understand that, Inspector? She is not a stripper. She's a good living woman. For myself, I don't care.'

Angel put up his hand. 'One moment please.'

He turned to the young Cadet who was by the door. 'Ahmed, nip out and fetch some milk for the cats.'

'Right sir.'

The door closed.

They both remained standing and faced each other across the desk.

'Now then, lass. What's this all about?'

'I was saying, Inspector, I'm not a lady in the old-fashioned sense. Olga *is*. And she's married to Peter, a highly successful and respected professional man. It wouldn't look good for him if the contents of the tape were discussed in detail across a courtroom and finished up in the newspapers. And I wouldn't want to think that the policemen in this station, and the barristers and solicitors and their staff are looking at the tape and sniggering. I don't know why you have to keep it. It is most unfair.'

'Why wasn't I told all this before?'

'It's embarrassing, Inspector. Even to talk about it. Olga had difficulty talking to me about it, and I'm a friend. A friend of both of them. Not a very good friend, I admit. As a friend, the best thing I could ever do for her is to leave Bromersley. And that's what I am going to do. The next best thing I can do is to recover that tape, for her sake, and give it to her husband. And that's all I am trying to do. I've done enough damage to them, I am doing no more. All this business has brought me to my senses. I shouldn't be here, vamping her husband. He would be happily married if it wasn't for me. I've tried to reason with him, but it only ends in rows. He won't say so, but he'll *never* leave his wife for me, so what am I hanging around for? So I'm going back home. Not to avoid publicity, God knows, I'm not camera shy. But Peter and Olga are decent people, they are entitled to their privacy. And they live in this town, I don't. I can go and get lost in Shropshire. It's no hardship for me. I've done it before, I can do it again. But Peter and Olga have a life together *and* a future. They don't need me around to muck it up.'

Angel's ears pricked up. 'You're leaving Bromersley then?'

She smiled and nodded. 'He's a nice man. But he's a married man. Olga's very lucky. But she'll be a lot luckier when I'm gone.'

'I wouldn't know about that,' Angel said. 'When are you leaving?'

'I've a taxi waiting. He's taking me to the station. There's a train in an hour. I'll be on it.'

Angel ran his hand across his mouth and made a decision. He reached down to the bottom drawer of his desk and pulled out an open brown paper package, holding it at one end he shook the videotape out onto the desk. 'Help yourself. I can put a blank tape in there,' he said, pushing the empty packaging carefully back in the drawer. 'I only hope there isn't a cry from the defence to play it, that's all.'

Lola Spedding reached out for the tape with both hands. Her eyes lit up as she grasped it with both hands and a big smile developed. 'Oh. Thank you. Thank you,' she cried.

Angel sighed and crossed to open the office door.

She rushed out into the corridor, she made a few steps on the tiles in her clackety high-heeled sandals, and then spun round and came back. She stood in the doorway, her eyes were moist. 'Oh thank you, Inspector. Thank you very much. You won't see me again. I promise. Goodbye.'

Angel's eyes followed her out of the office and up the corridor until she took the corner and was out of sight. He smiled to himself as he thought what a sucker he was for a pretty face. He supposed he had done the right thing and wondered whether he would see her again.

He was closing the door when a familiar, smiling face appeared. It was DS Gawber.

'You're back!'

Gawber nodded with a grin.

'Are you back from your course?' Angel said, 'And are you reporting to me?'

'Yes sir.'

Angel smiled. 'Come in. Sit down. Welcome back to the Wonderful World of Disney!' he added with a sniff. 'Profiling, wasn't it?'

'Yes sir.'

'Rubbish,' he pronounced.

'Oh no, sir.'

'Well, I hope you told them lads that we don't wear wing collars and spats up here anymore.'

Gawber laughed. 'Yes, sir.'

Angel rubbed his hands like a fishmonger on Good Friday. 'Well, you're like manna from heaven, lad. You couldn't have come at a better time. I'm up to my neck in it, and it don't smell of Chanel. I've got a job for you, it's this Welsh nurse murder. You won't know anything about it?'

'I've read bits in the newspapers.'

Angel reached over for a folder on the corner of his desk and pushed it into Gawber's hand. 'Aye. Well, assimilate that.'

The Sergeant opened the cover. 'There's a lot here, sir. It'll take me a while.'

'There's no time to dally, lad. The reading'll be easy. I've written every word in there myself. This case is as clear as a bottle of gin. All I want you to do is go out and make an arrest.'

CHAPTER 15

It was midnight. The sky was blue and the moon scarlet after another scorching hot day. Everything was quiet and still; there was not even enough breeze to make a Woolworth's windmill spin.

Angel came out of his bungalow with a carrier bag, a pair of gardening gloves and a torch. He switched off the kitchen light, pressed the button to set the burglar alarm, closed the door and turned the key in the lock. He looked around at the night scene from the back step; the nearby houses were all in darkness. Everyone was apparently in bed, and Angel thought that's where he would like to be. A distant Church clock struck twelve as he walked through a cloud of midges along the garden path to his car on the drive. He opened the door and put the carrier bag inside, then went round to the back and opened the boot. He pulled on the gardening gloves and lifted up two small bundles wrapped tightly in newspapers secured with string from off the back step. Holding them at arm's length, he put them carefully in the boot. Removing the gloves, he tossed them in the back and closed the lid. He made for the driver's seat while tugging at his collar to ease the shirt from his perspiring neck.

Powerful amber coloured lamps illuminated the deserted streets of Bromersley Town centre, and Angel witnessed the eerie sight of traffic lights going through their sequences with only his car to obey them. Three minutes later, he pulled onto the empty tar macadam square just inside the black iron gates of Jubilee Park.

The sky had darkened making the stars brighter. The lights of an airplane passed silently across the blue. There was still no breeze, and only the drone of traffic shushing past on the motorway a mile away disturbed the quiet.

Angel gathered up the carrier bag and the two newspaper bundles from the car, and set off on foot up the service road through the park towards Sycamore Grove. He passed the bush where he had so recently been summoned to investigate the incident of the young couple who had had the body of Fiona Thomas thrown at them so unceremoniously. He plodded on. Perspiration on his forehead irritated him, as he didn't have a free hand to wipe it away. He was soon under the black, overhanging branches of the trees at the perimeter wall of the front gardens of Sycamore Grove. He dropped the bag and bundles down by a bush. He turned back to look down the service road at the eerie outline of trees and the deserted bandstand two hundred yards away. There was no sign of life. He was breathing faster than normal, his pulse was drumming in his ears. He wiped a handkerchief across his forehead, licked his lips and decided he really must cut back on the haddock and chips.

Suddenly, he heard the snapping of dry twigs and the swishing of tree branches behind him. He froze.

A voice whispered, 'Is that you, Mike?'

It was Inspector 'Foxy' Moxon. He came towards him picking his way through the shrubbery. Angel could just about make out his round fat cheery face.

'Aye. You frightened the pants off me. I thought I was here on my own. You're early.'

Moxon chuckled. 'I wanted to get an idea of the layout. Thank goodness it's getting darker at last. My lads will be here soon. It's a straightforward plan and they're very good so it won't take us long to set up. I want to get to bed.'

'Don't we all? Did you notice any sign of life from those two houses?'

'No. Quiet as a grave.'

'Good. I've a little job to do. I'll be ten minutes or so.'

'I think I hear the van coming,' Foxy whispered and stepped out into the service road to attract its attention and guide it in position. The vehicle seemed to be making a lot of noise in the isolated scene.

Angel reached down to the carrier bag, felt around the contents and pulled out a pair of scissors. He put on the gloves, picked up the two small parcels by their string and followed the wall round to the door that opened into Sycamore Grove front gardens. He lifted the latch and pushed the door.

In the background, he could hear the gentle hum of the van's engine as it was being reversed into position. He hoped the noise would not alert the residents in the two houses. Detection at this point would devastate his plan.

He made his way silently on the lawned area through the Lowbridge's front garden, carefully avoiding the noisy gravel path, along the side of the house and down the steps towards the back garden. At the bottom of the steps was the coal grate that led into the cellar. Without a sound, he lowered the two parcels onto the ground, opened the grate and fumbled in his pocket for the scissors. He cut through several thicknesses of newspaper to open the end of one of the packages. The smell of the dead cat began to reach his nostrils and eyes. He held the open end of the bundle through the grate opening and shook it several times. Eventually the dead cat left the newspaper wrapping and slid silently down the coal chute into the coal cellar. Angel pulled a face, closed his mouth and fought off the urge to swallow. He screwed the newspaper wrapping into a ball, and threw it after the dead cat and closed the grate. Then he picked up the other package and made his way back up the steps. He turned to the home of the Wexells next door and dropped the other dead cat down their grate in the same way and then retraced his steps, along the grass to the door in the wall and back to the bush where he had left his carrier bag. He removed the heavy gloves and wiped his forehead and his eyes. The smell still lingered and he took a few deep breaths. Two rectangles of light through frosted glass showed him the way to the parked observation van. He pushed past two low branches to the open door, bounced up the two steps and went in, screwing up his eyes to get accustomed to the electric strip light in the roof.

Foxy Moxon was seated inside the van looking intently at one of a bank of four flickering TV monitors while talking on a mobile phone. He glanced up at Angel, stuck up his thumb to indicate all was going well, and then into his mobile, said, 'Yes, that's it, John. Perfect…Yes. Secure it there. Now, can you see some apple trees?'

Angel looked over Moxon's shoulder at the four black and white pictures developing and nodded approvingly. He dropped the carrier bag on a seat.

Foxy looked round at him and sniffed. 'What a pong. Is that you?'

'Aye,' Angel said wearily and got out of the van. He closed the door and looked out into the darkness. As he stood there looking at the distant outline of the bandstand, he felt a tickling sensation on his forehead; it was a mosquito. He smacked it away.

Two minutes later, Foxy Moxon came pushing through the low branches. 'It's all done bar the mikes. Can I get into the front gardens from this side?'

'There's a door in the wall just round the corner.'

'I'll be back in a minute.' Foxy rushed off with a roll of cable over his shoulder.

Angel yawned.

Unexpectedly a voice in the dark said, 'Is that you, sir?'

It was DS Crisp. He could make out his silhouette against the starry sky.

'Yes, lad.'

'We couldn't find the place. I couldn't see the van.'

'Where's Ahmed?'

'I'm here, sir,' he said eagerly. His big eyes and teeth shone in the dark.

'Are you all right, lad?'

'Yes, sir. And I've got my sandwiches and a flask.'

'This is not the Co-op trip to Skeggie, you know! Have you told your mother you'll be on duty all night?'

'She doesn't mind as long as I'm with you.'

Angel smiled to himself. He supposed it was intended to be a compliment. 'DI Moxon says they've nearly finished. Then we can get settled in the van.'

* * *

It was dark, silent and warm, there was no breeze to rustle the branches. The orange moon had turned yellow, and the sky was an unvarying dark blue.

Inside the observation van, Angel squinted, blinked and lowered his eyes from the four flickering screens. He looked at his watch, it was 4.30 in the morning. Loosening his tie, he undid the top button of his shirt, ran his hand around his Adam's apple and then wiped his forehead with his handkerchief. 'Sergeant,' he said quietly

There was no reply.

'Sergeant.'

He turned round to the built-in bench seat close behind him.

DS Crisp was slumped, his head back at an irregular angle, his mouth open and his eyes closed. His tie was slackened off and lay at an untidy angle half round his neck.

Angel reached back and shook his knee. 'Come on, lad. Come on.'

The sergeant opened his eyes and looked round. He looked surprised at where he was. He grunted, rubbed his mouth and then said, 'I wasn't asleep, sir. What's happening?'

'You drop off faster than fags off the back of a lorry. It's time we pulled the mikes in. It'll be daylight in a few minutes.'

Crisp yawned. He looked at his watch. 'Is that the time?'

Angel returned to watching the monitors showing static pictures of the four house doors.

In another bench seat by the rear doors, Cadet Ahmed Ahaz was slowly shuffling his feet. He screwed up his face, opened his eyes, blinked and then yawned.

Angel called across. 'Hey! Rip van Winkle. Good morning!'

Ahmed blew out a long sigh, rubbed his eyes and then mumbled. 'Morning, sir.'

'Help the sergeant pull those microphones in, lad.'

The sergeant and the Cadet nodded across at each other, then slowly shuffled out of the van into the breaking daylight. It was a delight to feel the cool touch of the early morning air on their cheeks and to breathe it into their lungs. Two magpies and a blackbird announced their presence and fluttered close by. The undemanding job of pulling up the microphones was a pleasant enough way for the two men to stretch their backs and there was enough light for each to see the other and smile understandingly as they silently coiled up the cable.

They returned to the van to find Angel with a paper bag of sandwiches and a vacuum flask of coffee complete with silver drinking cup spread out on the bench in front of him. He was examining a sandwich. The corners of his mouth turned down as he lifted up the top slice and peered at the filling.

'Mmm. Beetroot,' he muttered and shook his head.

He dropped the slice back, pushed the wad into the bag and put it in the carrier at his feet. He wiped a hand over his mouth and reached out for the coffee.

'Do you not like beetroot, sir?' Crisp said as he pulled out a bag of sandwiches from a plastic container.

'Not in sandwiches for breakfast lad. No.'

'Well, why did you let your missus make them up for you then?'

Angel didn't reply at once. He looked round the van, sniffed and then he said, 'She didn't make them up for me, lad. She's away, isn't she? In Derby, with her mother.'

'Oh yes sir. I had forgotten.' Crisp dug into his box and pulled out a sandwich. Then he added, 'Well, if *she* didn't make them up for you, who did?'

Angel grunted and hesitated. He swatted a fly off the back of his hand and missed. Then, reluctantly he said, 'I made these up myself.'

'But if you don't like beetroot…'

'That's all there was,' he growled. 'That's all there was!'

He glared at Ahmed and said, 'Look at these windows, all steamed up! All this condensation. Open that back door a bit, for goodness sake. My vest's as wet as a spinster's handkerchief.'

Nothing further happened until six a.m. when two young constables in plain clothes knocked on the door of the observation van. They were the dayshift. Angel immediately sent Crisp and Ahaz off duty with instructions to report back there at ten p.m. for another night's obo.

He then briefed the two young men on what to do in the event of any person leaving or entering either house with a large item that could be a human body. Five minutes later, Angel made his way through the bushes and low branches into the early morning sunshine and then down the service road through the park to his car.

He was at the police station in four minutes. He went into his office, leaving the door open and found a message on his desk under the paper-stapling machine. He pulled it out. It read:

To Inspector Angel. Your wife phoned last night. She could not get you at home. She said her mother is no better and it looks as if she may need an operation. The specialist is seeing her tomorrow and she hopes to have some definite news.

If so, she will phone back. She sends her love and hopes that you are managing. She asks you not to forget to feed the cats.

'Aah,' he groaned. 'That's all I need!' He pulled a face, screwed up the paper and threw it hard into the wastepaper bin. It made a ping sound as if it was a pebble. He began fingering through some of the papers on the desk, when he heard footsteps approaching. They stopped. He looked up. The burly figure of Superintendent Harker with the white hair stood in the doorway.

'Morning, Mike.'

'Morning sir. Did you want me?'

'No. No,' he replied thoughtfully rubbing his nose. 'Are you still on that obo?'

'Yes. I'm going home in a minute. Just came in to see if there was anything urgent.'

'Mmm. Are you still expecting to come by that woman's body?'

'Tonight's the night.'

'You hope?'

'We live in hope, John. We live in hope.'

'Mmm. I was thinking, if you *do* get lucky tonight, call me out. I'd be interested to see how this case wraps up.'

Angel pursed his lips. This was an unusual turn of events. 'Oh?' he replied. 'Wouldn't you rather stay in your comfortable bed with your missus, John?'

Superintendent Harker, noted for his observation, replied, 'Ah yes. Your Mary is still away at her mother's, isn't she?'

'She is. And I'm not very happy about it.'

'How's she getting on?'

'Not good.'

'Oh. I'm sorry. Er good luck.'

'Thank you, sir.'

'And good luck tonight.' The Super walked off.

Then Angel heard the footsteps stop, turn and come back.

'Oh, Mike.'

Angel looked up. 'Yes sir?'

'With old folk, these things can drag on for ages. Could be months. Don't bank on any compassionate leave. You know how things are. Must dash.'

'Oh yes. I know how things are.' And when he was out of earshot, he added, 'I know exactly how things are, O Master!'

He shook his head as he thought he had better get a positive result tonight or he would never hear the end of it!

* * *

'What you got then, Sarge?' Ahmed asked as he packed his vacuum flask and sandwich box safely under the observation van seat.

DS Crisp stretched out his arms, yawned and then said, 'Ham, I think. With some lettuce and tomato.'

Ahmed nodded approvingly and with a smile said, 'I got salami and smoked haddock.'

Angel's eyebrows lifted. He turned momentarily from the screens to glance at Ahmed. 'Somebody getting married? All that rich food.'

'No sir. They are things I like. My mother knows that. And they are not in together. They are labelled so that I know which is which. What have you got, sir?'

Angel smiled. 'Bacon butties.'

Ahmed said, 'Mm. We could swap some of our sandwiches. Give us all variety.'

Angel said, 'I'm not swapping mine for ham.'

Crisp said, 'I don't eat foreign food. And I don't want a greasy bacon sandwich in the middle of the night either, thank you.'

Ahmed looked aggrieved, 'It's not foreign food. We eat it all the time.'

'There you are. It's what I said. Foreign food.'

'*I'm* not foreign, Sergeant!'

Angel said, 'Hey you two! Keep it down. Take it to the United Nations, let them decide. Sergeant, do you know if these speakers are switched on? I haven't heard a dickey bird so far tonight.'

Crisp stood up and leaned over Angel's shoulder at the flickering pictures on the television monitors. 'Good pictures, sir. You can see the doorframes, the steps and everything. And it's pitch black out there!'

'Aye, lad. It's the sound I'm bothered about.'

Crisp looked up at the two speakers above the screens. He leaned forward and reached out to the side of one of the speakers. 'I can feel a knob.' He turned it causing a loud hum.

'That's it, lad, but turn it down a bit,' Angel said brightly.

Crisp obliged.

'That's better.'

'I'll do the same with the other.'

'Those idiots on the dayshift must have been fiddling around with them.'

By trial and error, they soon had both microphones set at the right volume, and the occasional small scratching sound in the gravel path and the breaking of a twig by a bird or small animal could be heard through the speakers.

'Listen. Must be a mouse or a rabbit or something.'

'Aye.'

Crisp stared at the pictures of the doors on the four monitors for a minute. They were clearly visible in strange purple and burgundy colours with a little 'snow'. 'Do you really expect someone to show with a body tonight, sir?'

'Well, I'll feel softer than an egg poached by Delia Smith if nobody shows up, lad.'

Crisp rested his elbows on the bench and his chin in his hands. 'But I mean, if I was a murderer sitting on a corpse, and I was safe in my own house, I wouldn't be in any hurry to bring it outside for the police to nobble me just because it whiffed a bit.'

'Wouldn't you?' Angel pursed his lips. 'Have you ever passed a dead cat in the street?'

Crisp considered the question. 'I don't suppose I have. I've never noticed anyway.'

'If you had, and it was in the middle of a heatwave, you would never forget it. There was one in the gutter on Henry Street on market day once. Now you know what a narrow, busy little road it is. I was walking along in a throng of folk, ahead of me there were crowds of shoppers spilling over onto the road. About fifteen feet this side of it, everybody left the pavement and walked into the road — some crossed over and stayed on the other side — the rest walked round it. Some made a whooping noise as the smell hit them, and held their noses. Some ran past. Not everybody knew where the smell came from. But everybody knew they wanted to get away from it — *fast*. Well, Sergeant, *that* was a dead cat.'

Crisp yawned. 'Mmm.'

Angel added, 'In a confined space like a cellar, after all this hot weather, a cat that's been dead for ten days is going to be an unwelcome contribution to the domestic ambience, believe me!'

'Mmm. And why would they mistake it for the smell of a corpse, sir?'

'Well, they won't know, will they, lad? Most folks don't know what a corpse smells like, and they don't know what a dead cat smells like either. All they might have gathered from the university of life is that both smell pretty damned awful. They would know if they have something in their house that stinks, wouldn't they? If it stinks, it stinks. And one stink is as bad as another, isn't it?'

Crisp was still resting his chin in his hands, his eyes nearly closed. 'I suppose so, sir.'

Angel shook his head. 'Trouble with you lad, you've no poetry in your soul. You've no imagination. And you've no gift of improvisation. No creativity.'

'Mmm.'

'And there's something else, too. In this particular case of murder, we're investigating, we've got a woman trained and paid for by the state — that's your taxes and my taxes — to be a nurse, committed to preserving life and healing the sick. She will have taken the oath to do no harm. Now this particular one is freely murdering whomsoever she pleases. She is playing god. She has murdered one person and by now, probably two. Now, I don't believe anybody should commit murder, and I have a personal objection to a professional nurse whose tuition I have partly funded abusing her training and the public's sense of trust and goodwill to murder whoever she chooses. And when I'm ninety-nine and in a bed dying, I expect to be able to depend on the lass in the blue outfit with the white hat running up and down with bandages and bedpans and pills, doing whatever she has to do. And not quake in bed with fear in case she's going to stick a needle in me to finish me off. You see, lad, I've got very strong feelings about that. So I want to *find* this nurse, and put her away so that she can't murder anyone else. Now I expect all that's got something to do with me being a copper. Well, if it has, I wouldn't be a bit surprised, because ever since my father was slashed in the face by that razor gang from Manchester trying to save his sergeant who was shot dead in a fight on the roof of Bromersley Brewery, I never wanted to be anything else.'

Angel paused a few moments and then he turned round to see DS Crisp.

The sergeant's head was slumped back on the seat. His eyes were closed, his breathing deep, regular and slow.

Angel pulled a face and shook his head. He looked down at his watch. It was three a.m.

He eased back from the monitors and looked towards the back door of the van. Cadet Ahaz was leaning forward in his seat, his arms resting on his knees, his eyes almost closed. 'Are you all right, Ahmed?'

Ahmed jerked his head upwards slightly and opened his eyes. 'Yes, sir.' Then he grinned.

'Good lad.'

Crisp yawned, stretched and then said, 'If it's going to happen tonight, sir…what *time* is it going to happen?'

Angel shook his head and then looked at his watch. 'It's three o'clock,' he said, frowning. It's about as dark as it's going to get. If it doesn't happen soon, it's not going to happen at all.'

Suddenly, there was a noise through the loudspeaker. It was the sound of a heavy door being opened. All three men froze.

Angel blinked and peered closely at the monitors, one after the other. Crisp leapt up from his seat and looked over Angel's right shoulder. Ahmed came up from the back and peered over the other shoulder. None of the three spoke or made any noise. They were as wide-awake as they ever could be.

Angel spotted some movement on a screen. He pointed to it.

They could see that the house door was open. A figure was struggling through it. It looked like a man carrying something large and shapeless over his left shoulder.

'This is it,' Angel said, slapping his mobile phone into Cadet Ahaz's sweaty hand. 'Phone the station, lad. Tell the duty Sergeant to advise the Super, Dr Mac and DI Moxon that we've got a body. They'll know what to do. Got it?'

Ahmed's eyes shone. His hands were shaking as he started pressing the buttons.

Crisp was out of the back of the van waiting for the Inspector.

The sound of the house door closing followed by slow, heavy footsteps on gravel came through the speakers. Angel heard it but didn't spare it a glance.

The two of them moved swiftly in the dark, staying close to the wall, to the green painted door twenty yards away. They waited, one each side of it. The footsteps in the gravel were getting louder. Their pulses beat like war drums in their ears. Angel could just make out Crisp's face and hands in the darkness.

The sound of the gravel being kicked around stopped. There was silence. After a moment, the sneck clicked and the door slowly opened.

Angel held his breath as the man carefully negotiated the opening. He could see he was carrying a shape that looked like a body over his shoulder.

As he came through the door, the man turned and reached up for the sneck to close it. Angel could hear his heavy breathing. He put his hand on his shoulder. 'Don't throw it this time, Tal. It's the police. It's Michael Angel.'

The man gasped, but said nothing. He just stood there motionless in the dark.

Angel said, 'She's dead?'

'Yes,' Tal Lowbridge said quietly and turned to face him.

Crisp said, 'Shall I cuff him?'

'No,' Angel replied.

'Shall I caution him?'

'No.'

'What about the house? Shall I go and find the wife and arrest her?'

Angel looked at a very quiet Tal Lowbridge. He could see the outline of his head, but he couldn't guess what was going through his mind. 'She isn't in the house, Tal, is she?'

'No.'

'There's nobody in the house, is there?' Angel said.

'No.'

'Where is she then?' Crisp asked.

Angel sniffed. 'Shove a brick in your mouth and listen. Take that body from him and put it in the van — *very carefully*. Give it into the care of Dr Mac when he arrives; he won't be long. And hand the van over to DI Moxon when he arrives. And tell Ahmed to join Mr Lowbridge and me in my car, straightaway. We're going to the station.'

Crisp took the woman's body from Tal Lowbridge. It wasn't heavy. Then Tal dipped into his pocket and pulled something out. He handed it to Angel. It was a bottle of capsules. 'Here, you'd better have these. I was going to bury them with her. These are what poisoned her.'

Angel caught Crisp before he got too far away. He gave him the bottle. 'Ask Mac, as a favour to me, to sort these out, urgent like, will you?'

'Right, sir,' he said, slipping the bottle into his pocket. He turned and carried the body away to the observation van.

'Come on, Tal. I've got my car. Let's go down to the station.'

CHAPTER 16

Ahmed switched on the lights in the Interview Room at Bromersley Police Station. Tal Lowbridge blinked as the white strip tubes flickered into life.

Inspector Angel followed them in. 'Get some teas on, lad. Then you can go home. We'll want three. The Super will be here any minute.'

Ahmed opened his mouth to say something and then closed it.

Angel indicated a chair to Lowbridge who pulled it up to the plastic topped table and sat down.

Ahmed came up close to the Inspector and said, quietly, 'I'd like to stay, sir, if that's all right.'

'Are you sure, lad?' he looked up at the big black and white clock on the wall. It showed 4.45. 'Look at the time.'

Ahmed's eyes shone bright with enthusiasm and he nodded quickly several times.

'All right lad. We'll need four teas then. Go on. Hurry up. Chop-chop.'

Angel looked down at the older man who had his head bent low and was peeling skin from his cuticles.

'Are you all right, Tal?'

He looked up and nodded.

Angel sat opposite him and pushed a tape into the recording machine. 'Superintendent Harker will be here in a minute. Then we can start. When he comes, just tell it how it is. It's for the best.'

The phone rang. Angel picked it up. 'Yes?…Speaking. Oh hello, Mac…That was quick. Yes…No, we haven't started…What you said before?…I see…Oh? Ingenious… Right…Thanks for being so quick…Yes, I'll tell the Super. Goodbye.'

'Talking about me?' Superintendent Harker appeared in the doorway. He had an even growth of black five o'clock shadow round his lip and jaw in contrast to his white hair, otherwise he was his usual immaculate self.

'That was Dr Mac with some info about the case. I'll tell you later, sir.'

Tal looked up.

'We are all ready for you, sir. This is Mr Lowbridge.'

The two men nodded at each other.

Cadet Ahaz came through with a tray. The teas were quickly distributed.

Angel switched on the recorder, gave the date, time, place, those present and then said, 'Right Tal, I've got most of the story. Will you fill in the gaps?'

Lowbridge was slow to start. He spoke with a very soft voice, getting more confident as he progressed. 'Well, *I* didn't murder anybody, you know.'

'Tell us what happened from the time Fiona Thomas rang your doorbell.'

'Ah. It's been a nightmare, it really has. Well, it was a week last Friday afternoon. My wife was out shopping and I was on my own. Miss Thomas rang the bell and asked for a room for the night. I booked her in and she signed the visitors' book. I showed her into room number 2 and took her order for supper. My wife returned, I told her what I'd done and that was all right. She saw the guest walking round the garden from the sitting-room window, looking at the flowers, and she went down to meet her. She came back almost immediately, her face white as snow. She said she recognised the woman, Fiona Thomas, a nurse she had known from the days when she had been nursing at Pontylliath Hospital.' Lowbridge stopped and looked at Angel for some reaction.

The Inspector nodded and waved a hand to encourage him to continue.

'Well, anyway, Violet rushed to the visitor's book to check the woman's address, and that confirmed it. It made her all of a dither. I had never seen her in such a state. I tried to settle her down. I said that maybe she hadn't noticed. But Violet was certain she had, and got more wound up when she saw her using her mobile phone.'

Angel looked at the Superintendent. 'Incidentally sir — excuse me Tal — I got a phone call yesterday from Pontylliath police. While seeking the whereabouts of Miriam Thomas, they came across a retired woman who had been working as a nurse with the Thomas sisters at the time of Derri Evans' death. Derri Evans is the male nurse who was killed by a patient in Pontylliath Hospital in 1981. She said that she had a particularly vivid memory of him being carried out of the cell, bleeding profusely and near death. She said that Miriam had said that it served Fiona right for taking Derri, the only boyfriend she had ever loved, away from her.'

The Super said, 'Was that the motive?'

Angel nodded. 'A neighbour said that the sisters quarrelled all the time. Their father had had a difficult job separating them, and when he died, their mother took on the role of peacemaker. After she died — only four weeks ago — there were no holds barred. And when she got that phone call from her sister, Miriam must have thought it was a golden opportunity to dispose of her sister and, at the same time, let Violet take the blame. Go on, Tal.'

'As I said, Violet saw Fiona Thomas making a phone call and thought that it might be to the police and that her happy and peaceful days in Bromersley were coming to an end. She hardly slept all night. And next morning, there was more trouble. Fiona Thomas didn't come down to breakfast. It got to be ten o'clock and so Violet went upstairs to see where she was. She came down all in a dither. She said the woman was dead in bed. I went back up to the room with her. She examined the body and couldn't find any bruises or marks or anything. Later on, she found that bottle of sleeping capsules on the floor under the bedside table when she was tidying round. She counted them out. The dose was two a night, and there were only two taken out of a full bottle of forty-eight.'

Superintendent Harker looked at Angel and said, 'What's this about sleeping capsules? I know about the diamorphine hydrochloride being injected between the toes. I don't know about any capsules.'

Tal Lowbridge looked across the table at the Inspector. 'I gave you the bottle.'

'That's right,' Angel said and then he turned to the Super. 'His wife had found them in Fiona Thomas's room, sir. They had her name on them. They were for a drug called Mogadon. They appear to be appropriately prescribed, labelled and the proper dose taken. However, Dr Mac tells me that the capsules had been opened and the contents replaced with diazepam. Two of that size capsule crammed full would be enough to shut a cow up for the night. In the case of Fiona Thomas, it would have given her a very deep sleep that would have enabled her sister to administer the fatal injection without waking her.'

Harker nodded, 'Ah. Right. Please continue Mr Lowbridge.'

Tal cleared his throat and looked at the Super. 'I was for calling you, the police, but Violet wouldn't hear of it. She said that we might not be believed and that there was still a warrant out for her arrest. She dreaded the thought of having to go back to Wales, the disgrace and everything, and then having to serve time in prison. She reminded me of my record too. I suppose you've dug that up. So after a bit of discussion, we decided to try and hide the death. We thought we could get away with it. Anyway, that was not to be, and later that day, sister Miriam arrived. Fortunately, I answered the door. She asked to see her sister. I said that she had left that morning. But actually, her body was on the floor in the cloakroom. Miriam didn't believe me and told me so. I told her to go away and she left in high dudgeon. I didn't tell Violet about the visit, I thought it would only distress her. But I did expect the police to arrive at any minute with a search warrant. But you didn't. Anyway, I helped Violet dress her, then hid her clothes, handbag and suitcase under the coke in the cellar for a couple of days. I burned them all, with some other rubbish, at the first opportunity.'

Angel said, 'You gave yourself away there, Tal. When I came round the boiler was still hot. I thought, who would light a boiler in this heatwave unless they had to? That's what made me begin to suspect you.'

Tal Lowbridge continued as if he had not been interrupted. 'Well, the following night I took her body to the park intending to bury it as far away from the house as possible. Well, you know how that ended. What you don't know is that when I got back home and told Violet what had happened, she went absolutely crackers! You have no idea what a putting up she gave me. She ranted and raved. I couldn't do anything right. It was all getting rather too much for her.'

He looked round at Angel and said, 'You called that night, and then you came back again on Tuesday.'

The Inspector looked back at him and nodded encouragingly.

Tal went on, his voice stronger. 'That was quite an ordeal. But we got through it. We didn't know whether you suspected us or not, but we lived in hope. But worse was to come. That afternoon, much to our surprise, her sister, Miriam, came back again. This time Violet answered the door and she pushed her way in. Violet recognised her straightaway, even after twenty years, and they took an instant dislike to each other. At first, she repeated what she had said to me on Saturday morning. She said she was looking for her sister, who had phoned her and told her she was staying with us, and she insisted on seeing her. Violet had to lie to her, of course. She told her that she had stayed the one night and then left. I supported her in this. But Miriam didn't believe us. Well, she wouldn't, would she? She didn't believe us because she knew the truth. She'd got in the house, through that unlocked downstairs window you pointed out to us, Mr Angel, I expect, and somehow killed her sister. And as the argument went on, it was obvious that she intended pinning the blame on Violet. She gave herself away again when she said she wanted to see the room Fiona had been staying in. Violet said she wasn't to go up, but she went anyway. And, of course, she knew exactly which room it was. After a few minutes, she came back down. She had apparently been looking for her sister's sleeping capsules — that's the bottle I gave you, Mr Angel. She couldn't find them and accused Violet of stealing them. Violet denied all knowledge of them, but I knew they were in her pocket all the time. Again Miriam didn't believe her, but then again, she expected a bottle of capsules to be there, and now knew they weren't. She was probably the only person in the world that would have known Fiona took sleeping pills. And she probably intended removing the bottle the night she came into the house and killed her, but was unable to find them because they had dropped onto the floor under the bedside table. Now when Miriam realised she'd been rumbled, she said that if Violet did not confess to poisoning her sister, she would inform the police that she was the nursing sister from Pontylliath Hospital wanted by them all those years back. Violet couldn't win! Miriam also tried to convince me that Violet had murdered Fiona during the night while I was asleep. That was ridiculous. Violet went mad and expected me to shut Miriam up. I tried but I couldn't. She wanted me to kill her. She said to protect our future! Believe me, I would have liked to. Violet screamed blue murder at me. Now I was being attacked on both sides. I thought Violet had gone off her trolley. I said if she didn't take control of herself I'd send for the police and that they could both take what was coming to them. Violet dug her heels in. She said she wasn't going to prison for anybody, under any circumstances. Miriam repeated her threat, so Violet let her have it. She told her she was a murderer, a bigot and a liar. I think those were her words. In reply, Miriam said she had not forgotten what had happened to her fiancé twenty years ago, and that Violet was responsible for his death. That was the last straw. Violet went for her throat and Miriam retaliated. The fight started in the sitting room, moved into the hall and then to the top of the basement steps. I tried to part them. They are both small but they fought like cats. Anyway, the fight ended with Violet being pushed down the basement steps. She landed at the bottom on the flagged floor with a crack. I can still hear the sound. She was very still. I feared the worst. Miriam went down to check her pulse and her breathing; she didn't say a word to me. I could tell by the look on her face that Violet was dead. Then Miriam dashed up the steps, and shortly after that, I heard the front door slam. I don't know where she went. I sat on the top step for a long time. I didn't know what to do. Eventually, I got up, tidied round, dragged Violet's body into the basement locker room next to the boiler room, and covered her in coats until I could think straight. I knew I was in serious trouble. I knew you would suspect me. The husband is always the chief suspect. Anyway, I was alone in the house. Fortunately we'd no guests coming in and I wasn't expecting anybody. I got through the next few days somehow. The nights were rough. I couldn't sleep. It seemed to get hotter and hotter. I had a fit when the doorbell went on Friday and it was you, and Violet dead in the cellar and you thought you could smell something. Oh. Last night, the smell had got much worse. I noticed it, coming out of the cellar for the first time and it was horrible. I decided I must get rid of the body!'

Ahmed's eyes swivelled and caught Angel wiping his mouth with a hand. The Inspector saw him and stopped momentarily and then lowered his hand and looked away. Then he glanced at the Super, who was listening intently to Lowbridge.

Tal continued: 'I decided I must carry on as normal to avoid suspicion. I remembered I had twenty schoolteachers coming to stay for the weekend. I would have to attend to them. Their rooms were ready and the shopping for food had been done. It was mainly a matter of cooking and serving breakfasts. I thought I could manage that on my own, at a pinch. But the smell from downstairs would surely give me away. It was unbearable by this time and getting worse by the hour. So I decided I must bring the body out as soon as possible and bury it somewhere in the park. I waited for it to get dark. It seemed ages. Then I uncovered her, wrapped her in a coat, and slung her over my shoulder. I didn't know you were waiting for me. Well, the rest you know.' Tal reached for his tea, finished it off and placed the empty cup firmly on the table.

The three policemen were silent.

Tal looked at the table top. The Super looked at Lowbridge. Angel stood up and looked at the Super. Ahmed looked at his foot and wriggled it.

The Super was the first to speak. 'Well, where's Miriam Thomas now? She's got to be found.'

Angel said, 'Yes sir. I have arranged for DS Gawber and a DC to be at a Building Society in Pontylliath to pick her up, charge her with murder and fraud, and bring her back here later today. That's if all goes to plan.'

'What's this? You've missed something out. I don't know anything about this.'

'Oh? Yes sir. When her mother died, Miriam Thomas planned her sister's murder and her own disappearance, and it turns out that it was to be financed with her mother's money. In that phone call from Pontylliath police I got yesterday, the Super there told me that Miriam Thomas had forged her mother's signature and withdrawn over £1,000 in cash and closed her account at a bank. Also, that she had worked the same trick on the Building Society in the town requesting the withdrawal of capital and interest in cash to close that account in excess of £20,000. It is, of course, very unusual for anyone to want such a large sum in cash. That's what made the Manager look again at the signature and then make enquiries. He then, of course, discovered that Mrs Thomas had died, and he immediately called in the police. However, it is a thirty-day account and Miriam Thomas could not in any case collect before the thirty days were up. She is expecting to be able to collect the money tomorrow — that is, now today.'

Harker stood up, towering over everybody. 'Mmm. Well. Good. If Gawber arrests her later today…Mmm. Sounds all tidy to me, Mike.' He rubbed his chin hard with his hand as he moved to the door.

Angel nodded. 'Sir.'

Superintendent Harker turned back, looked across at the Inspector and smiled. 'You see, there was no need to take those two houses to pieces. You didn't need a search warrant after all, did you?'

* * *

It was eleven o'clock the same morning.

Detective Inspector Angel had been home, had a shower, a shave and a bacon and egg breakfast.

He felt quite chirpy as he strolled into the office, even though he had been up all night. He wanted to see if anything urgent had come in the post and was fingering through some letters.

There was a knock at the door. 'Come in.'

It was Ahmed, wearing a big smile and carrying a piece of folded paper. 'Good morning, sir.'

Angel frowned at him. 'What you doing here, lad? At six o'clock this morning I sent you home in a car to get rested up.'

Ahmed grinned from ear to ear. 'I can't sleep with all this going on, sir.'

Angel blinked. 'What are you talking about? What *is* going on, lad?'

'Well, sir. There is so much happening.'

Angel shook his head and resumed looking at the post.

Ahmed looked sombre. 'And I've got a message for you, sir.'

'What is it?'

The young man placed the paper on the desk in front of the Inspector. 'It's from your wife, sir.'

Angel peered down at the paper. It read:

To Inspector Angel. Your wife phoned. She said that her mother is a lot better. She is going into a Nursing Home for two weeks. After that, the specialist says she should be well enough to return to her own bungalow. So your wife is coming home this afternoon. She sends her love and says not to bother about shopping. She is bringing something for tea and extra milk for the cats. Could you please meet her at the station?

A smile formed on Angel's face and it grew bigger.

'It's good news, sir,' Ahmed said.

'Ah. I'll say it is, lad. Maybe I'll get some decent grub now, eh?'

Ahmed smiled.

The phone rang.

He reached for the handset. 'Angel…Who? Gawber? Put him through. Now lad, have you got her?…Good. Everything all right?…Thank goodness…Right, lad. See you later today. Goodbye.'

'Was that Sergeant Gawber, sir?'

'Yes, lad.'

'He's got Miriam Thomas?'

Angel nodded.

Ahmed smiled down at him. 'That's good, sir.'

The phone rang again.

'Who's this?' He reached out for the handset. 'Angel… Who? Peter Wexell?'

Ahmed said, 'It'll be to thank you for returning that videotape to Lola Spedding sir.'

'About time too, lad. Yes. Put him through, Miss… Good morning, Mr Wexell. Nice of you to call…What?… No?…Disgraceful!…Yes sir. I'll look into it right away… Goodbye.'

He replaced the phone.

He turned and looked sternly at Ahmed. 'What do you think, lad?'

The young man looked anxiously at Angel.

'That was Peter Wexell complaining. Whatever next? Somebody's put a dead cat down his coal chute!'

THE END

MORE BOOKS BY ROGER SILVERWOOD COMING SOON

Don't miss the latest Roger Silverwood release,
join our mailing list:
www.joffebooks.com/contact

FREE KINDLE BOOKS

Please join our mailing list for free Kindle crime thriller, detective, mystery, romance books and new releases! www.joffebooks.com

Thank you for reading this book. If you enjoyed it please leave feedback on Amazon, and if there is anything we missed or you have a question about then please get in touch. The author and publishing team appreciate your feedback and time reading this book.

Our email is office@joffebooks.com

Follow us on facebook www.facebook.com/joffebooks

We're very grateful to eagle-eyed readers who take the time to contact us. Please send any errors you find to corrections@joffebooks.com